Th
Ratcatcher ot Berlin

by

James Stejskal

Library and Archives Canada Cataloguing in Publication
Stejskal, James, author
The Ratcatcher of Berlin / James Stejskal

Issued in print and electronic formats.
ISBN: 978-1-998501-28-1 (paperback)
ISBN: 978-1-998501-29-8 (ebook)

Cover Design: Paul Hewitt
Interior Design: Richa Bargotra

Double Dagger Books Ltd.
Toronto, Ontario, Canada
www.doubledagger.ca

This story is fiction. It is set in a divided Berlin, a city occupied by the victorious Allies — the United States, Soviet Union (Russia), United Kingdom, and France — after the defeat of Nazi Germany in World War II. While most of the characters in this book exist in my mind only, several who populate these pages are real, but their actions are as I imagined. So too, the intelligence organizations I name existed at the time. The words "Soviet" and "Russian" are used interchangeably throughout the story, because, at the time, they meant the same thing. Additionally, although I strived to keep the details of time and place as accurate possible, some incidents may have slipped to the left or right by several months. And finally, any and all errors are attributable only to me.

"the saddest thing about betrayal is that it never comes from your enemies"

— unknown

RESTRICTED SENSITIVE ACTIVITY
HEADQUARTERS
UNITED STATES EUROPEAN COMMAND

Executive Summary of 15-6 Incident Investigation of security incidents which took place in Berlin and resulted in the deaths of U.S. Army service members in Berlin during the time period January 1957 through January 1958. The deceased's names are published in a separate Eyes Only annex.

Unit Designation: Special Forces Detachment Berlin (S)
                     Cover Title: Support Detachment, US Army,
                     Berlin Command

Background.
The Berlin Special Forces Detachment is not assigned to Berlin Command. It operates directly under the command of U.S. European Command Support Operations Task Force Europe (SOTFE) in Paris.

SFD's presence in Berlin and its mission are classified Secret and Top Secret respectively.

Operational Context.

Circumstances. The incidents are described in separate classified enclosures with witness statements.

Recommendation. The deaths of the soldiers named herein took place under extraordinary circumstances. Further, no reliable disinterested witnesses in Berlin have been located. That, along with the refusal of the Soviet Occupation Government to provide any information on this case, has rendered further investigation impossible. With regard to the American soldiers under investigation, a famous lawyer once said, "no man was ever convicted based on testimony he did not give." This board concludes that no further action can or should be taken in light of the lack of evidence and the national security implications involved.

RESTRICTED SENSITIVE ACTIVITY

CLASSIFIED ENCLOSURES
REMOVED AND DESTROYED.
— VOCO CINCEUR
21 MAR 1961

DECLASSICATION
IAW EO 12356
BY JCS J-3/SO.
17 JUNE 2019

I can't leave tonight.
A war's begun;
I must stand and fight.
— after Farrokh Bulsara

1

---◆---

OBERST HEINZ STÖCKER didn't like driving on bad roads, but he hated having ten kilos of high explosives bouncing around in the trunk of the car, even if the Russian had assured him that it rarely went off prematurely. He was trying to think nice thoughts, but the grating voice brought him back to the matter at hand.

"We can do the test shot at this Kallinchen place?"

"Yes, colonel. Our facilities permit the use of explosives."

"And you have replicated the target exactly?"

"From the information we have gathered, we built a full-scale mock-up which we think you'll be pleased with, colonel." Stöcker addressed the man as colonel even though he held the same rank. Colonel Androv was, after all, a different kind of colonel.

"I hope so. We would have done it at one of our facilities, but the Americans watch them too closely."

Stöcker knew the Russians well enough to understand their concerns. The Allies had so-called "liaison" officers that seemed to be everywhere in the country looking and poking about the Soviet installations, the same as the Russians did in the capitalist West Germany. By any other name, it was spying. That said, he also thought the Soviets were a bit paranoid.

"No worries, colonel. The AGM/S has many resources and facilities that are completely unknown to the Americans."

"AGM/S?"

"The minister's working group, colonel. The 'S' stands for *Sonderaufgaben*, it's our Special Tasks directorate."

"You Germans have such precise names for everything. Ours are simpler and more to the point."

Stöcker waited for elaboration, but Androv wasn't going to satisfy his curiosity. Instead, he talked about the task ahead.

"To make this simple, we have chosen a tactic similar to one that was used before, not successfully, I should point out, but we have made some changes that will ensure it works this time."

"From the description you provided me, colonel, I assume you're speaking of Operation *VALKYRE*?"

"Very good, colonel. You know your history."

"Thank you, colonel. That is my job, but it was fairly obvious. And you are certain that your agent will have the necessary access to the target?"

"Colonel, I would not have chosen this plan had he not the ability."

"Of course, colonel. My apologies, I just want to make sure I have all the answers for the minister should he have any questions."

"You can be assured that Minister Wollweber has been fully informed of our plan, colonel. Operation *FEUERSCHMIED* has been approved at the highest levels and exemplifies the close comradeship of our two nations. Furthermore, the operation will appear to have originated from a third country. It will have no connection to us or you DDR-people for that matter."

"Fire Smith, an interesting name, comrade colonel. Why German?"

"Because the Russian was too difficult for your people to say." Androv seemed to relish his superior knowledge and smiled to himself as he stared out the window.

Kallinchen was a small village on Motzener See, a placid lake popular with the mostly high-powered East German officials who could afford and were allowed to purchase a beach-side cabin. But there were other "normal" people who lived nearby. Normal in the eyes of the *Stasi* because their lives were all well checked out and on file in the local office. About a kilometer outside the village was a forest that hid its own secrets. *Ausbildungsbasis Kallinchen* was one of the Ministry's most up-to-date training sites, an area that the locals knew existed, but dared not speak of or get close to.

The big Russian limo with official plates entered the village with a *Stasi*-appropriated West German BMW 501 sedan acting as escort vehicle close behind, more than enough of a reason for the mothers to snatch their kids off the streets had this been a normal place. But Kallinchen was not a normal place and visits like this happened often enough that everyone knew another government bigwig had shown up and ignored the cars.

On the other side of the village, a long, narrow road led them out into a heavily forested area. Marked as closed to all but official traffic, the track led to what was ostensibly a forest management facility complete with gate guards who wore the forest green-piped fatigue uniform of the East German Forestry Service. The three-meter fence with barbed wire on the top said something else entirely.

The red and white drop barrier was up as the cars approached. Management had been alerted to the approach and were ready. The cars went through the gate and swept by the main building onto an even smaller track. Off to one-side was an oval driving course, complete with several skid pads, and one section that faced a dirt berm. It looked like a good place to practice vehicular ambushes and do some live fire at the same time. The carcass of what appeared to be a large Mercedes rested on its steel wheels, brownish-red with rust, the glass gone, the body full of bullet holes giving evidence of at least one training session.

The cars stopped in front of a larger U-shaped berm. A one-story, flat-roofed building sat in the middle. A small party stood near the entrance to the structure, the technicians all dressed in pressed, clean, gray coveralls. Then, there were the officers, who didn't do the dirty work and only came out for the dog and pony shows when a senior showed up.

"Colonel Androv, this is Major Schildkröte, the head engineer on this project," said Colonel Stöcker. Major Schildkröte saluted and began his prepared spiel.

"Welcome, Colonel Androv. As you requested, we have constructed this facility to replicate the meeting room where the action will happen following the original architectural plans. Two long walls with no windows, one end wall with a ceremonial double-door entryway, and the end wall with five-meter floor to ceiling windows."

"Original plans? How did you find those?"

"They survived the war in the basement of the old Luftwaffe headquarters. We discovered them in the files."

"And is the actual target constructed in this fashion?" Androv ran his hand along the rough cement.

"Yes, poured concrete with marble cladding, but the stone was too costly to destroy it for this test. Our reinforced concrete is a good stand-in to demonstrate the explosive's effectiveness."

"I hope so, Major. We will have one shot for this to work and we don't want any mistakes." Androv turned to his aide who standing behind him. Stöcker didn't think the man looked like an aide as much as he looked like a hard case. Compact, about 1.75 meters tall by over 1 meter across, a bull-like neck and an Asian cast to his eyes, he looked like he could and would be happy to break most men in half with his big hands.

"Sergei, get the case, please." Even Androv was polite to him. As Sergei walked back to the trunk of the car, Androv said in a low voice to Stöcker, "He's SMERSH. Try not to make him angry." He clearly understood what the Russian meant; Sergei was his personal attack dog.

"I thought that organization was disbanded after the war?" The East German was too unsettled to even say the name of Stalin's old assassination bureau. Its methods were far beyond the pale of what even the AGM/S considered palatable.

"Well, yes, of course it was disbanded, colonel." Androv smiled, a genuine smile, a twinkle in his eye. "Of course it was."

When Sergei returned with the case, Androv said, "Major Schildkröte, let's see how this works."

"Yes, Comrade Colonel. Follow me, please," Schildkröte said and led the party inside to a well-lighted room. "We've provided the basic furnishings as your asset described them."

"I didn't mention an asset," said Androv, confirming there was an asset.

"No, Comrade Colonel. I just assumed."

"Don't assume anything, Major. Ever. That will get you in hot water and you wouldn't like that, I think."

"No, Comrade Colonel. So then, we've set everything up according to the instructions you provided." Schildkröte shuddered for a moment. He, like Stöcker, knew the Russians had special "facilities" in their Karlshorst headquarters that made the *Stasi* prison at Hohenschönhausen look like a petting zoo.

"That's better," Androv huffed.

Inside, there was a long, wooden conference table with chairs set all around it. Groups of lights hung in makeshift clusters simulating chandeliers. A long carpet lay underneath, a cheap industrial thing because no one wanted to sacrifice an eight-meter long, silk and wool Tabriz for an experiment.

"Sergei, the case. Put it on the table."

Sergei shuffled to the table and placed it on the table with a thump. A simple leather brief case similar to a carpet bag but thinner, with a leather handle and brass fittings.

"This is an exact copy of the device our man will use. Four kilos of explosive and one kilo of stainless steel bearings surrounding it. It should be quite effective. It will be fitted with a timer, but for today's trial you will connect it to an electric blasting machine for the manual test," Androv said.

"What type of explosive is it, Comrade Colonel?"

"A malleable putty explosive, similar to Nobel 808 but manufactured in China. It is dual primed with electric caps from China as well. Russian scientists showed them how to manufacture the explosives," Androv said.

"So, it will appear to have come from China?" Doubtful of Androv's claim, he was thinking that the Chinese, who invented black powder, probably already had a good idea of how to make explosives. But he wasn't about to contradict the colonel.

"Of course not. It will appear to have come from Pakistan." Androv didn't want to answer any more questions and turned to Schildkröte. "Place the briefcase on the floor under the table about one meter from the head of the table when it is ready. Then we can proceed." Androv turned and left, Sergei following protectively behind the boss.

Stöcker looked at Schildkröte and shrugged before he followed the Russian out of the facility. Schildkröte motioned to his technician who prepared the wiring.

———

Androv stood behind the car about fifty meters from the building where Stöcker indicated they would be safe. "The blast will be absorbed by the building's construction. The only places the shock wave can escape are the heavy doors, which should be shut, and the windows. Hopefully, the curtains will be drawn, but even if they aren't, the blast will take care of everything inside."

Androv just nodded pensively. At this point, there was nothing he could blame on the Germans. It was his game now.

Schildkröte joined them as did his technician who did the final circuit check and connection.

"The system is hot, sir," he said, holding the blasting machine out for someone to take.

"We're ready, Comrade Colonel. Would you like the honors?" said Stöcker.

"Just fire the damn thing," Androv said.

Stöcker nodded at Schildkröte.

Schildkröte yelled out "Take cover," waiting a moment as he counted the heads of his personnel then nodded to the technician who yelled, "*Achtung! Achtung! Los!*" and twisted the machine's handle sending nine joules of energy down the line. A muffled "crump" came from inside the building, followed by smoke and debris from both ends as the doors blew outward and window glass shattered and tinkled down. Dust sifted out through cracks in the roof and around the edges. They had left the curtains open as a worst-case demonstration, just to be sure of the effect.

The technician trotted forward and peered carefully inside before he announced the site to be safe.

"Well, let's look and see what destruction we have wrought," Androv strode ahead leading once again.

The inside was a chaos of rubble with the ceiling wood hanging down, and lights blown out, necessitating the use of torches to see. The table had been turned onto kindling.

"It looks not unlike Rastenburg," said Stöcker.

"The Wolf's Lair?"

"Yes, Colonel."

"I see one difference. The table is completely destroyed. There will be no safe spot in the room. I am satisfied that they will all die."

"And your man?" Stöcker said.

Androv looked at Stöcker contemplating whether his breach of security was worthy of a dressing down and decided against it. No one was close enough to have heard. "Even if he survives, he will be eliminated soon after. No witnesses. Let's get out here."

After shaking off the shiver, Androv's pronouncement gave him, Stöcker said "At your command, Comrade Colonel Androv. I suggest we stop for lunch before we head back. There is a wonderful place in the village called the *Alte Krug*. Its's owned by the Schulz family and they do a wonderful *Eisbein*…"

"*Eisbein?*"

"Boiled pig's knuckle, Comrade Colonel. Of course, they do a good borscht if you prefer, and their vodka is Stolichnaya."

Always the consummate liaison man, Stöcker was more concerned with prestige, food, and wine than he was about operations. He'd moved on, having chosen to put memories of the day's events, the explosives test and the frightening man called Sergei, away deep in his mind where he could easily forget about them.

2

———•———

BUCHANAN, HIDDEN AMONG the rubble of an apartment building blown up a decade earlier, waited. His long, dirty, German army wool coat was gathered close to isolate him from the winter weather. No snow yet, but a cold Siberian wind still whipped through the city and cut through his clothing like a scythe. He'd been in place observing for perhaps ten hours. From time to time, he allowed himself some coffee from a small thermos out of his backpack, but now it was cold. He was saving the cognac for the trip home. It wasn't far to cross the border back into West Berlin from here. About eight blocks as the crow flies, but he couldn't fly so it would take longer to weave his way back through neighborhoods — a mix of some streets in good condition and others not yet free from the destruction wrought by Russian artillery and British and American bombs during the war. Even in in Berlin's Soviet sector, most streets had been cleared of debris, but the buildings remained hollow shells, much like the one he was sitting in. Still, it was hard to believe that it had been twelve years since the war's end.

Several hours before, a big black car had arrived at the brown stone walk-up across the street. A stocky man got out and walked up the steps. The two men from the front seat climbed from the car and stood outside watching the street, obviously his security. That and his civilian clothing meant he was a Party bigwig or something. He couldn't read the license plates to tell if it was a government car, but he imagined it was. It was too big for anyone else to own it.

Many thoughts ran through his mind as he tried to puzzle together what he knew so far. The big man wasn't the first. Earlier, another man, taller and leaner, also wearing a long, dark coat like his own, but cleaner had gone in the same door. He'd walked down the street in the open, but he was wary, furtive even. Buchanan could see that. The man looked around like someone who thought he was being followed. Maybe there was a connection between them, but he couldn't tell. Two men in the same building, who cares? Did they even meet each other?

Buchanan had only one thing on his mind and that was to watch the house and report what he saw. Someone might be able to figure things out. His time was almost done and for all he knew, his replacement was already in position somewhere nearby. He started to move. Carefully because the big man's minders across the road were still attentive. He carefully moved along a half-fallen wall, slowly picking where to put his feet for every step, backing out slowly towards the rear of what was left of the building. Then he stopped. The door glass across the street flashed in the setting sun for a moment as it opened. The big man came out. Buchanan's Leica camera clicked several times as the man descended the stairs and got into the car. The doors slammed shut and the car did a U-turn in the street. As he shot several more frames, he hoped his hands weren't shaking and the film setting was fast enough to capture everything.

The car disappeared down the street and it was quiet again. Buchanan decided to wait. Minutes later, the door of the brownstone opened again. It was the wary man. This time, he didn't look about. His hat pulled down low, he just hurried down the stairs and onto the sidewalk. He turned his face to the sky checking for something. Buchanan thought he recognized him. The Leica clicked once more, and the man was gone. As Buchanan wound the film back into the cartridge and replaced it with a new roll, he thought about the man.

If it is him, he's a long way from home. He waited a while longer before he decided it was time and continued out through the ruins to head back toward what was left of Kreuzberg and West Berlin and then to his apartment and a warm bed.

3

MACK MAKINEN STRODE two steps at a time up the stairs of the headquarters building. He paused before he went inside to look up at the Alps to the south, the snow beckoning even in May. He was wondering what could be so urgent that it required him to pack all his stuff and be ready to move. He entered the Executive Officer's anteroom to find Richard Grossman, the duty sergeant, waiting.

"I was told the XO needed to see me," he said.

"Yes, sir. Go on in."

The door was closed. Makinen rapped lightly on the door, a silver wolf's head ring sharpening the knock.

"Come."

Opening the door, Makinen stepped inside and closed it behind him. Besides the Group XO, there was another, unfamiliar man in the room. Both sat at a briefing table littered with folders and papers. Makinen saw that most of the folders were personnel files.

"You wanted to see me, sir?" Not knowing the other man's rank on account of his civilian clothing, Makinen chose the formal interrogative.

Major Fuller rose and shook Makinen's hand.

"Yes, thanks for getting here so quickly. It seems several of us are needed elsewhere for a new job."

Nodding to his guest, Fuller continued, "This is Major Brock. He just got back from the States yesterday. You're going to be working with him. Major, this is Captain Makinen."

Brock stood as well. "Good to meet you. It's Mack, correct?" Brock was a big man, around six feet tall, Makinen guessed that he weighed about two hundred pounds.

"That's my American name. It's really Micha," Makinen clarified.

"Mine's Thomas. We're going to be working closely together. Come, sit. We need to talk about a couple of guys and whether you think they're capable of handling something of a delicate mission."

Makinen sat at the table with Brock as the XO went to open the door.

"Rick, get the dining hall to send up some coffee for us please."

Returning to the table, Fuller went to the opposite side and sat down heavily, almost wearily. He moved a large pile of folders off to the side and looked back at the rest and sighed. Fuller's eyes went to the walls and Makinen's followed, checking out the room. The room was paneled in wood, old wood from before the war. As second-in-command, Fuller had been given the second nicest room in the building. He had done very little to decorate it. An American flag hung behind him, as did the 10th Group regimental standard, rifle green with an eagle and crossed arrows over its head. The commander had an identical one in his office except it had a gold fringe. The perks of command. The only other decoration was a wood plaque on the wall, devoid of words, just a knife hung vertically, blade up. A V-42, the knife issued to the 1st Special Service Force in the last war. Makinen preferred to carry his own, a Finnish *Puukko* his father had fashioned from an old bayonet and given him to test out on several Russians. It worked so he kept it. Like his ring, it was his talisman.

"You've only been here at Bad Tölz for a couple of weeks, Mack, so I know you're not really attached to this place yet, right?"

"Not really although I was looking forward to the mountain climbing and the skiing. It's been a while."

"You're going to be waiting a while longer, I think. You're being re-assigned to Berlin, a new unit we've set up. Thomas will be the XO. As the first Team Leader, you'll also be in charge of the operations section. We're just getting off the ground."

Makinen sat back for a moment. "I think I heard something about this. The S-2 mentioned something about getting orders cut for a couple of guys to Berlin when I was getting my in-brief."

Brock eyed Fuller pointedly.

"We're going to have to knock some heads together. It's not good when our intel guy is talking about classified stuff in front of people that have no need to know. Not that you don't need to know, Mack, but we've put in a lot of effort to make this look like we're reducing the size of the unit here. Supposedly, we're sending "A" teams back to Bragg to stand up the new 77th Group, which provides us with the perfect cover to send six of those teams east. We don't want the Russians to figure out those folks will form a new SF detachment in the American sector of Berlin."

"But won't they figure it out once we've hung out our shingle?" Makinen reasoned.

"That's the beauty of it, you won't be Special Forces," Fuller replied. "You're assigned under cover to Army Unit 7781, that's where all the ash and trash outfits reside. So you'll be working on a compound with a whole bunch of administrators, mechanics, musicians, and supply folks."

"Musicians?"

"The Army Band is there," said Fuller.

"Of course. Where would we be without a band in the middle of a combat zone?"

Still, Makinen was intrigued. He could think of several hundred questions covering everything from "how would they conduct military training inside one of the biggest cities in Europe" to "where he'd be living," but one stood out:

"What's the mission?"

"Simple. On order, cross the frontier into East Germany and run guerrilla ops against the Soviets in their backyard. Delay them so the Allies in Western Germany have time to stop them."

"Wow," was all Makinen could muster. He glanced at the folders and was about to speak when Brock cut him short.

"There's just one detail you should know. When war comes, we'll be in civilian clothing or maybe sterile uniforms. Worst case scenario: Russian or East German uniforms. That a problem for you?"

Makinen knew the implications. If captured, you're dead — shot in the nape of the neck after a long, painful interrogation. Better not get caught.

"No, no problem. Colonel Bank had us to sign a volunteer statement with that requirement. I'm still good with that. Besides, the Russians usually shoot every commando whether they're in uniform or not."

Both men knew he was serious. Makinen's reputation earned in Finland during the 1939 Continuation War spoke volumes about his courage and tenacity, not to mention his skill as a soldier and his hatred of Russians. That hatred was a common denominator of the Lodge Act soldiers, immigrants who came to America after the war and joined up like him.

The coffee arrived, Makinen poured a cup for everyone and turned his attention to the folders. There were about fifty remaining in the pile. As he looked and sipped at the lukewarm, bitter mess hall coffee, he asked, "When do we leave?"

"We're flying out of here tomorrow morning," Brock replied. "After we go through the files, we'll get the rest of our gear together and packed. We sent an advance party six months ago — a supply sergeant and a couple of admin guys, the team sergeants, and thirty troopers. The commander's already on site. He seems to be spending most of his time with the Berlin Command staff getting things set up."

"What about civilian clothing? I have some, but I'll need more to fit in."

"We'll get that in the city. Yours is all American anyway, right? You'll need local stuff, German-made, preferably from the East — if they have any to buy."

Makinen sat back down, picked up a folder and began to read.

"So, these are the rest of the guys we need to choose?"

"Yeah," Brock said, although he made it sound more like *Ja*.

"We need to fill thirty more slots. The guys in these files are all SF-qualified, but some don't have the language skills we need and some just won't fit. If we can't find enough to fill our quota, we'll go short for a while. The guys need to meet all the requirements, we don't need to make the requirements fit them"

As Makinen glanced through the files, he was surprised to see the number of men who had served in the war. The unit designations 101st and 82nd Airborne kept coming up. A few from the OSS and 1st Special Service Force were also sprinkled in. Then came those who served with United Nations Partisan Infantry Korea, fewer, but still quite a number. He found himself wondering, which theater he would prefer: Europe or Korea.

No, not Korea, he thought. It was cold, like Finland — and brutal, also like Finland. He had no wish to fight in winter. Well, maybe he'd rather face the cold in Scandinavia than be surrounded by a million Chinese. But he couldn't be taken by the Russians either. The Reds were well acquainted with the Finnish *Jägers* and they had long memories.

Something caught his eye. "This Sergeant Thibodeaux, he's pretty young."

"He is," Fuller said. "But he has what we need. Speaks Hungarian, German and Acadian."

"Acadian?"

"Think Cajun French. You know, like from New Orleans." Seeing Makinen's eyes glaze over, he skipped along. "Never mind, it might come in useful somewhere. Anyway, he will join us later, his team is about to deploy on a mission, and they need his language."

Makinen did a quick calculation. "Probably not his French. Is Hungary in the cards?"

Fuller stared at him for a long moment and shook his head.

Brock jumped in. "Not something we talk about right now. Let's just say his kind of experience will be useful later."

Makinen focused back on the files, glancing over to see Brock watching him as if he knew what he was thinking. He shuffled the papers purposefully and as an afterthought asked, "So, who is the commander?"

"Jozef Ciernik. Polish-American lieutenant colonel. Served in Europe with General Gavin's 82nd during the war and was in Berlin. Served in Korea with the UN Partisan Forces."

Makinen couldn't place the name and, with his mind was buzzing with the perspectives of the new assignment and getting ready to go, he soon forgot it.

A venerable C-47 stood on the tarmac of Baker Army Airfield, its tail to the hanger. The airfield itself was small and basic: a single runway and not much of a taxiway. A couple of hangers on one side stood next to the control tower.

Brock and Makinen sat inside the rudimentary arrival-departure lounge under the tower with two other soldiers, waiting for the crew to finish their pre-flight checks before they could board. The two soldiers had been there when they walked in and regarded them coldly as they found their seats. Makinen saw both were technical sergeants from the insignia on their field jackets. He noted that their uniforms had only the Seventh Army patch and no airborne wings. *Damn Legs*, he thought.

"Tell me about the war in Finland," Brock said.

"What's there to tell? The Russians invaded and got their asses kicked, then the Germans tried their luck. We fought them as best we could, but by that time, our supplies were exhausted and so were we. We had to surrender. And then the Russians broke their treaty and invaded again, so we fought against them again alongside the Germans. We fought three more years before we were overwhelmed. We surrendered, but the Russians never got to occupy Finland."

"The war in a nutshell," Brock commented. "But what did you do? How old were you then?"

Makinen looked at him and appeared to be making some mental calculations.

"Seventeen and I was a soldier," he said. "I killed Russians, then I killed Germans, then I killed Russians again." He pulled a folding knife from his pocket and began to trim his fingernails, looking up for a moment to smile at Brock who wore a surprised expression.

You asked, he thought.

4

JOZEF CIERNIK PAUSED when he heard a sound, his foot momentarily arrested in mid-air before he slowly planted it back on solid ground. He was surrounded by darkness in a small green oasis called Friedrichshain. On one side of the track a hill rose, built from rubble piled around one of Hitler's Flak towers. Too big and solid to knock down, the easiest solution was to try and hide the gun emplacement, make it disappear and along with it, the war. On both sides of the city, the occupiers were doing their best to hide the vestiges of war, except in spots like Treptow, where the Russians had buried their dead under the statue of a victorious Soviet soldier rescuing a child from the Nazis. The women of Berlin were always moved by that statue, especially the ones who'd been raped by the Russians.

That spot in Treptow was several kilometers from where he was now. Where he was now — inside the Soviet sector — was a place he wasn't supposed to be, much less on his own. So the regulations said, but he wasn't one for regulations by and large. Especially when it concerned his personal business.

He stepped off the path and stood next to a tree. Watching. Waiting. No one visited the park at night. There was nothing to see or do yet, the park could still be dangerous.

He found himself remembering an episode from the last time he was here ten years ago. And not too fondly how the scene had shaped his present.

———————

The war had been over for six months, Winter was coming and for the second time in two weeks, he was locked in a cell. A suspect, not a jailer. The saving grace was that this time it was not as threatening as before. But he was still bored and a bit anxious. Boredom was not unknown to him — most of his career was about boredom — terror snuck in once in a while and made his life interesting. Being anxious just came from having little control over the situation.

A wisp of cold air snuck under the door, pushing the tiny dustballs across the floor like scampering mice. His hand ran idly across the top of the table feeling the grain raised by years of age and covered with a dark patina of use as well as neglect. The coffee they had given him was dark, cold, and unappetizing. He set the white enameled cup back on the table with a clink.

He was also annoyed. When he arrived at Tempelhof Airfield, a scramble of people awaited him. He saw them through the tiny oval window of the C-54 as the plane taxied to a halt in front of the hanger. All of them were at the bottom of the airplane's stairs, smoking and joking, awaiting his arrival like he was their big fish. Wet-behind-the-ears American MPs, like the children they were, barely out of high school and lucky enough not to have been thrown into the meat-grinder of the infantry. Then, there were the CI dinks, the counterintelligence folks, slightly older and cock-sure because they thought they were cool. After a brief ride in a big sedan to the compound, Jozef Ciernik was locked in a holding cell for safekeeping, a cold, dank, and dusty cellar — not unlike the previous cell — just slightly more comfortable. Then they left him to stew a bit.

A long wait until the CIC folks showed up to talk with him. In his mind, the Counter-intelligence Corps was populated by opportunist, pseudo-soldiers who pretended to be warriors when all they did was slink around in the rear areas and torment people like they were Salem witch-hunters.

He felt like he was sitting outside the principal's office in grade school, something he'd experienced once or twice. When CIC did show up, he felt like the principal had abandoned him to the caretakers.

"Why am I here?" he asked.

"It's standard procedure when a serviceman has been detained by the Soviets."

"How often does that happen?"

"This is the first time I know of."

"So, not so standard then."

"We're just following orders, Major."

"Where have I heard that before, junior?"

This whole episode started because the American Military Attaché in Warsaw — a "leg" colonel whose only idea of combat was buckling his trousers over his fat belly every morning — sent back a message about the encounter Ciernik had with the Russians.

Ciernik crossed his arms over his chest in an effort to keep warm. One other chair faced the wobbly, old table. A naked bulb hung by an electrical cord that looked suspiciously like an old shed snakeskin, looped halfway down to make it shorter. The muddy yellow light splashed on the table with a touch of brightness but left the deep shadows in the corners untouched. He looked for the rats, knowing they had to be around somewhere. *There were rats everywhere in this city.*

He was sure, almost sure, that it hadn't been long. But time drags, or speeds up depending on the circumstances, and he wasn't sure which he was in at the moment. The one thing the Russians hadn't returned to him was his wristwatch. A cheap army green Hamilton — maybe it was cheap, but it was issued so he didn't know for sure. It kept time though and, now that it was gone, he missed it since he didn't know what time it was.

The door handle rattled and twisted slightly then stopped, as though someone was about to enter, but had second thoughts. A moment later, the heavy door opened slowly, hinges squealing and protesting, until two men in civilian attire stepped into the room. The first was carrying a metal folding chair, which he proceeded to open and set on the floor, its back facing Ciernik, but he remained standing. The second man settled into the unoccupied chair. He slapped a slim folder haphazardly onto the tabletop.

"This is Mister Russell. He will be helping me with your case."

Russell briefly presented his credentials to Ciernik, who saw only the briefest flash of a shiny badge and identity card before the leather case slapped shut and went back into the breast pocket of the agent's jacket. He thought this might be the army's version of good cop, bad cop, which meant it would be amusing at best.

Stevens began again.

"Let's go over your story one more time from the beginning, major."

Ciernik caught the inflection. The emphasis on *your story* instilled that little bit of doubt. Stevens had done the initial interview and now he was checking the truth by asking the same questions endlessly hoping for the slight aberration that a false narrative might contain. Despite his annoyance, Ciernik was amused with their amateurish attempts to diminish his stature. The two barely out-of-high-school Army Counter-intelligence Corp agents referred to themselves as 'mister,' while he was 'major' not 'sir.' That meant they were either warrant officers or enlisted CI agents who didn't want him to think he was their superior. No, they were in charge for the moment. Ciernik didn't care. He spoke four languages and had studied to be a mechanical engineer. He would have finished his degree if his father hadn't suddenly died and left him to support his family. Then, being the eldest son, he had joined the army early in '41, but only when his brother had been old enough to work. He'd hoped to be the only one to serve. He had done well in the army, coming in well before Pearl Harbor and climbing through the ranks to make major by the end of the war.

Ciernik combed back through his life again. His family had immigrated to America — Ohio, to be precise — his parents were both Polish. They had left suddenly when things had become difficult for people like them. Once they arrived, they had spoken Polish at home, but his mother had insisted on his learning English without an accent and had stuck him with a tutor, a neighbor who was a teacher, to perfect his elocution. His father, who came from the far eastern reaches of the country, had taught him to read, write, and speak Russian. He'd also learned German along the way. After his platoon sergeant decided that he was too smart to be a regular grunt, he became an infantry officer before going to airborne school. When Germany surrendered, he accompanied General Gavin's 82nd Airborne Division to Berlin where he was working as a liaison to the Russians. That was July 1945.

He thought back to the cellar in Poland. Nothing, but endless questions and a dreary, damp cold. November in central Poland was never pleasant, especially without a blanket. Even less so when under Russian interrogation. He'd had to think about what he would tell them, how much of his true story and how much of the lie. There were lives at stake here, he had to get it right.

He drifted back into the conversation only when Stevens spoke.

"Your relatives' village is Bran-zee-zix?" Stevens stumbled twice trying to get the pronunciation right, which is what woke Ciernik. "And you said it is about sixty kilometers northeast of Warsaw? Yes?"

"It's Brańszczyk." The name rolled off his tongue smoothly, unlike Stevens's attempt which sounded like a sneeze. "And, yeah, roughly sixty clicks."

"Okay. Tell us again what happened before the Russians picked you up."

"I flew to Warsaw from Tempelhof with a bunch of State Department types. They were being posted to the embassy there."

"Wait. You were on official travel or what?" Russell interjected.

"Permissive TDY. General Gavin personally signed off on my request. Once there, I hired a car and driver and we went out looking for any of my relatives around Brańszczyk, which is where my mother said they lived."

"Why did you hire a car when you could have used an Embassy car and driver?"

"They didn't have enough cars and it was a personal trip."

"Were you in uniform?"

"Yes, I thought it better to show my true self."

Ciernik drifted back two weeks to the drive. It was 1945, half a year after the war had ended, and the devastation across Poland had still been visible everywhere. Warsaw was not quite so bad as Berlin, with the exception of the Ghetto, but the countryside was only beginning to recover.

The old Opel sedan was in fairly good shape considering it had survived the war and they'd covered the ground quickly. He'd decided the best idea was to visit the local church to see if the priest had any ideas about his family. But before they got to the centre of the village, he'd seen a small tavern that seemed busy. He'd put his hand on the driver's shoulder and flashed some money.

"Stop here. Wait for me and I'll pay you extra. Give me a couple of moments to talk to these people."

Ciernik had climbed out of the car and crunched over the hard-packed snow to a group of local men who stood near the entrance. They had been startled and anxious to see a man in a strange uniform walking towards them.

He had introduced himself as an American soldier and explained in fluent Polish what he'd been looking for, staying formal but being as friendly as he could. That had seemed to change the mood. The locals had crowded in to hear him as he talked. Several asked when the Americans were coming to Poland and why he — a Pole — wore an American uniform, but he talked only of his search. All seemed well until one of locals cast a glance up the street and whispered, "*Milicja.*"

The locals began to melt away as two men in long, grey woolen great coats walked towards them. They both wore Polish insignia on their hats and carried Russian submachine guns. By the time they'd reached Ciernik, the locals had all entered the *tawerna* or disappeared around the corner. His driver, it seemed, had also disappeared.

"Greetings." Ciernik said. He had not been concerned. He was, after all, an American officer, an ally of the Soviet "liberators" of Poland.

"What are you doing here?" had asked one of the two in badly accented Polish, he noted.

"Looking for friends." Ciernik said.

"You will show me your papers."

Ciernik had recognized it as a command rather than a request. He'd pulled his Allied Occupation Forces Berlin identification card from his coat and presented it.

"I'm American Army, an officer." He said in simple Polish. He knew specific ranks would make no impression on the soldier.

The man had studied the card's four language description and authorization to be anywhere in Germany at any time without being hindered. Ciernik doubted he could read.

"But here you are in Poland. Where is your authorization to be here?" Again, bad Polish. He was tapping the card on his other hand.

Ciernik had fixed his eyes on the wall, entranced by his own recounting of his story. He glanced up at Stevens. "I realized these men weren't Poles — they were Russians. It was the first man's accent, he wasn't a native speaker."

He remembered what he'd said to the Russians. "I was told authorization was not necessary," emphasizing the "not." Tension now rising, uncertainty twisting him up inside.

The militiaman had studied Ciernik for a moment and then looked back at the identification. The second security man had stepped back and scanned the neighborhood just out of arm's length, his PPSh-41 at the ready. It was an ugly little pig of a weapon, a submachine gun with a drum magazine that held seventy-one rounds of 7.65 x 25mm ammunition.

"What happened next?" Stevens said, bringing him back to the present.

"They took me to what looked like the local constabulary office, though there weren't any signs outside. I was put into a holding room while they made a telephone call. I didn't hear them. I could just see them through the doors. Then, I was taken to the basement where I spent the night in a cell.

"The next morning, a couple of guys in civvies came to see me. They were clearly not Poles, even though they both spoke good Polish. They talked to each other in Russian and they obviously didn't realize I understood them. One had my identification card and kept looking at it. It was clear he had never seen one before. The other one persisted with questions about what I was doing there."

"What did you tell them?"

"Nothing other than my name, rank, and serial number and that I was searching for old family friends. They kept asking the same things over and over again. They wanted to know why I was there and who I was. I heard them say they weren't sure if I truly was an American army officer because I spoke Polish so well."

"How did they treat you?"

"Not badly, other than leaving me in a cold cellar like this to sleep for five days." Ciernik looked around pointedly.

"No worries, Captain. You won't be sleeping here," Stevens said, offering a half-hearted attempt to allay his concerns.

From the look on Russell's face, Ciernik wasn't sure if he could believe him.

"Who do you think these men were?" Stevens asked.

"The heavies. They looked like the kind of guys who decide who gets shot or not. In other words, Russian intelligence officers, probably NKVD. The other two on the street must have been low-level security of some type. Definitely not Polish."

"You're lucky, you know. The embassy told us they lost an assistant military attaché a while back. He went out into the countryside and never came back. They're still asking the Russians about him," Russell said.

"What did they say when they let you go?" Stevens interjecting again.

"Nothing. I did hear them on the phone talking to someone. They seemed worried that my ID card was signed by Marshal Zhukov's deputy in Berlin, General Gorbatov. In the end, they drove me to Warsaw, dumped me in front of the embassy, and left. I managed to find my driver later and he gave me my luggage back. Said he was sorry, but he didn't want to risk getting arrested by the communist militia. They always asked for money and if you don't have any, they locked you up until your family paid. I told him they were Russians and asked what he thought of them. He said they were worse. He was truly frightened by the Russians."

"And what about you? What do you think of the Russians?"

Ciernik looked at them with barely concealed malevolence. His patience was ebbing as he slowly stood up and stepped around the table. The two CI agents backed up, close to the wall, like hyenas who had mistakenly awakened an old lion from its slumber.

He smiled benevolently knowing his prey couldn't evade him and let them worry a moment before he spoke, an unmistakable edge to his voice, "Listen to me closely boys, I am an American. How do you think I feel about Russians?"

As he walked into the room, the MP in the chair outside the door stood up, unsure of what to do.

"At ease, son," Ciernik told the MP as he walked out. "Take a load off. We're done here,"

He'd returned to the States shortly after that. His wartime experience had been mostly forgotten as he'd continued his career. But then he'd gotten the offer he'd been waiting for, an opportunity to command a Special Forces unit in Europe. And he was back, doing what he needed to do to fulfill that long held commitment.

He shivered in the dark, never quite liking the cold even though it was part of his life.

A long, slender figure came towards him, quietly flowing down the path like a spirit. Dressed in dark colors, a long coat swayed gently. It stopped and waited, looking about furtively.

Ciernik stepped from the shadows. There was a gasp as the woman realized someone was near, then she relaxed, arms dropped to her side as he grasped her shoulders firmly, and kissed her cheeks lightly.

"Maja, my dear Maja," he said in Polish, whispering the words. Holding her face in cupped hands, he gazed deeply into her eyes, so close he was inhaling her breath, cloudy vapor, as she exhaled. "I've missed you. How are you, my dearest?"

Her face brightened with a broad smile; nervous but happy to see Jozef. Happy because it had been so long, nervous because she didn't want anyone else to see them together.

"I'm getting settled in. Roman is in a good job now, so they've given us a nice apartment. But I don't think you can ever see it. All around us live other military officers and diplomats, hardly any Germans. One of the other wives told me the police watch the place all the time, even if we're all trusted. And you, you're an American. If they saw us, there would be trouble, no matter what the story was."

"They won't know I'm American." Ciernik paused a moment, then thought it better to change the subject. "Do they treat you well?"

"Well enough. No, I can't complain. They protect me and have given me what not very many women back home have." There was a quiver in her voice. Jozef wasn't sure if it was nerves.

"Privilege, you mean?"

"That's harsh. But, yes, I suppose so. I don't have much to worry about." After a beat, she added, "Except maybe you."

He chuckled, his own bravado. "I promise I will be careful, Maja. There are people who worry about my past too. You know they all have long memories."

"And the present. We also have the present to worry about."

"Yes, that too. But I don't want to lose you again."

They both were silent, absorbing the stillness that enveloped them. It was as if the surroundings calmed their souls.

"I can't stay long. Roman will get home soon and I told the housekeeper I was going out to buy some food. I still need to do that."

"Otherwise, they'll be suspicious," he said. "Yes, I know. They'll think you have a boyfriend." He smiled at the thought.

"They'll say it's too soon for me to have a boyfriend in Berlin. They'll wonder and then ask more questions. Just like back home."

"Was it that bad there?"

"Not really, but there was no trust especially where I worked. Everyone is suspected of being an informer. Here it's worse. It's like the war never ended, only the enemy has changed."

"I'm not the enemy, you know that."

"I do. But they will assume the worst. You haven't married, have you?"

"Why would I do that, Maja? I don't need anyone else."

Maja laughed lightly, almost to herself. "It's funny, you know."

"What?"

"That it's too soon for me to have a boyfriend, so my neighbors will think something else."

"What else?"

"That I'm a prostitute or maybe dealing on the black market, I don't know. They always think the worst." She held up the envelope filled with 500 Ostmarks he had slipped her in his first embrace. They were worth almost nothing in West Berlin, but in the East, they often meant the difference between having food or not. "I don't really need these, you know. Roman brings home enough money and we have special diplomatic ration cards."

"Still, you might need money. Just hide them somewhere. When can I see you again?"

"Next week. Roman said he must go to Dresden on Monday. He'll be gone all week to participate in a conference. All the Warsaw Pact representatives will be there. I can get away. So, Tuesday. Does that work?"

"Tuesday." He thought a moment. "I will make it work. We'll meet here again, but I think I'll have a place we can go."

"It will be safe? I hope so. I really want to see you. Inside. Not here all bundled up."

"Go now. I'll see you next week." He kissed her cheeks again and held her close, relaxed, warm in his arms. Not tight, scared like before.

She looked into his eyes. "See you soon, dear. I love you." Then turned and walked away.

"I love you too," he said. If she heard him, there was no sign. *I love you*, he whispered again as she disappeared into the night.

5

"WHAT DO WE have?"

"A stiff in the wire."

"Come on, let's do a little better than that. I mean, I don't think the commanding general likes graphic descriptions. More verbal decorum, if you please." Chief of Berlin Base, Ted St. John was nothing if not proper.

"Why? I heard the general racked up quite a body count in the war and they were mostly our boys. So, he must be used to corpses hanging about."

"Let's assume he's moved upwards a notch into a more genteel society where such descriptions are abhorred. He has to deal with those folks from State and Congress all the time. More polite language then."

"Well, I'm not briefing him."

"No, you're briefing me. I get to talk to the general and I don't want any of your vocabulary rubbing off on me."

"Kind of My Fair Lady-like, boss?"

"Didn't you have a leave request in my basket, Palmer?"

"Yes, sir, I did, Chief. Alright then, what we got is a deceased American. He was found on our side of the border, dumped just past one of the inter-city crossing points, which was totally unmanned at the time. The *Berliner Polizei* called in the MPs, and I have a friend in there that knows to call me for things like this."

"How do we know he's one of ours?

"He's not one of ours. He's army. There was an ID card in the wallet. His name's Buchanan. David Buchanan. He was a CIC agent. One of the MPs who searched the body found a roll of film stuffed in his sock. I told the MPs it was a national security matter, so our photo lab is developing it. It was wrapped in a piece of paper with some notes."

Palmer handed the paper to his boss.

"Cause of death?"

"Either strangulation or a bullet. Wire marks on the neck and a small caliber hole in the back of his head. Pretty sure it was the bullet."

"Have we told the CIC folks yet?"

"No. Given our relationship with them, I thought you needed to know first."

"Good call. You might get to take leave yet."

––––––––––––

Palmer enjoyed taunting his boss, a staid Ivy-leaguer, whose full name as his passport stated was Theodore Horatio Edwin St. John. The name told you everything, St. John's privileged upbringing, his parents, where he went to school… But Charlie Palmer didn't push too hard because St. John had connections… As a cum laude graduate of Yale, former Office of Strategic Services officer in Switzerland during the war, Agency plank owner, close confidant of Allen Dulles, and now Berlin's Chief of Base, St. John knew people. The important kind. His parents must also have had humor, albeit White Anglo-Saxon Protestant humor, because they named him "Theodore Horatio Eduard," which everyone in Greenwich shortened to "THE Saint." But no one Palmer knew called him that, because Theodore Horatio Edwin St. John preferred to be called "Ted."

The tech finished with the photos a couple of hours later. They were acceptable but not great, and Buchanan's notes didn't add much. They could locate the building easily enough, the house number was visible in one shot and someone, probably Buchanan, had scrawled "Bornitz" on the note. Palmer knew there was a Bornitz street in East Berlin. The picture of the car was simple. It was a big Russian ZIM, only a government official would have access to that. As for the bigwig himself, it was hard to tell, the man was an unknown, at least the office didn't have anything on file that matched him. A second man was next to him, maybe a subordinate, his face was clearly captured on film, but he didn't look Russian. Also an unknown. The license plates on the car were East German government, not Soviet Occupation Forces. The note had a series of question marks next to the word "Bigwig." That photo would go in the TBI or "To be identified" file. As for the third man, St. John had no clue. Buchanan had just written "am col" in his notes and the face was blurred.

"What is 'Ay Em Col period' supposed to mean? Does he mean morning? And what's Col supposed to be?" he said, half to himself.

"If I were to venture a guess, boss, and this is just a guess, I'd say American colonel."

"So, he recognized the guy as an American officer? He could have given us a name."

"Maybe he wasn't sure, didn't know it, or didn't want to compromise the name if he was picked up."

"Perhaps, but now Mister Buchanan's dead and we're left wondering who this guy is. Very unhelpful of him."

Palmer doubted Buchanan had deliberately gotten himself killed just to make their quest more difficult.

"Do you think CIC can add anything to this? They or the MI detachment must have tasked him to do this surveillance. What have they said?" Palmer asked.

"I haven't told the CIC folks anything. I was going to speak with their commander, but I need some background."

"Do you think we should talk with CIC first?"

"Yes, and now that we have the photos, I think this would be an excellent time for you to go see them," said St. John.

Palmer wanted to ask why he had to be the one, but inside he knew St. John would obfuscate and make excuses, because St. John disliked the CIC chief that much. The boss delegated certain things and talking to army intelligence was one of the things Palmer usually ended up getting stuck with.

Charles Palmer — Charlie to his friends — had accepted the fact that he was a johnny-come-lately in the outfit. He had not attended the Hotchkiss school, nor had he sculled an eight-man shell on the Charles River, nor been inducted into a posh Harvard university frat in his youth. And he certainly wasn't married to the daughter of a Texas oil-man who made it clear to the boss, Ted St. John, that the road he traveled in life would be well-paved as long as he cherished, or at least tolerated the Wellesley woman he'd met and whom the father pawned off to him at the altar many years before.

In Palmer's case, that he made it through state university was something of a surprise itself. Coming from his hometown of Hastings, Nebraska, he didn't win a football scholarship and had placed in the bottom of the top half of his senior high class, so no one expected anything more from him than to take over his father's business. But the last thing he wanted to do was stay in his hometown and that was probably the fault of one man — his high school English teacher. Mister Wellington had encouraged him after he turned in a research paper on the war correspondent Ernie Pyle, saying that journalism was a noble profession, one that he too had followed before retiring at a young age to become a teacher in his home state. What Palmer learned later was that Tom Wellington had indeed been a journalist, but his work had been done overseas under the aegis of a shadowy organization known as the Office of Strategic Services. Wellington said his boss at the time, a guy called "Wild Bill," ran the organization as if it was a fraternity that had to work hard and party harder. The expectations of success were high, sometimes too high.

Wellington filled him in on a few more things when he returned home on summer break after his sophomore year. His former teacher was in mentor mode, probing for details on his scholastic achievements and his non-existent love life while treating him to an ice-cold beer at Wally's, which was Hastings' best bar. Between bites of his cheeseburger, Wellington enthralled him with tales of adventures in Casablanca and Istanbul during the war and gave him well-thumbed copies of *The Mask of Dimitrios* and *The 39 Steps*. Wellington provided the match for a fire Palmer didn't know he had inside.

Starting his junior year of classes, Palmer was excited about the prospects of journalism, writing novels, and becoming an intelligence officer. The last prospect was a bit daunting. Wellington had told him to worry about grades and he'd help with finding a newspaper that might need help, but he was elusive about the spy stuff and said, "You need some experience in the real world first. Go get a job in the big city. Forget about corn fields and cows." It all sounded good except to an impatient kid who wanted to jump the queue and go straight to the head of the line.

His first semester was going well and by November, Palmer thought he would graduate on time. He had sent out several job queries, but his mailbox remained empty and at one point he contemplated walking into the local military recruiting station, such was his desire to avoid returning home to Hastings. So, when his paper, "Shakespeare under the Influence of the Greeks," was returned ungraded, Palmer started to worry. There was just an ominous "see me" penciled on the cover sheet. Professor Gerald Scott was not a man of many words; his usual response to a well-written paper was "you can improve this." If a student received a failing grade, his paper would be marked "rewrite" in red script and, even then, an acceptable rewrite would be met with a grade of "D" or if you were lucky a "C." But Palmer had never heard of a student being called in to Scott's office and in preparation for the meeting he went through every possible permutation of what could have gone wrong before he even knocked on the professor's door.

Scott spoke in that sort of British accent that can only be affected by a pretentious American from New England. But it was only through the small details that Palmer divined that Scott was actually a gentleman from South Carolina who had an imperceptible drawl, but a very precise, patrician enunciation.

For an English professor, he sounded about right — he carried something like a pompous disdain for all other humans.

"Sit down, Mister Palmer." Scott directed. There was only one choice open to him, a ragged armchair that was free of books. The other was acting as a temporary storage facility for every spare paper, book, and box that would fit onto it.

"I liked your paper," Scott said. "overall, your performance in class has been very strong. You've been studying international relations along with your English program, is that not correct?"

"Yes, I'm hoping to have enough credits to add a minor to my major."

"But nothing in humanities?"

"No, I didn't think it'd add to my resumé," said Palmer.

"Your resumé? If all you want is a degree that's true, but if you want to be well-rounded, you should seek other challenges. You might try adding courses that would help you understand human behavior, especially if you want to understand the people you write about and not just the events around them. The alternative way to learn is to be a bartender, but you're too young, the pay is lousy, and life is too short."

And so began his first course in human direction. The subtle art of choosing someone and working to influence their actions, to grow and cultivate their interests, and move them onto an azimuth they might think is one they have chosen. Unlike recruiting an agent — someone who has already been radicalized, disappointed, made greedy, or subverted by something — and persuading them to give you their secrets. It was the craft of molding a person to be the ideal candidate for a mission.

But Palmer only realized everyone's interest in him was for something other than a career in journalism when Wellington showed up for what Palmer believed to be an impromptu event at the professor's house just before his graduation.

Scott had laid on a meal that surpassed what a simple teacher-student dinner should have entailed. There were huge Porterhouse steaks, not on the hoof as of yesterday but properly aged, and several bottles of wine. Unusually, there was also fresh lobster, not a normal dinner course for a casual meal in Nebraska. Scott said he had an "in" with the chef at the Blackstone Hotel who had fresh crustaceans flown in daily on ice from Boston. How the lobster traveled the additional sixty miles from Omaha to Scott's home in Lincoln was left a mystery, but they were much better than local Platte River crawdads in Charlie's eyes.

They finished the dinner with another new experience for Palmer, crème brûlée, after which Scott invited his guests into the study, part library, part storage closet for an after-dinner drink — single-malt whisky, naturally — and the conversation turned from literature and football to Charlie's aspirations. Charlie didn't see it at the time, but it was a classic, double-team, recruitment pitch with Scott extolling the virtues of service and Wellington telling more adventure stories. The bait they had agreed to use was simple — travel, adventure, and money. Okay, not so much money, but a decent paying job with security. They concurred that Charlie was the kind of man the Agency needed: not an Ivy Leaguer, but a guy from the street with a well-rounded public-school education — the fact that he had double majored and learned German on the side were pluses. But the real kicker was he possessed an innate ability to assess his fellow man; to know what drove them, what they feared, what they needed, and most importantly, how to make them do something he wanted them to do.

"Now then," Wellington said as he set the hook, "if you're interested, there are some guys that would like to talk with you. We've already primed the pump a bit, but it would mean traveling east to do the formal interview and tests. And it's all on Uncle Sam's dime." Which appealed to a relatively penniless Charlie Palmer. They had the paperwork ready for him to sign. And they would even send it.

"Just a formality," said Scott, eyeing Charlie over his reading glasses and puffing away on a briarwood pipe with a paternalistic smile on his face. "As Tom said, we convinced some key people in the system that you are a candidate they should consider for the program."

"It's a program?" said Charlie.

"Very much so, Charles. It's a strategic program that recruits the best and the brightest for the country. I am — I should say — Tom and I are what are called talent spotters in the trade. Having worked in the business, we know the kind of person needed. We look for the right kind of man for the job. That's what we think you are — the right kind."

He later found out that he was different from most of the other candidates. The others tended to come from Ivy League schools and, as one veteran explained to him, invariably "thought alike, spoke alike, and behaved with predictable similarity." He was expected to break that mold, and his first assignment was Bonn, where his ability for handling agents was quickly recognized. With several recruitments under his belt, including one hard target, he was destined for good things. He wasn't a household name in Headquarters yet, but if he played his cards right, who knew? Then came Berlin, not a hermetically-sealed, denied area like Moscow, but a fishbowl of espionage rivaled only by Vienna, Istanbul, or maybe Hong Kong, but with its own brand of danger — a bit of the wild West thrown in for good measure — and the reason why he carried a pistol on the street.

Palmer felt at home in Germany and especially Berlin. Not so much with the people, who he felt were haughty, cold, and officious, but the feeling of being in a good fight, for a good cause. His father fought in Europe and that's what he had called it, "the good fight." He'd come home and gone back to work, proud of what he had done. His mom had even worked at the nearby Naval Munitions Depot during the war. She never let dad live down the fact that she earned much more money than he did, $45 a week compared to his $70 a month. The good ol' days.

Palmer was now making four times what his parents did, so he couldn't complain. On top of that, he got overseas pay and what the State Department folks called the "unhealthful post provision" allowance — and Berlin could be unhealthful at times, just not quite in the way the Foggy Bottom green shades thought about it. He wasn't in it for the money though. He enjoyed the game and, as far as he was concerned, he was a journalist, although his reading audience was a bit more exclusive. An investigative journalist to be precise, finding out what was happening behind that thing the British Bulldog had called the Iron Curtain. The real story. That's what it was all about, because you couldn't believe the newspapers, *Neues Deutschland* in the Soviet Zone or *Bild* in the West and Axel Springer's *Die Welt* leaned so far into anti-communism it couldn't be trusted to tell the complete truth. Both sides relentlessly used the press to push their agendas, and no one was above fabricating their own version of reality. It was just a slight variation on Orwell.

That said, in his job, fabrication was a cardinal sin. Whether it was an agent making things up to keep his case officer happy or to make more money, or an Agency officer padding his case files or accounts, lying was anathema to Palmer who prided himself on verifying everything he reported to the Nth degree. If he couldn't make sure it was true, his reporting was heavily caveated, or he just didn't send it. Which always pissed off St. John because he was all about the numbers. The chief was a statistics man who went by the quantity of reports sent, not whether they made any sense. Almost any old crap would do, but Palmer wouldn't write it down if he thought the story was false, contrived, or just BS — that way the boss couldn't give it to a secretary to type up for him. Besides, he was saving the government's cash. Each character on a page cost real money to transmit, so he wasn't going to waste cash on trash.

But today's job wasn't about meeting agents or writing intelligence reports, it was about keeping up relations with the neighborhood or the "community" as folks in the business called it.

Major Shaun Myers looked more like an accountant than a military officer in charge of counterintelligence. With his large fish-eye glasses, thinning hair combed over a bald pate, the baggy uniform — he had a somnambulant way about everything he did — everything about the man screamed imposter. Maybe that's why his underlings called him "Yawn" Myers. Maybe that's why he hadn't been promoted. Senior officers were frightened by the witch hunters. That's what Myers was. He chased witches, rumors of witches, the scent of burning sulfur — anything that might lead him to the traitors who sold secrets to the devil. It didn't take much to start Myers on a chase, just a hint of impropriety and he would open a new file. Which is why he had files on hundreds of people he didn't trust. If he'd been married, he'd probably have a file on his wife's parents. Myers didn't worry Palmer because the army officer had no jurisdiction over agency people. Besides Palmer didn't have any baggage that he could think of at the moment.

Myers didn't bother to stand when he came into the office, so Palmer flopped into the gray GSA-issued armchair by the window.

"What's up that the Agency comes to see us lowly CIC folks?" Myers said.

"I'm sorry to inform you that your man, David Buchanan, is dead. Murdered apparently," Palmer said. He paused for a reaction.

Myers took off his glasses, rubbed his eyes, and pulled the sheet of paper he'd been typing on out of the Remington on his side desk and balled it up. He spun around in his chair and lofted the crumpled paper ball toward a trash can.

"I suspected something when he was late reporting back. What happened?" Myers said as he put his glasses back on. It was obvious he needed them to see because the paper missed the can by a good three feet.

Palmer was even more impressed by Myers' reaction to the news. One of his guys had been killed and he asked, "What happened?" without a shred of emotion.

"Not sure. His body was found right on the inter-city border. Was he yours and was he working on something on the other side?"

"He's ours or he was ours. If you're asking 'was he operational?' the answer is yes. He was working on a special project. And yes, we knew it was dangerous. Buchanan wanted the mission, so I gave it to him."

"May I ask what it was?"

"No. It's a counter-intel thing. You know I can't share that with you," said Myers.

"That's too bad because I thought we could help."

"I don't see how."

"No, right now from your vantage point, I doubt you could see. But it seems we have some photos that you might find useful."

Myers had played a few card games in his life and realized what was happening. "So, you guys got to him before anyone else. What are they of?"

"We got to him first, yes. And the pictures show interesting things. I would be happy to share them with you, all I need is a little information." Palmer had decided it served no purpose to tell Myers the truth of his relationship with the MPs. Nevertheless, it amazed him to no end how easy it was to get something with just the right kind of pressure. Manipulation worked on friends as well as enemies.

6

SERGEANT THIBODEAUX WANDERED the halls of the cavernous building, a drab, three story, concrete structure built after war's end. It was one of many such structures on the compound that housed the units and troops of the American occupation forces. He knew the layout intimately, but he found himself going over it in his head, just to stay alert. Thibodeaux was the Staff Duty, a boring name for boring work. He was essentially the security guard who made sure the building stayed secure through the night. Logistics on the ground floor, offices on the first floor, and team rooms on the second. He rattled door handles one after another to ensure all the doors were locked, spun safe dials to make sure they were secure, and manned the telephones in case the balloon went up or the commanding general had a bad dream. It was the second hour. Only ten more hours until relief.

Thibodeaux hiked up his trousers a bit as the gun belt he wore pulled them down. He preferred his pistol tucked inside his waistband in a suede holster. *It just fit better.* He would have liked to carry his own pistol, a Browning High Power, but he couldn't on duty.

He mused over the significant detail that he was the unit's last line of defense. If someone tried to get into the building, he had only two fall backs. The first was the alarm, the second was his weapon. So far, it had never come to using either, although one geographically-challenged, inebriated soldier from another unit came perilously close to dying when he pounded on the entrance door late one night. He was politely led off to his barracks by two of the building's occupants after being thoroughly but unobtrusively patted down for weapons.

If a Russian *Spetsnaz* kill team wanted to break in, the situation might prove different. That is, if they could even find the place. It was a good thing the intelligence warnings were reliable. He continued to wander through the building.

The ground floor housed the supply and medical sections, arms room, gym, and day room. Its central hall cut through the building and a single stairwell provided the only access from top to bottom to each floor. A few rooms were on the top floor for the younger, single soldiers who lived in the barracks. For the "kids," as the older troopers called them, it was an easy commute to work, especially after the trials by beer that were known to happen on weekends.

Thibodeaux spun the dials on every secure door and container before he scratched his initials on the check sheet as he made his rounds. Staff Duty rotated among all the junior non-coms in the unit, which meant he had the night shift once every two months or so depending on the roster the sergeant major kept. Boring, but it was a necessary evil. Who knew when a Russian commando might swim through the drain pipes and pop out of a toilet to surreptitiously open all the safes?

Then again, it could be worse. One asshole of a sergeant major down in Bad Tölz was known to put a paperclip under his office carpet and would check the next morning to make sure duty person had cleaned up properly. When one guy put all the paperclips under the SGM's carpet and said he thought that was where they were supposed to be kept, the stupidity ended. Well, except for that guy who put them there. He ended up with ten years of extra duty or something ridiculous. Berlin wasn't like "Tölz." It was relaxed on the spit and polish discipline, but ready to go to war quickly, living as they were right on the ragged front line of a new world war. Everyone was just waiting for Nikita to get wound up and declare war. For the moment, there was just staff duty. Which everyone agreed was … boring.

Each team had a big work room on the top floor. One wall was covered with maps and diagrams of bridges and power plants. Heavy curtains could be drawn over the documents for those few times a stranger might be brought in; a stranger being anyone from the unit other than team members and the commander or sergeant major. No outsider got to see the team's plans or maps and that included anyone from the other teams. No one. It was called compartmentation.

Thibodeaux completed his round and typed it up in the log. Routine security check. "NSTR," he typed—*Nothing Significant To Report*. He could have written more about the floors being clean and the plumbing in good order, but the document was preordained to go into the files never to be seen again, unless something catastrophic happened on his shift. He'd save his creative writing for a better cause.

Anton Imre Thibodeaux, an unlikely mix of Acadian and Hungarian parentage raised up in New Orleans, had escaped what he thought was a dead-end future by joining the army after his high school graduation. Had it not been a question of money, the university might have been an option, but he had no clue what he wanted to do, and his single mother really didn't want him hanging around the house while he figured it out. The local army recruitment office lured him in with photos and brochures. Slowly, the recruiting sergeant threw out little morsels of how wonderful a military life would be for a poor boy like Anton and how a world of possibilities would open up. The man must have come from somewhere deep in the mountains of Tennessee because he spoke with an accent so deep Anton had a hard time understanding it.

So, he was wary. Anton had heard the same spiel from guys on the street who were trying to sell him good deals on stuff that he wasn't about to buy into. Finally, he tried the aptitude test, which the sergeant said had no obligation tied to it, just to see what those possibilities might include. After the test was scored, the sergeant talked with his colleague a bit and then disappeared into the back. A couple of minutes later, a tall man came out of the back of the office wearing what Anton recognized to be a captain's rank, apparently to vouchsafe what the sergeant had told him. He actually held out his hand and introduced himself with a name Anton would have forgotten had it not been on his name tag. Montgomery, it was. On the other side of his uniform, he had two colorful lines of ribbons and some badges that looked pretty, but meant nothing to Anton. They would later.

The captain said, "Welcome and congratulations on doing such a fine job on the test. Sergeant Fields here says you're interested in the army and the test results say you are eligible for just about every specialty we have." He was smiling the broad smile of a used car salesman about to stick you with the biggest lemon deal ever, Anton thought. It didn't matter what side of the tracks you came from — the hustle was always the same.

"So, what do you wanna be?" said Sergeant Fields.

Not "What do you wanna do?" but "wanna be?" Like it was a life altering proposition.

In his early teens, Thibodeaux had thought about becoming a forest ranger or a marine biologist, but neither of those were in the brochures the sergeant had given him. But there was one other thing he'd thought about. It came from a movie he'd seen downtown at the old Prytania Theatre. It was called "The Red Beret." A bunch of Brit soldiers jumping out of aeroplanes and shooting up Germans all over Europe.

"I want to be a paratrooper," he said.

———

When Captain Mack Makinen came bursting through the door at 6:30 a.m., he was surprised to find the staff duty on his feet. More usually, the duty NCO would be leaning back in the chair, feet up on the desk, half asleep or maybe aiming an air pistol at a target someone had set up in the corner for practice.

"Thibodeaux! You're up and raring to go this morning."

"Nothin' else to do, sir. Ready for my day off. Then right into the weekend."

"Don't call me 'sir.' Big plans?"

"Nah. Do some PT, shower, and head downtown to see what kind of treasures I can buy off the Germans." Thibodeaux had made it his business to accumulate as many antiques as he could comfortably afford, everything from war memorabilia to Meissen porcelain. He'd learned a bit from a shop owner in the French Quarter where he worked a summer and kept in contact. With a bit of a markup, he could send stuff back and make enough money for college or that car he was thinking about.

"Well, see you Monday then. We've got a day of city training planned."

"Roger that, sir."

Makinen hadn't stopped moving and was across the basement hallway and up the stairs leaving Thibodeaux's last words echoing up the staircase behind him.

7

———◆———

PALMER WAS BEGINNING to think Major Myers might prove difficult to work with. Army people seemed to have an inherent distaste for civilian intelligence officers. Time would tell.

"Show me the pictures and I'll think about it," Myers said. His pupils were pinpoint like those of a ferret coming out of its hide into the sunlight. He took off his glasses and looked closely at the photo Palmer handed him.

"This was the first photo on the roll," said Palmer.

"I see a number, 212, what of it?"

"Bornitz Straße 212. That was the address your man was watching," said Palmer.

"Maybe it was. I need more," said Myers.

"And I have more, just throw me a bone here. Why was Buchanan watching a house in East Berlin?"

Myers put his glasses back on and sighed.

All the better to see you with, my child, thought Palmer, wondering how harmless Myers really was.

"We have an on-going investigation. All I can say is we got information that that address was being used by the *Stasi* as a safe house for meeting agents from the West."

"Anything more than that?"

"*Nichts. Rien.* Nothing."

"Okay, we can play a little ball then. Here's another. Know this guy?"

"Can't tell. His face is blurred."

"Your guy wrote a note that had the letters and I quote, 'A.M.C.O.L.' Any ideas?" Palmer said.

"He probably meant American. Do I get to see the notes?"

"You can have them; we made a copy. American, huh? That's what I thought, too. And the 'C.O.L.' — what's that mean?"

"No clue," Myers said, shaking his head and looking down.

You were a bit too quick with that, Palmer thought before moving on. "What about this one?"

"It's a Zis-110 with East German government plates."

"Great, we're on a roll. And this guy?" Showing the photo of the first guy who got out of the car.

"Not a clue."

"And this one?" The second.

Myers took a long hard look at the photo, turning it in the light at different angles, before he looked up at Palmer.

"That's an easy one. He's Michael Storm," he said.

"Who's Storm?"

"I thought you guys knew everything. We've heard he's a news reader for *BERU, Berliner Rundfunk*, the radio station in the Soviet sector. He's East German, but they never mention his name on the air," Myers said. He polished his glasses with a piece of calico fabric and put them back on. Judging by the handkerchief's age, his mom had probably given it to him in high school.

"A journalist? If that's true, then why the incognito stuff?" Palmer said.

"He's as much a journalist as a person can be in the East, no doubt. I'm sure he gets told exactly what to say. And maybe they want him to do stories without being recognized."

"Okay, so what's he doing at a *Stasi* safe house?" Palmer asked.

"I dunno. Maybe they were doing an interview."

"The Ministry for State Security doesn't use journalists to do interviews." Palmer waited for a response that didn't appear to be forthcoming. Myers just sat in his chair with an expectant look on his face, as if the Agency man would answer the riddle for him. Instead, half to himself, Palmer said, "So what was he doing there?"

"Your guess is as good as mine," said Myers. "By the way, did you find Buchanan's pocket flask? He had a nice old one."

"No. Maybe the MPs grabbed it."

The next face he met was an expectant St. John.

"It's a mystery, boss," said Palmer.

"One possible American maybe meeting an unknown guy and an East German journalist at a reported *Stasi* safe house. So, the only thing we have that is definite is a murdered American CI agent," said St. John.

"Like I said, a mystery. I think Myers is hiding something. I asked him about the 'C.O.L' in Buchanan's notes and he dodged the question really quick."

"So, the blurry guy might be an American officer?" said St. John.

"A colonel no less, and there aren't many of those in Berlin."

"He could have come up from the Zone on temporary duty or on leave." St. John always referred to West Germany as the "Zone," a reference to the areas created by the Potsdam Agreement after the war, as in the American Zone of Occupation. Not the "West," not the FRG, not even Germany. Just the Zone.

"We should check Tempelhof and the Duty Train," said Palmer.

"Not just those, you'll have to check all of the entry points, Check Point Bravo, Tegel and Gatow Airfields, and the Frog and the Brit duty trains as well."

"I think I have my marching orders, then. I'll make up a roster of all American colonels that were in Berlin that day."

"Both lieutenant colonels and colonels. He didn't specify what kind," said St. John.

"Of course, all the colonels. What else?"

"Send the photo of the journalist to the station in Bonn. See if they can dig up anything. If he really is who Myers thinks he is, he may have popped up somewhere else before."

"Done. I'll follow up. *Sonst noch was?*" said Palmer.

"Something else? No, nothing for you. See, I do speak German," St. John said, proudly displaying his scant command of the language. "But I need to go tell the general that he may have a small loyalty problem."

A small loyalty problem, he says. He makes it sound like his car needs a tune-up when the engine is about to seize. No, it's much worse than that. And it's not just loyalty betrayed that is a problem, it's the public relations nightmare that follows when the traitor is found out. Not to mention morale, because when a fellow government employee — be they soldier or spy or secretary — defects or sells his country's secrets, the whole organization suffers. The investigators come around and ask all sorts of obvious questions to find out who knew what and when, or why they didn't. And, of course, everyone around the traitor will be suspected of high treason for the rest of their career, if not their whole life. Paranoia feeds on secrets and then it eats itself.

But no, St. John calls it a loyalty problem, like a fan who forgot to wear his bright red Nebraska Cornhuskers team jersey to the football stadium or something. Sacrilege.

And there is a problem. And I think we may have a way to solve it.

Palmer gathered up his notes, locked them in the five-drawer, Class 2 safe, and inspected the city map on the wall one last time before heading out the door. Yes, Maria, the office secretary, could just as easily have called the Autobahn checkpoints, airport ticket counters, and train stations to gather the names, but it would cleaner and more discreet if he did it himself with some of his casual contacts and friends.

On the way out, he said to the chief in a deadpan voice, "I'm off on the hunt, boss."

All he heard as the door slammed was a faint "Tally-ho."

8

FROM BEHIND HIS desk, Captain Makinen was staring at the wall. More precisely, he was staring at the big map that showed the city of Berlin, tiny in the middle of a big East Germany. There were many flags stuck in the map, colored so the viewer could understand what he was looking at. Red flags for known Soviet military locations, green for NVA — the East German army, and black for the really important stuff. Black flags indicated his team's target set, more precisely, the targets Makinen's Team Six were assigned to destroy. Of the about two hundred flags, only seven were black and four of those were inside the city. The other three were not far outside, locations that could be reached on foot and attacked within forty-eight to seventy-two hours of the launch order depending on how the opening hours of the war went. The seven black flags didn't worry him too much, it was the 190 some green and red flags because each one designated a military unit that could threaten the success of their mission. That didn't even begin to consider the other million plus heavily armed Soviet soldiers that would be pouring over the Polish border and heading west to attack NATO. It was a prospect Makinen didn't enjoy thinking about, but it was his mission as team leader. The scenario was not unlike what he'd experienced in 1940, a war against a force far superior in numbers but not in training and resolve. This is where his team along with the unit's other five teams would thrive. *Or die trying.*

He was often the first into the team room — between he and his team sergeant, getting in early was almost as much a competition as seeing who could put away more booze in the evenings or get the most bull's-eyes at twenty-five meters with a pistol. Alone in the room, he wasn't thinking about how the task should be accomplished, or even planned, that was why he led a team of highly trained specialists. To start with, there was Master Sergeant Richard Becker, all-round bad ass — Jedburgh in World War II, 10th Special Forces in the early fifties, etc., Becker's career was legendary. Although Makinen was the senior officer and team leader, as with most SF Teams, it was Becker who actually led. He just cut "his" captain slack because Micha had once been an enlisted guy fighting the same enemies. Another guy, Rolf Kreutzer, one each Sergeant 1st Class in military speak, took care of the intelligence side of the house. Whether it was teaching proper tradecraft or running his local sources, he was the one who knew what was happening in the neighborhood. From there, it was the hard trades: two engineers who could build a school house or destroy a bridge; two medics that were one diploma short of being called doctors, but could still handle a Kalashnikov; two communicators who could run their own clandestine radio station from a basement; and two weapons guys who could build guns from scrap, one of whom could recite the lessons learned from Battle of Cannae in Polybius' original Latin. These were the ones who figured out how to execute the mission — that's what sergeants do. Officers were just for window dressing and to sign requisition orders.

Sitting in his GSA-approved, gray Naugahyde-covered, swivel chair, Micha "Mack" Makinen was contemplating the bigger picture. He'd been in this fight since 1939, first in his homeland and now sitting in the middle of what potentially could be the biggest battlefield of all time. Absent-mindedly, he felt the ring on his left hand, a gift from his father, following the contours of the wolf head with his fingertips, its silver smooth, well-polished from many such moments in his life. It was his talisman, a connection to family and home, his ground to life. *We who are about to die.... No, to hell with that. A whole bunch of you commie bastards will go down first. And Op Strangle was what would do it when the time came.*

9

————•◦•————

COLONEL JOZEF CIERNIK was not a physically imposing man, perhaps five feet nine inches tall, in reasonable shape, a little jowly, nothing special. If you noticed him at all and if he was in civilian clothes, you might mistake him for an everyday man, a nine-to-five kind of guy, probably a father that vacationed at the beach with his family every summer. Just a normal Joe.

On closer inspection, his eyes told a different story. An intensity in them hinted at the things he had seen, things most people would never experience. The ribbons on his uniform — when he wore one — some awarded in one war and the rest during a so-called police action said even more. To those who knew him, he was everything a commander should be. He knew when to manage from a distance, when to say what but let his people figure out how, and when to take charge and lead. Inside the man, it was hard to say. He didn't tell tales. Everything about him was under tight control.

They were six, squeezed into a room meant for three. Including the commander, Ciernik, there were his deputy, Major Thomas Brock, the unit's top enlisted man, Sergeant Major Carl Lynch, the recently arrived S-3 or operations officer, Captain Peter Thacker. Then, there were the members of Team Six, Captain

"Mack" Makinen, and his senior non-com, Master Sergeant Richard Becker. Three chairs, but one of them was the colonel's and no one was going to sit in it even if the boss was sitting on his desk. Brock found one and Lynch the other, leaving Thacker, Makinen and Becker standing. *No matter*, thought Becker. He was used to standing in front of desks, often being screamed at for some perceived infraction or another. That wasn't the case today. From the corner table, RIAS — Radio In the American Sector — was playing jazz medium loud, the windows were closed, shades drawn, and the probability of being listened to was about nil this deep inside the old Prussian officers school complex. It had been seized early after the war and turned into one of about seven American military facilities inside the western sector of Berlin. This building was given to the unit soon after they arrived, but only after a thorough rehab and pest control work. Once the specialists declared the building secure and free of bugs, they moved in.

Nevertheless, Ciernik was circumspect in his briefing.

"The specifics are outlined in the project folder you have. There are two copies, one for the headquarters section and one for your team, Mack. Both will be logged in and out of the S-2 safe every time they're needed and locked back up every night. I'm telling you this because it isa Top Secret code-word and if it gets out all of us, every last swinging Richard will be going to Leavenworth. Got it?"

Met with heads nodding their understanding, he continued.

"Note the code-word." With his finger he indicated a word in capital letters, EMBER. "That goes on every document created. And for Christ-sake, don't use carbon paper."

Everyone smiled nervously. After an accidental discharge of a weapon, the fastest way to get tossed from the unit — and probably the army — would be a security violation.

"This is our mission statement. 'The unit will establish a network of mission support sites inside the Soviet zone of occupation.' This is directed from the top, so we don't have a choice of locations. Those are provided and the ones in East Berlin are in your area of operations, so you're on the hook. At least they didn't give us street addresses, only general areas."

"They want us to put in caches, right?"

"Cache sites, yes. Buried, hidden, wherever they won't be accidentally discovered and where someone can get to them again."

Cache, spoken like the word cash but with an entirely different meaning. A hiding place for ill-gotten gains, loot, illegal substances, or, in this case, weapons and equipment of war.

"Who are these sites supposed to support?" Makinen said.

"More a what than a who. Contingencies, that's all we know. We put them in, and someone gets to use them when the time is right."

"For when the balloon goes up," added Brock.

"What are we putting in them?" Said Becker.

"Sterile weapons and ammunition, explosives, fuse, detonators, and medical gear," Thacker said.

"No commo gear?" said Becker.

"Some back-up sets. I assume those are for the ones they have already, but who knows?"

"It's all part of a bigger program," Ciernik said as he reached behind him for another folder. He held it up. The cover was blank except for the red Top Secret markings on the top and bottom of the page and in the center of the page a single word in black caps: KIBITZ.

"Where does this align with Op STRANGLE?"

"It doesn't. STRANGLE is our primary mission. KIBITZ is an additional task we've been saddled with by higher. Make it happen and then — forget about it," Ciernik said. "We just happen to be the best equipped to handle it, because the spooks sure can't."

"That means they don't want to get caught inside the Soviet Zone of the city doing this."

"Which leaves it to us. We aren't so risk adverse."

"Like the old OSS," said Becker. "We did this all the time."

"We are the OSS now," Lynch said.

"One more thing," Ciernik said. "We need to send someone across to meet the leader of underground, which they've code-named STORCH. We need to give him a new communications plan."

"Let me guess. The agency can't do it," Brock said.

"What I'm about to say stays with us only. This mission came to us directly through our headquarters in Paris from the agency's War Plans Staff Europe. That's their unconventional warfare office. He's the one who knows who's who in the underground on the other side. The agency's Berlin Base is unaware of us, or this particular program. Besides, I am told they don't have more than a couple of officers who can work in the Soviet sector."

"So, BOB doesn't know we're here? Are we going to tell them? We might cross wires otherwise," Lynch said.

"I've requested permission to brief them, but the seniors haven't given it yet. Until that happens, we'll be on our own. Anyway, WPSE has given us one name. He's the resistance leader."

"So, who gets the honors?"

"Gentlemen, you know your people best. You choose. But I would suggest someone who knows what he's doing but hasn't been read in on all of our operations."

"Someone expendable?" Lynch said.

"Not expendable. Someone who has the best chance of getting in and out successfully, but also won't or can't reveal too much if they are captured."

Thacker looked at Makinen, who looked at Becker.

Becker already had his answer. "Thibodeaux is my number one candidate. He's new, but he has recent experience in a denied area. Hungary."

10

HAVING TURNED IN his duty pistol and the log, Thibodeaux headed for the door. He'd changed into his running gear, deciding he'd wear a jacket to shield him from the weather. It wasn't quite bitter cold outside, but he didn't want to push his luck too far. Black watch cap and some decent, soft gloves he bought downtown. He had a small canvas rucksack that was usually big enough for the things he needed — which were basic — to get him from his apartment downtown to work and back when he was running. Otherwise, it was hop on the S-Bahn in civilian clothing and make his way around town like any other working-class rube. The only people who had cars were the ones with more money than he made. *Maybe next year*, he thought.

"Where you off to?" The booming voice belonged to only one possible source, the sergeant major.

"I'm running the Teltower Kanal then home. Hopefully, I'll make it to Nollendorf Platz later today to do some shopping,

"Souvenir hunting again?" Sergeant Major Carl Lynch said.

"I'm still looking for Otto Skorzeny's *Fallschirmjäger* helmet," Thibodeaux said. He'd already scored a few high-profile items, but he was still hoping for treasure.

Lynch had descended the stairs until he was eye to eye with the young sergeant. "I need you to do something for me if you have time."

"Sure, Sergeant Major. What is it?" Having time just became a priority.

"I need you to check on a friend of mine and drop him a message. Very discreetly." Lynch handed him a small, dark green, rubber capsule that looked like a waterproof Boy Scout snake bite kit. "Don't open it, I sealed it." He pulled out a small map segment and explained where to put the capsule. Then, he handed the paper to Thibodeaux and pointed at a spot. "Now, there's a gray *Bundespost* telephone connection box on this corner a couple of blocks away. After you leave the message, put a horizontal mark on its north side — the thin side. Just a small black slash with something, about two inches long."

"When does it need to be there?"

"Any time before midnight tonight."

Thibodeaux took in all the information and stared at the sergeant major a moment, trying to decide whether or not to ask more, then went with the simplest question. "I won't get arrested, will I?"

Lynch smiled his big, down-homey smile and said, "Only if you screw it up, son." As he turned to walk back up the stairs, he threw down one last tidbit, "And, by the way, don't mention this to nobody."

The canal gave off its usual frigid greeting, the air turned even colder and heavier as he stepped onto the path that paralleled the water's bank. His breath left a contrail behind him as he ran, passing the occasional dog walker who felt runners like him disturbed the perfect equilibrium they had achieved. They were even more perturbed when he yelled at them to clean up their pooch's *Hundekot,* a chore most native Berliners felt was better served by immigrant street sweepers. In cases like this, Thibodeaux generally sided with the Turks and Slavs, the *Gastarbeiters.* But he didn't flip the old woman off as most American soldiers would have, he just kept running while she barked at him doing a good imitation of her stupid, football-sized mutt.

He'd get serious in the next mile as he neared the area the sergeant major told him about. He ran on, passing the big power plant across the water on his right, small green parks carved out of residential blocks, then along the new construction site of the Steglitz Clinic and the Free University. The path pierced between tall apartment blocks before he branched off towards the garden colonies of Schöneberg. He didn't want to get too close to his objective, instead orienting himself on landmarks before turning off to find the metal box Lynch had described to him. Then, another dogleg before running to his apartment. He had enough information to walk a different route later, one that would allow him to service what he knew to be a clandestine dead drop and load signal that the sergeant major had tasked him with putting down. The question was: why?

11

————•◆•————

AT THE END of the third day, after traipsing around Berlin from Reinickendorf to RAF Gatow to Lichterfelde to Neukölln to Wannsee and then back to Dahlem, Charlie Palmer had a list just as the Chief of Base had requested. It was a list of lights and birds, all the lieutenant colonels and colonels who were in town that day. He thought. He'd done his best, including visiting all three RTOs — rail transport offices — then Check Point Bravo, Flughafen Tempelhof, and checking the manning rosters for all the units in the city from the Berlin Command from the top on down and sideways, because there were a number of units that weren't listed anywhere and a whole bunch of officers who worked in the U.S. Mission, which was in its own world. The roster's part was easy because there was a civilian secretary working at the headquarters who was sweet on him. He owed her a nice dinner out, but he'd get his op fund to pay for that.

"How many?" St. John wanted to know.

"Assuming we found them all, full colonels six, light colonels seventeen, in all twenty-three with TDYers. And that includes air force and army."

"What about navy?"

"The navy doesn't have colonels."

"Right. I knew that. Just testing you. Have you checked them out?"

"When would I have had time to do that? Besides, isn't this a CIC case?"

"It is, but with… that guy in charge, we need to look at it."

"You're saying Myers isn't capable of bringing this case to a successful conclusion?"

"He doesn't have a moth's chance in a flame-thrower contest. Besides, the general asked me to take it on as a personal favor."

"And if we find out who it is, what happens then?"

"The COB," he said, "the U.S. Commandant of Berlin that is, gets a real bad problem taken care of before it bites him in the ass."

"Meaning he doesn't want to lose his shot at being promoted to three-star."

"Something like that," said St. John, who knew a thing or two about getting promoted.

"So, I think we need to start with how this all got started. Like how and why Myers got the info on the safe house to begin with. How's the easy part. The why might be tricky."

Might be tricky. That was already clear to Palmer. The why could be anything and mean anything or mean nothing. It could look like one thing and be just the opposite, a mirror image of the truth or a lie. And to get Myers to divulge the why would require either direct questions, which probably wouldn't work, or deception. The problem was that Myers was a counter-intelligence officer and despite most people's tendency to think of CI as an oxymoron, he was well-versed in seeing through subtly-laid verbal booby-traps and cleverly rigged mind games.

Palmer had a trick or two of his own up his sleeve. For one, he listened more than he talked. Contrary to popular belief, extrovert intel officers who talked a good game missed a lot of what was happening around them because they never shut up. It was the introverts, the listeners, who got it. Second, he didn't ask many questions. Never answered them either, if he didn't want to. Rather, he turned them around in a way that suggested they be looked at from a different direction, taking the conversation off tangent to reveal what he wanted to know. It also made his partners feel as if they'd been drained like a bathtub once they realized he'd acquired the information he sought, if they ever realized it at all.

Palmer gave Maria a job to do and she was happy to do it. He knew that anything that got her out of typing the chief's expense reports and his other drivel made her happy. So, she was calling around town to all the units and their spouses asking if this colonel or that one might be missing a watch from the party that just happened to have occurred the night Buchanan was killed. After two hours of calling around, she'd accounted for eighteen officers well enough to eliminate them from the list. That left five. A call to the manager of the temporary officer's quarters at Harnack House eliminated the two who were up from the Zone on temporary duty. That made three his new lucky number.

12

IT WAS NEARLY pitch black as he walked the path between the small garden plots. Small cabins sat inside fenced-off plots, mimicking a lilliputian village tucked inside a hidden valley. Most of them were dark, not hooked to the power grid, the owners had gone home to their even smaller apartments at night after several hours of pruning, planting, and drinking warm *Schultheiß* beer during daylight, and schnapps in the evening. It was too late in the year for any serious gardening though. Everything was in stasis, waiting for the warmth of spring to begin the cycle again. And the drinking could be done in a warm, cozy pub.

Anton Iskander Thibodeaux was bathed in the shadows. It was a place he was comfortable in and had been since he had felt he was alone on his surveillance detection route, the one he'd mapped out in his head during his earlier run. It wasn't a provocative route, but he did allow for some channelization that gave him good opportunities to check his back. Nobody was there, he was pretty sure of that. The scratching of tree branches in the breeze, car noise, and snippets of music and voices came to him from the surrounding apartment blocks that towered over the city gardens. The buildings filled with their human occupants seemed much further away from where he stood isolated in this sanctuary, one of many inside the city, places that kept people sane, he thought. The rest of the city was still recovering from the war, there were still ruined buildings — some districts worse off than others, especially in the East — shattered by British and American bombings or Russian artillery fire. The greenery, the plants and animals, the lakes; in his mind, the only place better to be was the Grunewald, in the western part of the city. That is, if you didn't mind the occasional pack of wild boars chasing you down the trails and through the woods.

He wasn't here to relax and he walked on, not the hunted but the hunter, careful in his movements, watching and listening for anything that seemed out of place. It might be a much different story in the Soviet sector, but he wasn't worried about threats. There was no predator that he couldn't deal with here. He had only one job, get to the spot, place the drop, and move on. Just don't be seen doing it or, if you are, do it in a way no one knows what happened. Misdirection, deception, that hidden imperceptible moment when the magician does his trick. No one sees, no one saw. There was no one here to see his slight of hand, it was too dark, too isolated. He walked on, coming close to a fence, brushing along its wooden slats with his hand. A metal pole. A gate. The fence began again and then, just inside, came a raised flower bed. If you were close enough you might have seen his left hand cross over, pause a moment, and return to his pocket. But probably not. The drop made, he walked on into the blackness of the night. One last task for the night, his antenna was still out, checking for visual clues or, more importantly, that gut-instinct that would tell him to break off. He saw the box where he was to put the signal about the same time he felt the danger. A van parked behind him, the sudden feeling, the hunch that something was off. But he had nowhere else to go. He was locked into the narrow path at the street's edge. He would blow off the signal. Something wasn't right.

The two men who came out of the shadows were fast, faster than he was. He cursed his lapse as his arms were quickly pinioned behind him. The night went even blacker as a hood was thrown over his head. A punch in his shoulder, a burn, and he felt himself wobble, suddenly his will to fight ebbed. He could still hear though. An engine cranked, he knew the sound, a Mercedes starter. A sliding door rolling back to a full stop as the truck lurched from its place, then quickly stopped next to him. Head pushed forward, a hand on his shoulder, arms held tightly, his shoes scraped the ground, then he fell forward onto something soft, a mattress. Not a word was said, he couldn't speak. A sharp crack, the door smacking his ankle hard, legs kicked, feet pulled inside, and the door slid forward again, finally closing. He pulled himself into a fetal position. All he could do was try to protect himself like an armadillo from a coyote. Head spinning, his world went black.

He awoke to hurt. He fought upward like a diver in the ocean who let his precious breath go too soon. But there was no light to swim to, just darkness. His body angrily swore at him in a language he'd heard before but not in such intensity. His brain throbbed, a steady hum hurt his ears from the inside. He was troubled — not panicked — because he couldn't see. He tried to touch his eyes, but he couldn't. He kept swimming, up, slowly, until he felt the rough rope binding him. Something dark around his face, he blinked, eye lashes brushing something soft, blocking the light and his vision. He wondered why. He was in the Allied Zone when he loaded the drop, not the Soviet side. Who would have any reason to? He rolled over on the hard surface. He kicked with his foot, and it bounced off the tense surface. Not a bed. His sniffed the fabric, his nose next to it smelled the canvas, a cot. He rolled again and smelled the dankness of damp stone and plaster. A cellar, maybe an old house. He tried to sit up by swinging his legs over the edge.

A scrape of a chair. Someone got up, muttering. A sharp pain in his arm, the same spot, a hand holding him. It became darker as the world swirled like a merry-go-round. Dizzy. Black.

He didn't hear, he felt the door open. The air moved. How much time had passed, he had no idea. It was cold, dampness permeated the air.

He could feel them close by. Sound, footfalls on the stone floor. Metal on metal, a knife being sharpened?

"*Wieder bei uns?*" Back with us?

They're speaking German, talk German back. But he remained silent. His excellent German was tinged with a bit of an Acadian accent and was often confused with someone from Alsace. He also knew this was not a time for the standard name, rank, and serial number. He had no idea who was in front of him, where they were from, what they wanted. Best to wait.

"Tell us why you went into the park last night. We saw you there."

No beating around the bush with these guys. Straight to the point.
Silence.

The rush of air he didn't hear, the pain he did. A rubber pipe — he assumed it was rubber — slapped his upper arm hard, a sharp, biting whip against his back. Searing pain across his shoulders, waking up the bruises of ten minutes ago.

"*Wach auf. Verfluchte Hund.*" Wake up. Damn dog.

"Who are you? What do you want?" Anton said, wincing from the burning that penetrated deep into his muscles.

"Answer me."

"I don't know what you're talking about. I was walking, stopped at the bar. Why am I here?"

He was almost pleading, an affectation he learned. He could have responded angrily, but he didn't. He wasn't a tough guy. Not here. He was just ordinary, nothing special, *langweilig—boring.*

The minutes blurred. *Or hours?*

He smelled burning tobacco, sweat — his sweat, their tobacco. And maybe his own fear. He didn't know what the hell they wanted or what more they might do to find it. As a soldier, he knew he was bound not to reveal secrets. Even if he told all, that might not protect him. What did he know that might be important, besides his whole reason for being in Berlin? Was it just his appearance near the park or did they suspect him of leaving a message? The sergeant major told him not to tell anyone, he assumed that meant everyone to include people who were beating on him.

More questions followed, not so much the pain. Hours, days? No sleep, no food, no water, no opportunity to take a piss even. Just stupid questions about his mom, his dad, where he lived, why he was in Berlin. Thibodeaux had three lives, two of them he needed to hide — his real background, especially his training, and the reason he was in Berlin — he told them the third tale, the one that put him in Berlin. That lie was his truth as he told it, the innocuous job he had, the boring life he led, everything but the true story. He repeated the reason he was outside last night, his cover for action, why he did everything he did, except what he actually did. That question never came up, he had no contradictions, no mistakes they could exploit. Yet, they persisted. The questioning stopped and he heard the shuffling of people leaving. It was quiet. He still felt a presence, a hand on his head. Then the hood was whipped off. The light blared, he winced, then opened his eyes again. A man stood in front of him. He looked like a Cossack. Rough wool clothing, rougher face. Slavic, it was a face he didn't know, a big mustache and stubble of a beard. Big hands shoved him over onto his stomach and he felt the rope release its bond. He lay silent, then he heard the door close. He didn't know what time it was when they left, but he waited before he moved, not sure if he was being watched from the other side of the wall or door. He walked to the door, silently across the cold floor. His shoes were gone, but he still had socks.

He looked through the tiny, grated window and saw the expanse of a warehouse. A huge space filled with old wood crates, and steel gantries. It looked abandoned. At the other end, a door. Looking around the periphery of the door to his cell as best he could, he saw no one. He was standing close, then stepped back, his weight came off the door, it moved, just a bit. He stared at it for a moment. Grasping the handle, he pulled, lightly at first, and when it moved more, he stepped to the side and pulled further. It swung open.

He stepped out and looked all around him. There was only one door he could see, it was across the open bay of the building. He walked toward it, stiff from being tied up so long. Quietly, his eyes searching everywhere. He couldn't believe it. The door was coming closer, he didn't want to rush, not yet. Then, he was there. Another small window to look through. A corridor to another door. He saw the sign. *Ausgang.* Exit. Daylight and green beyond.

He pulled the second door open and stepped inside, his nerves jangling, almost there. *But how much further?*

One step, two steps. Quiet. He stopped and listened. Another step.

"*Stehen Bleiben.*" Don't move.

He bolted. Hands of men from in the shadows grabbed him from behind. The hood went back on. Handcuffs this time. They walked him back, then around, finally another door. And sat him roughly in a chair. He waited, two sets of hands on his shoulders, he was not going anywhere.

Finally, he heard a new voice, one he hadn't heard before. This one was calm, relaxed. The others had been angry, urgent, demanding, relentless.

"Have you been truthful with us?" it asked.

"Yes, of course. What do you want from me?"

There was a brief silence. The hands left his shoulders and he heard movement, footfalls. One, no, two people walking across the floor. The door opened and closed. Not a word. Movement close to him and the hood was pulled from his head. His eyes were blurry. He felt his hands released and he rubbed his wrists then his eyes. He looked again. Becker and Makinen were standing in front of him, arms crossed, not too close, just in case he reacted. To the side, a small table with a platter filled with *Brötchen* and cuts of meat and cheese. A glass of water lured him. He grabbed it and drank it all in one draught.

"You did good. Sorry you had to go through that, but we had to know." Master Sergeant Becker said. "You okay now?"

Thibodeaux wasn't upset; he was relieved. "Had to know what?"

"How you would react," said Makinen.

"A test?"

"Yes, a test. You did fine."

"What for? Does everyone get the same treatment?"

"Eventually they do, yes. But there's something we need to do very soon, and you'll be part of it," Makinen said.

"What about my day off?"

"That was Monday. It's Wednesday morning now. You might get some comp time later, but we need you to get ready. Top will take you home. Relax and come to work mid-day tomorrow." said Makinen as he moved toward the door. "And one other thing…"

"I know," said Thibodeaux. "Don't mention this to anyone."

13

MAJOR GENERAL CORNELIUS Barksdale, Commandant of Berlin, sat at the head of the long table in the center of his office, a place Ted St. John called the throne room. The general's chair stood imperiously on a wooden dais that made him seem taller and more omniscient than even the two silver stars on each of his shoulder straps indicated. Somewhere, there was probably an army regulation that dictated how high his chair could be elevated over the others. St. John imagined it would say a four inches lift for a brigadier and major general, add another four inches for a three-star, and a full general would be entitled to a full foot. You weren't supposed to notice things like that as a commoner. He wasn't even sure how many commoners even got to see the great man.

That was probably why the general's chief of staff — whose activities St. John knew were accounted for on the evening in question — asked him what rank Palmer held when they were met at the door. Ted told him not to worry; after all, Ted was a super grade and could get away with that.

"Frank, it's okay, he's with me. And he's a GS-15. That's the same rank as one of your bird colonels in our speak. That's the one above you, right? He just looks young. What are you, Palmer? 25 years old?"

"29, Chief." Charlie didn't mention that he was only a GS-13, the equivalent of a major.

Having had his face rubbed in it, Lieutenant Colonel Frank Barnes was not pleased. It had taken him eighteen years to make 0–5 and that was with West Point and two wars under his belt, which made him forty-two. Granted, he'd never seen combat, but he knew how to run an ops center, write memos, and make coffee better than most. And for those reasons, he held a grudge against spooks who seemed to skyrocket up in rank based solely on their ability to trick people into selling out their country like used car salesmen or arrange assassinations of third-world potentates. In his book, that wasn't fair play. As far as he was concerned, gentlemen didn't spy and didn't read other people's mail — unless it was his wife's because, technically. she wasn't a person. So, begrudgingly, he showed the two civilian intruders to their chairs at the opposite end of the table and retreated into the shadows.

The general began because, after all, he was the one who beckoned the Agency base chief to his office in the main headquarters building. Also because he was concerned.

"Mr. St. John and?" He paused, waiting to be told.

"Palmer, sir." Palmer spoke politely.

"Mr. St. John and Mr. Palmer, I asked you here today because I have a problem." He never used the royal "We" because he was in charge. No spreading of glory for this man. Blame — well, that was a horse of a different color.

"I discussed this Buchanan incident with my Chief of Staff, and I'm concerned. I talked to the Joint Staff at the Pentagon about it too. Secure line, naturally. Nathan — I mean — the Chairman expressed his concerns as well."

Effective name drop, St. John noted. The Chairman probably didn't know him from Adam.

The general continued. "We agreed that we can't let the Reds murder our people. The Soviets are trying to run us out of this city again. First, it was Stalin's blockade, now that commie-bastard Khrushchev wants to try and force us out again. You told me that, didn't you, Ted?"

"Yes, sir. I did." St. John was pleased the general remembered his first name as well as the intelligence assessment he had written up for the folks at Langley. Berlin was a huge sieve for East Germany's communist economy and through it the lifeblood of the country was slipping away to West Germany. If they didn't staunch the outflow of workers crossing the intercity frontier to West Berlin soon, the East would wither and die like a plant without water. The only way to stop it was to force the Allies to abandon their little "Outpost of Freedom" and retreat to their homelands. But Eisenhower wasn't about to let the Soviets push them out, even if the French didn't agree with him and the British angled for some nebulous compromise.

"So, what I want you to do is this. Find the guy that killed Buchanan and take him out. Remove him from the board," the general said.

"Do we have the legal authority?"

"This is an occupied city. It's my call as the commandant."

"Do we really want to do that? If it's a Soviet who's responsible and we take him out, we're guaranteed a tit-for-tat brawl," St. John was going with the unwritten codicil that the Agency and the KGB didn't kill each other's officers. He was also questioning the legality of the whole thing.

"I thought you said it was the East Germans?" the general blustered, now standing, all five feet seven inches of him, plus the extra four inches provided by the stand.

"It probably *was* the East Germans, but they don't dare have a bowel movement without the Russians' permission," said St. John.

"So what if they do have to ask permission? Our man's dead and since when do you folks play by the rules?"

"Generally, when it's a matter of self-preservation."

"So, you're afraid the KGB might come after you?" the general said. Used to getting his way, he stood with his hands on his hips, doing his best imitation of what he thought George S. Patton would do. All he was missing was a holstered Colt revolver with the ivory grips.

St. John, on the other hand, was doing what he did best. He glared back trying to find a good answer, knowing full well he could be asked to leave the city quickly if he didn't do what the general wanted.

He started to speak….

Palmer interrupted, offering an escape route. "We could make it look like an accident."

St. John and the general both looked at Palmer with what might have been newfound respect, but the general still had questions.

"But an accident won't send them a message. They need to know it was us. We want them to understand they can't mess with us Americans."

"They are paranoid, even if they can't prove it, they'll understand and get the message. It'll just be indirect," said Palmer.

The general chewed over that for a while. "Okay, come up with a plan and brief me before you go anywhere with it. Understood?"

It was just then St. John realized he was now stuck with devising an active measures plan to whack an East German or a Sov and briefing that plan to Headquarters. A worried thought made him rethink the wisdom of having allowed Palmer to tag along in the first place. *Of course, dropping the whole thing in Palmer's lap and going on leave was an option.*

The general waved them out with a sweep of his hand, "Thank you, gentlemen. By the way, there's one last thing, the Chairman gave me an early warning. POTUS will be in Paris in several weeks for a Heads of Government meeting with Prime Minister Eden, President Coty, and all the other little NATO countries. But after that, he's going to come to our little town. Secretly, no announcement, so get ready."

"POTUS?" Palmer said on the way out.

"President of the United States. POTUS is an old newspaper telegraphic code," said St. John. "And how exactly do you intend to *accidentally* kill whoever it is we have to kill?"

"Give me a minute, I'm still working that out. Besides, we still need to find out who is responsible."

"And find a traitor at the same time," said St. John. "Look at it this way, Palmer, at least we're back in the game." St. John was starting to get enthused about the idea of messing with the communists.

"I wasn't aware that we were out of it."

"Well, I was getting tired of just doing this intelligence stuff. Now we can play a little game of hard ball with the Russkies. This place is too boring."

"I guess. Might be fun. Who knows?"

14

AFTER HE LEFT the building alone, Palmer contemplated the wet, gray cobblestones in front of him, step by step, trying to take in his surroundings as well as not to slip on the uneven surface. On one hand, being distracted by the stones while trying to watch for surveillance was a disadvantage, on another, it was as good an excuse as any to use to look around from time to time. Which was exactly what he was trying to do. Walking through the Tiergarten, only now beginning to take shape again as the green space it was before the war, Palmer was thinking about the plan he didn't yet have and it complicated things having his mind occupied with murder, retribution, and the upcoming secret visit of the president.

He had wondered, what do we do during a presidential visit? Historically, not much, St. John told him. Agency people don't protect VIPs with anything other than the threat information they collect and share with the Secret Service. Early warning, you might call it. We collect intel from everywhere; like one giant Hoover sucking up everything and anything that might be useful and usually a whole bunch of what's not. Sorting through it all is the key. And the pain. The only saving grace was that the Agency folks could always be ready to go to ground and hide until the visit was over.

St. John later said it was called Operation PRIMROSE. Palmer suspected that whoever had the job to think up codenames must not have consulted with the White House on that one. The main attraction was the POTUS whose radio call sign was "Providence," so at least the Secret Service had some sense. For Berlin Command, the whole thing was an enormous inconvenience. One might think that a visit by the president would be a good thing, an honor to host the head of the most powerful country in the world. That is, if you're not on the receiving end of an advance team of petty bureaucrats who believe themselves supremely entitled and, more importantly, who think they outrank everyone. All they had to do to get their way was say, "The president would like this." and it becomes so. Even if the Prez doesn't really want something, they say he does for their own damn convenience.

Palmer was beginning to think the office had a bit too much on its platter. Beside finding a possible American traitor, knocking off a communist killer, and listening for signs someone might make trouble if they found out that Ike was coming to town — a lot to ask of people who were just trying to do their day job — they had to collect intelligence and decode Moscow's intentions for world domination.

He headed south off what was left of the Bellevue Allee and the remains of the *Bendlerblock* rose before him. Not long after he had arrived in the city and the first time he'd seen it, he was surprised the former headquarters of Hitler's Army had survived the battle for Berlin in 1945. He decided the Russians must have needed the office space.

He could see the building complex well because the forest had been denuded of trees, their wood fed into fires during the long, cold winters after the war. Approaching a small stream, he was met by a set of stairs, not many, three in fact, but with typical German efficiency there was a handrail on one side leading to a footbridge over the water. Strange, he thought looking around. There was nothing but cleared ground around him. Many of the villas and embassies that had stood south of the park before the war were gone, blown out of existence by Allied bombers and Russian artillery. Maybe some safety expert decided an old person might fall, he decided.

He reached for the rail to hoist himself up the stairs. He stopped midway, his hand slimed by some gelatinous substance on the rail.

What slug left this here? He shook his hand, freeing it from most of the disgusting mess, and wiped the rest off with a handkerchief. He paused — an epiphany — and a plan began to swirl about his brain.

Br'er Rabbit and the Tar Baby…a trap. "That's the ticket!" He said out loud, surprising himself.

He knew who Rabbit would be — the killer — but who could play Tar Baby?

Palmer stopped momentarily, stored the plan away in his orderly mind closet, and went back to focusing on the surroundings. It would do him no good to compromise the meeting, his source or, for that matter, himself thinking about old folk tales.

He looked across the barren park, shorn of its cover, the trees stubbled and shredded by the consequences of war. There weren't many people around, but he still felt vulnerable. Most of the black marketeers had been cleared out, but he could see a few sellers and buyers milling in front of the burned-out hulk of the

Reichstag. People still risked coming for the goods they couldn't acquire anywhere else. That is if they had the cash or something good to trade. He didn't linger on the sight long, his eyes were swiveling, not his head.

His father mentioned keeping his head on a swivel when he was fighting the war, always looking for an enemy ambush, a machine-gun position hidden, or a sniper carefully camouflaged in the hedgerows of Normandy. In combat, it didn't matter if people saw your head swivel, because if the enemy saw you, you were already dead. You needed to be sure no one had that chance to kill you. But, in this business, you didn't do that because anyone watching would know that you were watching back. Only criminals, police, and intelligence officers do that, not normal people. Most folks on the street were oblivious to what was happening around them. So, he did his best to find natural ways to look around, behind him, without sending the signal that he was aware. They had taught him well at the Farm and he'd practiced it on the streets of Bonn, where he learned the hard way not to assume anything. Blend with the masses, all the men in gray, the women in black, do nothing that didn't make sense and bore the trackers to death.

He decided the Tiergarten was too open — more cover was needed and plunged back into the built-up, urban jungle of the city. This section of Berlin was a mix of rubbled buildings and those few somehow untouched by war. It was in this terrain that he felt comfortable, a place he could lose himself in and anyone who might be following him.

His route took him east, stair-stepping through the streets, the dark blue sky of evening dropping over the town like a dense blanket. It turned to night early in these latitudes. Earlier in the year, he generally went to work and came home in the dark. Now, he had until just after dinner. He was hungry, but food would come later, after he'd finished what he came to do. South of Potsdamer Platz, he crossed Zimmerstraße and entered the Soviet sector evading the active control points not far from where Buchanan was found dumped like so much trash.

Enabled by a quick look-back at an intersection, he checked himself one final time and entered the churchyard almost sure he was alone. He felt clean, no lingering doubts, no pit of the stomach anxiety. At least for that one moment because you were never totally, unequivocally, one hundred percent sure. If you were sure, then you were stupid. Besides, the place gave him the chills, tombstones and monuments to people long dead were hidden in the shadows. He'd used this site once before and just had to hope there wasn't a phalanx of *Stasi* heavies waiting to swoop in and arrest him. He stood near a monument, a tall winged angel, its marble blackened with the passage of time and the smoke of wars past. A tall figure moved confidently toward him. *Right on time*, Palmer thought. He stepped out to greet his asset.

15

————◆————

SEVERAL KILOMETERS AWAY, Anton Thibodeaux realized his only reason to be in the Soviet sector was a death wish he hoped would be long delayed in coming. That and his overwhelming desire to pull the wool over the *Stasi's* eyes getting into hostile territory and out again without being noticed. The pre-war S-Bahn car rocked back and forth on the uneven parts of the rail-line as they moved towards the East like a drunken sailor walking down the Reeperbahn.

Makinen had told him what needed to be done. Meet a man, take some contraband and don't get caught. Sounded like a Chandler novel. He'd done the training, given by old OSS/Agency vets who had run things against the Fascists — whether German, French, Italian, or Croatian to name a few — back in the day, and he had done similar things in Hungary.

He was running black or almost black. A skillfully forged East German identity card was in his pocket but, other than that, he didn't have much of a cover story. Despite what the intel officer had said, he wasn't sure challenging the DDR customs officers so directly was the best idea. He also knew that although travel was not restricted between West and East, an American would always be regarded with suspicion, as would a

West Berliner. He thought he'd return on foot across one of the less travelled routes he knew of that were often unmanned and unwatched. If he made it in at all.

Anton was dressed in his best work clothes, stuff he'd bought through some of his dealer friends who brought things out of the DDR to sell to the "rich" people in West Berlin. Looking around him, he saw many of the people were dressed like he was, down to the cheap ersatz leather briefcases and metal lunch pails. Instead, he carried an old German army rucksack, well-worn and shabby, suitable for a worker. There were the two "*Wessies*" who dressed like they were taking a stroll down the Ku'damm. He stayed close to them hoping that when the checks did come, the officials would spend more time on them, hoping for a payoff.

The train clanked slowly across a bridge with a wide street below. When he saw the big sign with the words "*Anfang des Demokratischen Sektors von Gross-Berlin,*" he knew he was in another world — the communist side. *Beginning of the democratic sector of Greater Berlin. That's a laugh,* he thought with a smirk. He looked around to see if anyone registered his reaction, but no one was paying any attention.

The train lurched forward as the brakes squealed, slowing down in approach to the station. The first stop in the East was Friedrichstraße Bahnhof, but he didn't get off since checks were most intense on that platform. Some people got off and the officials came on, two of them moving toward him through the car, gray uniforms with green trim of the customs police. One checked documents, while the second watched the passengers. The newspaper in Anton's lap became his focal point, watching, but not being seen to be watching. The door opened and the first man called out for documents to be displayed and, obediently, everyone pulled out their ID cards or passports as did Thibodeaux. What he hadn't counted on was that the West Berliners had gotten off, leaving him without cover. With a pleasant smile on his face — just a worker coming home — but a steadily rising heart rate as the officers approached, he waited. They seemed to be moving quickly. He hoped the inspectors would just pass him by. They didn't. He was too young to be working in the West, military age. Maybe that was what spiked the policeman's interest. He took Anton's ID.

"Home address."

Thibodeaux rattled off his pseudo address.

"Where do you work?"

"Borsig, in Tegel." He pulled out his Borsigwerke identification and his dirty hands told the tale of a machinist who had little time to clean his fingernails before climbing on the train.

"Why aren't you in the military?"

"I was. Mustered out because of my back."

"Disability card?"

"At home. I don't want to lose it over there."

"You should always carry it. Tell me, why don't you get a job in your own country?"

"I hope to. I'm waiting to hear from Zeiss in Jena. I've applied to them. That's my dream job. Working with optics. Binoculars, telescopes, and such," Anton said, gushing out his story.

The officer's eyes glazed over. "Good luck with that." They moved on.

Anton tried not to smile. His theory worked — a decent cover story generally overwhelms the questioner. This time at least. His legend wasn't deep enough to sustain a protracted interrogation session with the *Stasi* in the bowels of Hohenschönhausen.

He disembarked at the next station, Oranienenburger, and started the second leg of his journey on foot. The thrill of passing the first inspection gave way to the tedious routine of surveillance detection. He'd run similar routes in Budapest, but that city was confused with a revolution about to begin, and no one was acting normally. Security in East Germany was far better, the police and state security, the *Stasi*, had things well in hand. The place was oppressively controlled with watchers everywhere. Worse than when the *Gestapo* were running things he had been told.

Much of the rubble in the Soviet sector had been cleared, but vast tracts were left empty, shells of buildings and no funds to rebuild. It was dirty and seemingly grayer than West Berlin. Not too far to the south, Anton saw three huge gasometers, looming spheres where the city converted coal to gas. Smoke billowed out of the plant's chimneys, obscuring the night sky and what city light was behind it. The furnaces below painted the cloud with an ethereal orange glow. He shuddered and walked on.

He employed all the tricks he had learned from the agency and incorporated some of the ideas his teammates had tossed out, the smart ones at least. When he at last turned into Bonhoeffer Straße several hours later, he thought he was clean. He had run into no unusual people, had no coincidences, and doubted there was any static surveillance — except the old ladies who were perched like owls in their apartment windows. *Just look harmless,* he told himself.

Number eighteen, a dingy, gray walk-up on a plain, gray street. All the buildings in Berlin were tinged with the dirty soot of the cheap, lignite coal used to fire the electric plants or make gas. During winter it was bad, a yellow haze hung low over the city and colored everything with its monochrome dust.

He walked past the stairs and turned into an alley, more a tunnel barely wide enough for two people, through the damp, grimy passage to where a back entrance hid in the darkness. He grabbed the handle and turned it slowly until the pressure on the frame released and it sprung inward slightly. Unlocked as it was supposed to be. Anton stepped inside and closed the door, the square glass windows, loose in their frames, rattling slightly. It made enough noise to make him look over his shoulder to check that he hadn't been heard. As his eyes accustomed to the dark, the interior details slowly emerged.

Following the contact plan, he took the stairs up to the second level and lightly pushed the door to the apartment on the left. It swung open freely on well-oiled hinges, revealing a corridor as dark as the stairwell. He stepped inside and shut the door softly, pausing to sense the surroundings. It was dead quiet. He smelled several days' worth of stale air, cooking oil, boiled sauerkraut, and human occupation. It reminded him of his bachelor uncle's house in the lower 9th Ward back home. Except for the sauerkraut.

The scrape of a wooden match broke the silence, and a flame flared in the next room. It settled to a constant glow, wavering a bit as the light spilled through the open door and illuminated the hall. Old paintings hung on the wall, a dark wood cabinet stood at the far end, a couple of old hats piled on top, and what he could see of a long, threadbare carpet lay on the floor, wrinkled like the shed skin of a snake.

He peeked around the door jam and found himself looking at a living room. More specifically, an older man sitting in an armchair who peered back at him. A couch and another chair stood around a low table where a candle burned, its flame flickering. The light played on the man's face. Maybe mid-forties, Anton thought. His sweater draped loosely around his shoulders showed how thin he was. A small, travel-sized chessboard sat on the table, a game obviously in progress. But Anton saw only one teacup.

"Are you Frederick?" The man said.

"Are you König?" said Anton. The response to the challenge given, he continued, "I've come a long way, I hope all is quiet here."

"It is. The door would have been locked if it wasn't. You should call me Rudolf by the way."

Anton placed his rucksack on the couch cushion and went through his "mad minute," a review of security and emergency procedures. That out of the way, he pulled a small radio, an Ilmenau 210, and two cans of corned beef, out of his rucksack and put them on the table, being careful not to disturb the game in progress.

"These are for you, Rudolf. And you can call me Klaus."

Rudolf picked up the radio and looked at it closely. "I could have bought this here, in fact, I have a similar one. And I hate corned beef."

"Give your old radio to a friend. This one's special. It has a short-wave transceiver to pick up and send messages. And the corned beef isn't corned beef." Anton fitted the opening key, turning it around the can until the top popped off. A package was stuffed inside. He pulled it out and unfolded the wrapping to expose a tape recorder.

"There's a spare in the other can. You can record your message on the tape, connect it to the radio, and send it to us. It plays back ten times faster than it records."

Anton went through the procedures and laid out two small message pads from a hidden pocket in his coat. One-time pads with fifty random five-letter groups printed on each page, one for receiving, one for transmitting. "Unbreakable," he explained, "as long as you don't use them twice. One message, one page, then burn it when you're done. From here on out, all your contacts will be by radio." He detailed how information and orders would be passed once the balloon went up. "And you need to find a good place to hide the recorder and the pads, so they won't be found. Not in this apartment."

"It isn't mine anyway. Only a safe place. What if I need something or have an emergency?"

"First, do you have a telephone?"

"No, I use my neighbor's."

"Do you trust them? If someone calls, can they get you a message?"

"Yes, but it would have to be something easy and safe. She's an old lady."

Anton pulled out another envelope. "Good. There are a few simple code words, and your emergency contact plan is in here. Memorize them and burn the instructions. If you use it, we'll be in contact within twenty-four hours. Give me her number just in case."

"What is the plan after that?" Rudolf said, scribbling down the number.

"I don't know. It's in there, but it's only for you and my people in the West."

"But you're from there."

"I am and I'm not. Because I can travel, they tell me what I need to know for each trip. But not everything. That way I can't reveal too much if I'm picked up."

"Then tell me why you are here."

"To check on you, to make sure everything is alright. You are alright, aren't you?"

"Yes, but I need money."

"I was ready for that." One last envelope came out of the bag. "Six months' pay in advance. Further payments and anything else you might need will be left in Dead Letter Drops. You'll receive a radio message with instructions and directions to each DLD. They will be used only once. Got it?"

"Yes. What else?"

"Your mission," Anton used the word *Aufgabe*. In German, its meaning was totally encompassing, meaning: mission, task, purpose, role. "Your mission is not to collect intelligence. It is to be ready for war, yes?"

"Yes. We are ready, but we need equipment and specifics of what we should do. What are our targets, for example?"

Anton had left the best part for last.

"This is how we are going to support you." He outlined the concept of KIBITZ without giving its name, the general mission, or the locations of cache sites. No specifics, not yet. Those would come on the cusp of war. The teams had put too much effort into the selection and emplacement of ten sites inside East Berlin and no one wanted the weapons and explosives being pulled out and used early or compromised before the time was right.

"Questions?" He said finally.

Rudolf sat back. "No questions. Well, maybe one. Your accent. Where did you learn German?"

Anton thought he had spent a lot of time getting a proper Berliner accent into his speech, but a long discussion often brought out nuances of a second language. "My mother is Hungarian. It's her fault." Anton, nonplussed, stood and gathered his rucksack, checking to make sure he had all his stuff. The meeting was over.

"No fault. You just need to be aware. You Americans are always so sure of yourself. Like thinking you can plan something without anyone noticing." Rudolf sat back.

Surprised Anton said, "What have you heard?"

Rudolf smiled. "Did I surprise you? You didn't know, did you? Funny, our people heard about it last week."

Anton wanted to say that his bosses didn't tell him everything, but didn't. That would show lack of control. So, he improvised. "You heard what? You heard something, but don't you think it's amazing? A few lies here and there, disinformation spreads faster than the truth."

Rudolf looked at Anton a moment with an expression somewhere belief and skepticism. But also uncomfortable. "Whatever your people are doing, tell them to beware."

"Why? Is something being planned?"

"Not exactly. I mean, nothing specific that I know of. One of my contacts said something strange to me. He said, 'The King's Bishop is bad.' He always speaks in chess riddles."

"What's that supposed to mean? Which king?"

"Your king, I think. Listen, I don't trust anyone in this city. You shouldn't either."

Anton calmed himself. Rudolf's earlier criticism stung him, and this new information worried him. He didn't know what to make of it and deflected by looking at the chessboard closely. "What will be your next move?"

"It's Black's move. What would you suggest?" Said Rudolf.

Anton paused. "I'm not very good. Maybe, knight to G2, to capture White's pawn."

"Going for my rook? Look up King's Pawn openings when you get home. My checkmate in four."

Anton grimaced. "Told you I wasn't good at chess. I guess I should be going now. Goodbye, comrade."

"I'm not a comrade. I'm a freedom fighter," said Rudolf, standing suddenly with enough vehemence in his voice to tell Anton he had made a mistake.

"I'm sorry. I don't mean you're a communist. You're a fellow soldier like me."

"Maybe I can forgive you this time, Klaus." But Anton saw how he hated the word.

They shook hands, Rudolf's was soft, uncalloused, not a laborer's hand.

Anton turned and took a couple of steps but paused at the hallway, looking back at the chess set. "That's why you're called King, isn't it? Because of that."

Rudolf relented and smiled. "More than that. It's because I'm a Grandmaster."

16

AS HE MADE his way west through the streets, Anton kicked himself inside for antagonizing König. He had been lucky so far, but small mistakes could lead to big disasters. It might be as simple as an asset who decides his handler doesn't value him or a suspicious police officer who hears something strange in his voice. He reviewed what he had said over in his mind trying to pick out the words that could have given him away. It wasn't a *mir, mich* grammar thing; it was what was underneath, his *Aussprache*, his pronunciation. If he was going to do this again, he must sit down and learn with a Berliner who could critique him. He needed to better understand the people he was working with.

At the moment, he had bigger catfish to fry. Getting out of the Soviet zone intact was what he needed to be concerned with, and something didn't feel quite right. He'd left the apartment building using the rabbit warren of passageways, typical for an old Berlin residential block. Mercifully clear of most debris, he was able to make his way through to a parallel street and head into the city center, a dystopian patchwork of restored blocks, rubble piles, and cleared zones ready to be rebuilt once funding became available.

He thought he'd gotten away from König's place without being surveilled, but his unease grew. He didn't have a set route. He'd planned several in case he ran into check points, so he felt confident he could change to a more aggressive pattern of stair-stepping through streets with a couple of deliberate reversals. There was still no one behind him. Or in front. No cars either. Just quiet dark streets. He stopped, stepping into a doorway, just to listen and watch. For five minutes, he saw nothing except a man walking a crooked line to somewhere. A drunk probably on the way home. Anton decided to continue and headed in the direction the man had come from.

Ahead, he saw a sign for a movie theater and for a moment thought about losing himself inside until he saw what was playing. *Kampfgefährten,* the title on the billboard said. *Battle comrades.* A soldier embraced his young son on the poster, not Germans, but Koreans. North Koreans. He would not sit through a propaganda movie. That war should have been finished long ago. Instead, it simmered like a stew.

A block later the sight of a tiny *Kneipe,* a corner pub, came into view ahead of him. He checked the street signs, Oderberger and Kastanienallee, and knew exactly where he was — the Prenzlauer Berg district — still a ways to go from from a quiet place where he could safely cross the border.

What the hell, he decided and, needing a drink, stepped inside.

The *Berliner Biere* sign with a logo of a bear holding three beers above its head on either side of the entrance signaled what was on tap, not that there was much choice. The words "*VEB Getränkekombinat*" across the bottom reminded him he was still in a place where there were people's collectives for everything from farms to beer breweries to pubs. More a government monopoly than anything else — the people never seemed to benefit from the setup. He knew Berliner, it was a typical brew, no better or worse than the bitter dishwater they served in the West, where equally bad Schultheiss and Kindl ruled. He didn't like any of them, preferring the smoother Czech Pilsners. Those were hard to find, and he wasn't about to be picky at this time of night in this part of the city. Nor was he going to try any of the schnapps, reasoning they were probably distilled in someone's bathtub. He looked at his watch. Nearly eight p.m. He'd sit for thirty minutes or so to see if any strange people came looking for him before starting out again.

The interior of the Kastanien-Eck was as dreary as the outside. And, like almost any other establishment in the communist East, it looked like it was struggling to make a profit — although he wasn't even certain what the word "profit" meant under communism — for a bar with a clientele who looked almost as lean as the sparse decorations. It was mostly men who inhabited the bar. One woman was seated at the *Stammtisch* with two elderly men, better dressed than the rest of the people. It was interesting that in this supposedly egalitarian world a *Stammtisch* even still existed. *Some people really were more equal than others.*

He ordered a beer, dropping a single *Ostmark coin* on a pewter countertop that had somehow survived the war. When it hit the metal, the aluminum coin made a flat sound that was as hollow as the East German economy. He grabbed his glass and headed to a seat at a small table in the corner that had a good view of the door and the windows. Aside from the low chatter and an occasional burst of a laugh or an exclamation, it was quiet. The lack of music, undoubtably because the government-approved stations were so bad, left the atmosphere stale, almost oppressively so. Maybe he was used to the West where the laughter and the music were louder and the talk looser, but he sensed the patrons here were guarded in what they said when outside their homes.

A cute, richly endowed, young woman came out of the back of the bar and walked through the tables, putting empty glasses on her tray and speaking with the guests amiably. Eventually, she made it to Anton's table. His beer was almost gone, and he kept his hand wrapped around it protectively. She saw that and smiled. "No worries, I won't steal it from you. Want another? We have a great dinner tonight, eel in green sauce."

Despite feeling that he was about to retch, Anton smiled back. "No, I'm good. I have to go soon anyway."

"Too bad," she said. "You're new around here, aren't you? Haven't seen you before." Her *Berlinerisch* came so fast and thick that he almost missed what she said. With no music to blame it on, he almost panicked. König's comment about his accent had shaken his confidence. *Breathe, slow down.* He went with a generic, "Just got into town." He hoped she didn't ask anything more and decided to avoid that by gulping down the rest of his beer and handed her the glass saying, "But I'll be back now that I know you're here."

He wasn't sure how his forward approach would be met, but it seemed to catch her off guard. She froze as he stood up, pulled his jacket around him, and slung his rucksack over his shoulder. He smiled. She smiled. The last thing he heard was "I hope so." He was happy to be gone; his nerves were frayed.

Once outside, he took a moment to settle himself. The intersection gave him a good chance to look in all directions before he launched off again to the West. He'd work himself through the neighborhoods to the chosen cross-over and hope no checkpoints interfered.

Unease. He'd felt it before on the street, but never quite like now. He wasn't sure if was just anxiety or some kind of premonition, like a spirit chanting "Beware." He didn't know why, but he heard his spirit voice again tonight, telling him to be careful. He'd heard it in Budapest several times. He was more comfortable on the street there; his Hungarian was more than up to the task. In fact, several of the underground fighters asked him when he had left Hungary to join the American army. He didn't elaborate — he'd always been told that it was unwise to give up too much of your life story when working with foreigners. You never knew who might try to use it against you.

They hadn't spent much time in the capital, and when they did go, it was never more than two of them and almost always with one of their Hungarian counterparts. Several times, he'd gone into Budapest alone to case a hard target, but that had been rare. Most of the work had been in the forest, teaching the underground how to use Soviet weapons and sabotage tactics. It hadn't enough to help the revolution when it had finally kicked off in October 1956. They had been the only American team in country, the pilot team. Other teams had been supposed to follow, but when the President had decided not to support the uprising and the Secretary of State, John Foster Dulles had said Hungary "was not a potential ally," they'd been ordered out of the country. They had parachuted into the country five weeks before, so there were only two ways home: walk a week to get to the border or a variation of the versions they'd used to get there — so they had been picked up on Lake Balaton by a black SA-16 Albatross that landed under a half-moon. He could barely hear the airplane; it was so far out in the water. Their Hungarian counterparts had taken them out to the amphibian in two motor boats, quietly rowing until they were far enough from the shore to start the engines. They'd cruised out to where the plane had waited, bobbing gently in the water and loaded their gear in the bay then climbed up the ladder one by one, wishing those staying behind luck but knowing that they would not see many of them again.

With the door closed and everyone settled, the pilot had turned the big amphibian into the wind and punched the throttles forward. The fuselage had glided through the smooth water, small waves smacking the aluminum hull loudly as speed picked up, then he'd pulled back on the yoke slowly and broke free. Heading south, the plane had stayed low until the shore approached and he'd lifted it higher, but not so much that you couldn't hear the tips of the pine trees smacking the skin as they'd turned west.

He had felt at home in Hungary, even when running counter surveillance on the streets, maybe because of the time he'd spent preparing, paired with his language skills and lineage. Berlin was still new to him. He wondered if he should have begged off this mission because of that.

No, you volunteer no matter what and hope for the best.

Anton's confidence had been shaken, but now wasn't the time to worry about it. The proper *Aussprache — pronunciation —* wouldn't be worth a picayune if he got stopped at this time of night. He ducked into an alley. It was time to go black.

17

---◆---

"I'M DOWN TO two, boss." Palmer said at the door to the chief's office. His own cubicle lay close by in the sanctum, righteously called the bullpen. That was where the real work was done. At least the stuff on paper, the work of documenting meetings, writing reports, tallying up expense accounts, ticking hours until the next diplomatic event, agent meeting, dead drop, or brush pass.

"Two what?" Said St. John.

Palmer sighed impatiently. No one ever seemed to know what he was thinking when he said something. He was tired of always having to explain the full context behind his comments.

The rain was pattering overhead, hitting the copper roof of the BOB building in rhythmic splashes. He reminded himself not to have a metal roof on his house even if he could afford it. *Maybe slate...*

"Down to two colonels," he said. "There were only two colonels who could have been in the East at that time. I've eliminated all the others from the equation. That said, one of the others still might need to be careful. He was with a girlfriend at the time."

"In the West or the East?"

Typical. St. John always going for the dirt.

"The West. His wife thought he was involved in a planning meeting, but he wasn't."

"Did you tell her?"

"No, but I told him. He hates us now."

"Of course he does, but we could always ruin his career. So, who were the two?"

"One each Brad Monroe, Light Colonel. He wasn't at work and no one can pin down where he was at that time."

"What's he do?"

Cupping his hands around his ears, Palmer swiveled his head back and forth miming an antenna.

"What that supposed to mean?" St. John said.

"That he's NSA." Palmer didn't like saying the name. Some things were not supposed to be mentioned. The NSA, whose name was furtively whispered in Washington as "No Such Agency," was one of them. Nor was the fact that the NSA was turning Berlin into America's largest surveillance site in Europe, setting up a listening post atop a pile of rubble dumped in the Grunewald after the war.

"Oh," said St. John, apparently oblivious to the rule. "That would make him a perfect target for the Russians."

"It would, but I don't think we should tip our hand yet. At least, until we find the second guy."

"Who is he?"

"Don't know yet. There's a colonel listed on the manning roster but without a name attached."

"Meaning?"

"I believe it means he's under cover. There are a couple of units in town that aren't on the books," said Palmer.

"The army isn't telling us something…"

"The only reason I figured it out is that they need an accurate count of assigned officers for Congress. They haven't figured out how to hide those numbers yet," Palmer said.

"Well, if you found that tidbit, you should be able to find him."

"Couldn't you just ask the general?"

"He won't tell me. The only reason he tolerates our presence is because he's got orders that he must," St. John said. "Or when he needs his dirty laundry taken care of."

Berlin was still an occupied city. Occupied by the Allies after the war, that is if you counted the Soviets as allies. Unlike West Germany, Berlin was still under nominal control of the military governments, not the Germans. So, the army could get away with not telling anyone — including the CIA — what they were up to, which irritated St. John. The army's intelligence officers tended to show up where they had no business being … at least in his view of the world.

St. John almost turned to return to his office, but pivoted back to Palmer.

"Didn't you have a meet last night?"

"I did, with B/1. It went well, no problems and he's happy for the moment." The "B" was for BLACKGUARD while the number "1" meant he was the first in the series.

"Did he give you anything worthwhile?"

"Not verbally, we didn't have time. I'm breaking out his written report right now."

"And…?"

"Mostly stuff for the analysts: facts and figures on the army, some personnel changes. There's interesting tidbit about a leadership struggle going on."

"Between whom?" St. John lived for dirt on any of regime's leaders.

"Right at the top. Wollweber and Ulbricht had a bit of a knock down drag out."

"Where did he get the info?"

"Wollweber himself apparently. He is pretty sure the government is trying to get rid of him."

"B/1 is close to Wollweber?"

"They were in exile in Moscow together during the war. Came back to form the new government in 1945."

"So, the head of *Stasi* tells his bosom buddy, B/1, that he's going toe to toe with the head of the Central Committee?"

"From what I've read so far, that's pretty much it," Palmer said.

"Two things. First, that report needs to go out immediately. Second, tell B/1 he needs to find out what it all means."

"I'm on it. There are a couple of pages to decipher, but it'll be done soon. Then, I'll set up a message for him."

"Blind broadcast, right? We don't have time to wait for the next scheduled meeting. When is your next anyway?"

"Not for five weeks."

"Set one up for earlier than that. Maybe a week."

"Do we want to risk one so soon?"

"Yes. If there's going to be a food-fight, we need the details before it happens. You need to see him soon, no later than five days."

Palmer hated moving targets. The scheduled meet should have been a month off. Then St. John said a week. Now, 30 seconds later, he said it had to be even sooner. He shoved his papers to one side on his desk and started to make notes on some foolscap before he committed the message to B/1's one-time message pad for transmission. *Time to write a nice love note to my asset ... and find a new place to meet.*

18

ANTON STEPPED OUT of the alley just far enough to check out the street in both directions. Across the Invaliden Straße to his front was a cemetery. From here, it was less than a half mile to the West and he could almost smell it. A short walk among the dead and he'd be at the church and beyond that, Bernauer Straße. Then, he was home free. The street was empty, so he walked across quickly and through the open gate. No one ever locked the gates these days — too many people used the place for black market deals and romantic trysts. He could never understand that. *Who would want to fool around in a cemetery?*

It was a curious thing, he decided. How these places were always quiet. Even if the city around them was loud, inside the walls, the sound seemed to be absorbed by the green lawns and trees, even the stones themselves. Most of the trees here had survived the war and the tombstones and memorials were for the most part untouched. Some were tilted off kilter, but didn't seem worse for all that had happened here. That was strange because the Russians and Germans had fought hard for the center of the city.

He didn't like cemeteries. He'd avoided them since he was little and only went when he was forced to go visit this dead uncle or that dead aunt for some family thing. The only thing worse was going to the hospital to visit a relative when someone said, "you should go, it might be your last chance." The answer to the why part was always a bit nebulous, but it was also when he finally understood what the color "ashes of roses" looked like when a saw someone on the verge of crossing over. *Enough about death*, he thought as he moved forward, off the path, through the headstones, stopping every five yards or so to listen and peer into the darkness for intruders. He sensed a pair across the way, far enough not to be a problem. They were busy anyway, on the ground, entangled in each other. It appeared they were lovers, at least temporarily, because he heard no protests or words of anger. Nothing in fact, just movement beneath a dark pile of clothing. He moved further into the yard and began to see the outlines of the church steeple against the brighter sky of the West, lighted with the lights that were still rare in the communist East, and a suitable reminder that his salvation lay beyond the cemetery. Then, he remembered he would be required to return to the dark side in order to finish his mission sometime in the future. First things first.

The clatter of a S-Bahn train echoed through the neighborhood — he was surprised it was running this time of night. Moving forward, he tried to watch his steps, hoping not to fall into an open grave. He'd already seen one protected with a couple of boards, but there could be one the diggers had neglected to cover, and he didn't want to find it.

He came to a second gate and a second, much narrower street, but he needed to cross to get to the church. The wall was low enough that he could see along the street. He saw a pair of *Volkspolizei* at the intersection about a hundred yards away. They were facing the West, not watching his direction, so he decided to chance it and trotted across to the yard behind the church. He glanced toward the officers. Still oblivious, he was safe for the moment and passed through the entrance gate.

Into the arms of another *Vopo* policeman. Older, broader, quite portly in fact. In the dim light, the cop resembled the good soldier Švejk, a man who would rather be sitting on his favorite stool in a bar rather than on the cold street walking a beat. His wool coat billowed like a potato bag, unlike some of the younger, trimmer officers he'd seen. A constricting Sam Browne belt seemed to be the only thing keeping the *Bulle* from exploding out of his uniform, but the old Luger P-08 pistol in a clam-shell holster on his waist was still worrisome.

"Where are you going in such a hurry?" asked the cop.

"You scared me," Anton said. He bent over to breathe, anything to buy a couple of seconds, and stood straight with an affected exhale. "I was going to church." He indicated the building just tantalizingly out of reach.

The cop snorted. "At this hour? I believe you like I believe my wife. What's in the bag? Show me."

Somewhat relieved, Anton dumped his little rucksack on the ground and knelt beside it pulling out the half-crumpled newspaper he'd picked up in the bar and a can of Brazilian corned beef — the only real one he had brought with him — setting everything on the ground.

"What is this?" The policeman said, picking up the can.

"Beef."

"Beef? In a can? Really? That's something. Never seen it in a can before. Herring, yes. Sausages, yes. Never beef."

"It came from Brazil," Anton said, pointing vaguely toward the west. "A friend gave it to me."

The policeman tossed the can from one hand to the other while studiously and silently studying its flight path.

Anton broke the silence after a couple of seconds. "You can have it if you want."

The cop deftly pocketed the can in his great coat.

"Get lost, junior. Go to church."

Anton picked up his rucksack and dutifully headed off with purpose. He spotted an entry on the south side of the apse — the rear of the building which faced the East. It was closer and a better bet than trying the front entrance which faced the heavily travelled Bernauer Straße — it was probably watched by the *Vopos* or the *Stasi*, maybe even both. Stepping into a small, covered alcove, he hoped the door was unlocked.

The door was old-world construction. Heavy, dark wood with black, wrought iron strapping and pointy-headed bolts holding everything together securely. It was the kind of construction meant to keep marauders and ne'er-do-wells from breaking down the doors. Anton quietly turned the handle back and forth a bit and felt no resistance. Twisted a bit more to the right and heard the metallic slide of the bolt releasing its hold. *Apparently, the clerics don't expect raiders at this time of the morning.* Looking behind him as his paranoia dictated, he saw all was clear, even his "Švejk" had disappeared. He pulled the door open, expecting it to protest. Instead, it rotated on well-oiled hinges. Turning back to the doorway, he was about to step into the vestibule, but for the second time in five minutes, found himself looking into a shadow-cloaked face close at hand. A beard hid the thinness of the man in front of him. Dark rings under his eyes described weariness, the gauntness of an old man with many concerns.

"May I help you?" the clergyman said. Anton breathed a sigh of relief.

"I'm sorry. You surprised me. It's late. I was looking for a place…" Anton let his words dangle. He didn't have a good answer.

"To pray? No, to sleep maybe?"

"Yes, to sleep. It's cold and I don't have anywhere to go."

"Yes, yes," he said, a tired voice. "Come in, son."

The Church of Reconciliation sat like a forward outpost on the intercity boundary. Despite lying at the base of a U-shaped bump in the trace of the frontier that pointed into the East, it was the closest church to the West of any in the Soviet occupation zone. He'd seen the church's tall Gothic-revival steeple many times from the other side. In fact, its front door opened on Bernauer Straße, effectively placed on the border between the godless East and the god-fearing West. He'd never crossed into the East near here — somehow this time it felt like a good choice.

He'd been anxious and paranoid all day and decided this would be as good place as any to seek sanctuary and wait things out. After all, it was early Sunday morning.

The pastor led Anton through the nave to a room near a stairwell that spiraled into the steeple. Opening the door, he ushered Anton into the small space, not more than ten feet square. Two chairs, a couch, and a small table were the only furnishings. He recognized the images of Martin Luther and Philip Melanchthon on one wall from his youth and the Lutheran church where his parents took him to until he decided he wouldn't go any more. The image of Christ on the opposite wall completed the trilogy.

Anton stared at the paintings, the faces slowly disappearing into the aged, dark varnish.

"They are copies," as if Anton might contemplate theft of the church treasures. "You may stay here until morning," he said indicating the couch as a bed. "I am father Wilhelm, by the way."

"I'm sorry. I should have introduced myself. I am Klaus," Anton said extending his hand.

They shook, the pastor regarding Anton's eyes carefully as they did so.

"You're safe here, son. You should wait for the end of the early service tomorrow and leave out the front with our congregation. Many are people from the French sector and the *Vopos* never check them." With that and a tired smile on his face, he disappeared, shutting the door softly behind him.

Above the door, the cheap wall clock ticking away told Anton that he could snatch a couple of hours sleep before the early service. Close enough, he thought, only a couple of minutes difference from the *Glashütte* that adorned his wrist for this trip. He'd left the Waltham his dad gave him behind. As he settled back on the couch, his now empty rucksack serving as a pillow, he only wanted to make it through the sermon and quietly slip across the frontier and go home. And for the first time in a long while, he said a silent prayer.

19

PALMER WAS AT his desk doodling on a piece of paper, when St. John breezed into his cubicle.

"Tell me how we're going to do this," he said.

"I assume you mean eliminating the guy who killed Buchanan?" said Charlie.

"Yes. Killing people isn't really something I have had much experience with. Anything else, I can handle."

"I haven't killed anyone either, but the first thing will be to find out who bumped Buchanan off."

"You think it's the American colonel, whoever he is?"

"My gut feeling tells me it's not him. Probably a security guy. And Russian. The East Germans would have arrested Buchanan, I think."

"And you really think you can come up with a way to kill the assassin and not have it blow back on us?"

"Pretty sure, but it'll be tricky, boss," said Palmer.

"How so?" said St. John.

"Well, once we figure out who it is, we'll need to arrange a trap to lure him in. Then, maybe we can kidnap him or something. The Soviets will think he's defected."

"He won't come easily, whoever he is. And if he dies in the attempt?"

"Then, he's dead and we make him disappear."

"You have no problem with killing someone?"

"I'm not going to kill him. We need someone else to do that kind of stuff, whatever we come up with."

"All right, you may not do the deed, but you'll still be responsible. How do you reconcile yourself with that?" St. John asked.

"People die every day. Besides, the end justifies the means."

"Perhaps, but in the end, it will be our house that burns."

"Only if they find out it was us."

"How do we set the trap and who do we get to grab him? I can't ask Bonn for a kidnap team — headquarters would shut us down. It's the army's problem, not ours."

"I'm still working on that part."

20

"HOW'D DID THE meeting go, T?" said Captain Makinen. "We were a bit worried when you didn't check in Saturday night."

Anton Thibodeaux wasn't fond of being called "T." He preferred Anton or Sergeant Thibodeaux in formal settings, but he let it slide.

"It went well enough. I gave him the equipment and talked him through all the instructions. It was weird though. I mean, I know we're not really doing intel collection, but he told me something that one of his contacts picked up. He said, 'your King's Bishop is bad.' I mean, he said he thought it was our king, whatever that means."

"Top?"

"Incidental collection. It's permitted. I'll give it to the S-2 and he can run with it."

"Okay," Mack said. "What else, Anton?"

"Only that this time I didn't feel comfortable over there. I mean, I did at first, but then I pissed off König a bit and he called me out on my German. After that … I was too nervous. Anyway, now I know why he can't come to the western sector."

"Why?"

"He's too well known. He's one of the regime's reigning chess masters and is therefore a national asset. He needs permission to travel."

"So, this famous guy is one of the agency's secret assets?" Becker said from the other side of the team room.

"Yeah, but maybe they believe that's good cover. Anyway, he is connected with the underground." Makinen paused, clearly thinking about what he needed to say next. "You may have to go back over. You okay with that?".

"I suppose. Before I go, I need to practice my German with someone."

"Spend some time with Hilmar. He can help."

"Kullek? Why him?"

"Because he was born here. He speaks *Berlinerisch* and knows the city well. Even got the Iron Cross here in the war. He won't talk about it, but Uncle Adolf personally gave it to him in the Grunewald. I think he was fourteen then."

"*Hitler Jugend* then."

"Actually, he was *Volkssturm*, the people's militia, but don't mention it. He only talks about it when he's drinking."

"How'd he get into the army if he fought against us?" Anton asked.

"The same way I did. We both fought the Russians, not the Americans, and the army needs people who know the Soviets," Makinen said.

"And the East Germans," Becker said.

"And the Hungarians," Anton said, musing. "Maybe I should be back at Tölz where I can concentrate on the country I know best."

"Bad idea. We need you here. You might have had a rough time of it Saturday, but you made it in and out, and you recognized the problems. Each of us is our own worst critic. Just remember that with your experience in Hungary, you're far ahead of most of us doing this urban warfare stuff," Becker said.

"Was that my pep talk, Top?"

"Moving on to other matters…." said Makinen.

"Hold on, sir. I have a question," said Anton. "Is our team the only one doing this or are the others?"

"I can't tell you that," Makinen said. "I mean, I don't know myself because this is all compartmented. We get instructions from Thacker, the new S-3 and we submit our plans for review and, I assume, deconfliction, so we don't cross wires with anyone. Beyond the command element, no one knows the whole picture."

"So, they'll tell us if we're going to run into anything out there, right?"

"I would hope so. Why?"

"Because I felt like someone was watching me after I left König's place."

"You sure you weren't just paranoid?"

"Yeah, I'm sure. It's a feeling I get when I'm being watched."

"A feeling?" Becker asked. "How so?"

"I don't know how to describe it."

"I know what you mean," Makinen said. "It's the feeling that alerts the prey when a hunter stares too long. I saw it from the other end of the scope."

"I felt it in Budapest a couple of times. Once, I was walking with one of the resistance guys. Nighttime. Then I got it, goosebumps, the hair on my neck went up," said Anton.

"What happened?"

"I told my partner, and we hid in an alley. Two guys were following us. They turned out to be ÁVH."

"The secret police," said Makinen.

"Yeah."

"How did you figure that out," Becker said.

"Their identification cards."

"They showed them to you?"

"Not willingly."

"Okay, I don't think we need to know any more about that. But you did good then and you did good this time. Just keep listening to your gut and you'll be okay. Just remember, there are no coincidence in this business," said Makinen.

"I wanna know what happened to the ÁVH guys," Becker insisted.

"I don't remember," Anton said.

Some things were better left unspoken.

21

ANTON WAS EARLY to work that morning, the team room empty except for his team sergeant who looked up from reading some documents on his desk.

"Thibodeaux, the boss said that we might need you to go over again. You up for it?" Becker asked, dispensing with greetings.

Anton said, "Yeah."

"You don't sound elated about it. Still re-living the last run over?"

"I'm ready. The last one is done and gone. No sense in overthinking it."

"Worried about getting caught?"

"Getting caught? Of course, I'm worried, but I can't just quit." *Yeah, you prepare for every problem, but deep down you just had to believe nothing would happen. Otherwise, you'd never volunteer for this stuff. Or maybe it's the adrenaline.*

"You can say no anytime, Thibodeaux, but you'll be heading home pretty quick after that. No pressure."

"I ain't going nowhere, Top."

"Good man. We're going to have six people moving in the Soviet sector tomorrow night. Two from each city team, so we need to stick to our assigned areas of operation."

"Who else from Team Six?"

"Rolf, but you're both going in separately. Hopefully, you won't see him. Just coordinate your routes in and out."

"I can do that, but shouldn't you tell me what I'm supposed to do over there?"

"Hold your horses. I had to make sure you were good to go. I need you to service a drop."

"Put one in or pick up?"

"You're dropping a radio for an asset we can't meet personally. Here's the casing report for the site," Becker said, handing him the write up, map, and site sketches.

"More corned beef radio, then."

"Not quite. It's bigger. A full agent comms package, a SP-15, a West German radio transceiver set. In fact, that's it on the table." Becker pointed at a canvas chest harness with four pockets each the size of a thick paperback book. "You will have to wear that in along with the rechargeable battery belt, so I think the S-Bahn is out this time."

"I would have to agree," Anton said. He hefted the two belts and looked at Becker. "Heavy. It's what, fifteen pounds total?"

"Thirteen. Beats carrying a rucksack, and you get to leave it all there."

"When I'm carrying a rucksack, everyone knows what I'm doing. I'll have to wear this under my clothing and walk normal."

"Practice with it then."

"I will. I think I should also take my toys, just in case."

"I thought you might say that," Becker said. He pulled a dark blue cardboard box out of his desk and pulled the top off. "I recommend you take this. You know it?"

"One of my favorites — the High Standard HDM/S. I know it well. You're not worried about me carrying an American weapon?" Anton picked it up and made sure it was unloaded. He held the pistol up in the air examining its long, slim suppressor.

"Thibodeaux, if you get caught with a weapon, it ain't going to matter where it came from. It's quiet and it works. Just take lots of bullets and don't get caught."

"Just checking, Top."

"Right. *Alors, bonne chance et reviens en un seul morceau après.*"

"I'll do my best," Anton said, starting to leave. He turned back "I didn't know you spoke French."

"It's our secret. I was born in Strasbourg. When you're back, I'll have you over for dinner, maybe *Cervelas à l'alsacienne.*"

"Sounds good, but I'd be happy with a shrimp Po'boy."

"I don't do seafood this far from the ocean."

"What about eel? There's this place I found in the East…"

"Eel? Not just no, but Hell no. I don't eat river-worms, especially when they're communist."

———

Anton felt better on the street this time. Since he'd crossed the lightly guarded frontier into the Soviet sector, he hadn't seen Rolf or anyone else from the unit. Nor were there many uniformed police, but because there were always so many spies, spooks, undercover police, and criminals working this city, it was hard to tell who was who sometimes. He'd heard tales of close calls, someone who ran into a completely unrelated op while trying to do his own — you don't want to get close to anything that might draw attention, but it was a reminder of how alive Berlin was with illicit activity. East Berlin was not the place where he needed to see anything strange going on.

Evening in Berlin meant early darkness, except in high summer. The street lights on the east side were dim where they existed at all, making his job easier and harder at the same time. Easier to disappear, but sometimes harder to detect surveillance. He used the light and the dark to his advantage — he was confident that he was free of trackers as he closed in on his objective — the drop site.

When servicing a dead drop, there were three places where the opposition could nail you to the cross. The first was on your way into the site. That was a difficult proposition — if surveillance moved in and jumped the wrong person early, the agent making the actual drop might be alerted and abort his run. The second was to nail him on the way out after the drop — again, surveillance had to have their ducks in a row because the agent could bolt and evade capture. The best place to nail the agent was right when he stuck his fingers into the drop site. Then, a really good camera loaded with high speed film caught the spy with his hand in the hole as he looked around for surveillance. The guilty face always looked great during an espionage trial. With that, you could embarrass whichever agency or country owned the operation. Once you nailed the agent, you'd wait for someone to pick up the package. That's exactly why some clever spook developed a load signal — a location somewhere on the way out of the area after the drop was made. That way, if you'd arrest that putz before he had put up the signal, the recipient knew something had gone bad and could avoid it. However, there were no good ways to ensure you'd nail both the sender and the receiver, especially the first time they used a site. There was even less of a chance when the recipient of the drop hadn't been given the site location.

Which was why Anton was a bit more confident about this run. No one had used Site *TAUBE* before and, unless he had really bad luck or some block warden observed him in the act, he was fairly safe. To add to the difficulty, he wasn't inserting a tiny concealment device in a wall or dropping a fake dog turd on the ground, he had to shed his bulky harness with the battery belt and stuff them into the drop site without attracting attention. No simple feat. If anyone was behind him and saw he spent too much time in a spot, they'd come back and go over it with a fine-tooth comb. He needed to be free of the hounds and ready to load the drop quick.

He found an alley where he could get ready for the "operational act" as the instructors had called it. The day before, he'd practiced with Becker timing him as he shed the gear until he could pack it into a small bag in the shortest time possible and not look like a damn fool — maybe more like a dog shaking off water after a dip in the pond. His coat came off, followed by both harnesses. Everything laid tightly into the shoulder bag he carried in less than a minute. Not ideal, but it would have to do.

When he was finished and back on the street, he took a moment to make sure he was clean before he entered the danger zone of the actual drop. The whole run was dangerous, but this spot could get more than one person rolled up and stuck in a bad place. He owed that much to anyone courageous enough to need to retrieve and use the equipment.

The site was a park. *At least it wasn't a cemetery.* The cache location was behind a wall that isolated the underground cavity from wandering children. He found the space described in the casing report — a hollow concrete cistern under large flagstones — and quickly stuffed the heavy bag into it, replacing the cover that fit the opening perfectly. He brushed dirt and debris over the spot and, although darkness prevented him from being completely sure, hoped it was enough to conceal the spot. He backed out through the brush, his crepe-soled shoes quiet enough on the ground, but each rustle or twig snap unnerved him enough to cause him to stop, listening to the city and the quietness that surrounded him. He rechecked his gear. He didn't want to leave any tell-tales, and he certainly didn't want to lose his pistol. A quick self-pat-down assured him he was still armed, pistol, short knife, papers, emergency funds all accounted for, and he turned for home. Not a straight route mind you — too much determination in a westerly direction might be worthy of someone's attention — so he meandered.

As he walked, he realized that none of his nervousness had reappeared. He was calm, unworried, at least until the hair on the back of his neck stood up. *That feeling again,* he thought. *Someone is out there.* He walked on, stair-stepping through the neighborhood, using natural look-backs and rational direction changes to check his trail. Windows were useless — it was too dark and the glass too dirty to show anything but phantoms. Before long, a figure emerged. Far back, but it was the same figure repetitively in a place where there should be no repetition. No coincidence in this business, he remembered well his instructors saying. This time, he knew what he saw and it made him angry.

Last time, he had been in Budapest with his partner, Károly. He remembered how they had lain in wait for the two guys who were following them. His partner hadn't even hesitated, he knew what they were. ÁVH — the bad guys who had learned all their heavy-handed tricks from the KGB and had used it on his family and friends. Their mistreatment were the reasons why he had joined the underground. The two had walked into the alley with their cudgels at the ready, but not ready enough. Károly had his own weapon drawn, an Izhevsk suppressed TT-33 pistol. Anton had never seen him fire it before, but Károly had stood with his off hand holding the heavy suppressor while he aimed the weapon. The first goon had rounded the corner and Károly fired. The bullet had hit the man in the face, a barely audible *pffft* announcing its presence. The 7.62mm Russian bullet with an "X" that Károly had had painstakingly inscribed into the tip using a fine jewelers saw — turning the slug into a dum-dum — did its job and cooked the man's brain like scrambled eggs. He had fell backward dead as Károly had pumped the suppressor back and forth with his off hand to reload — the weight of the suppressor attached to the slide kept it from cycling the action on its own — and had fired again, hitting the second man in the back as he had turned to run away. He'd only taken a step and had fallen forward to the ground, his face hitting the sidewalk hard. One more round in the back of the neck for each had finished the job.

"Just like they do to us," Károly had said.

Back in their forest camp, after Anton and Károly had reported the results of their mission to the commander, they'd sat on the edge of a campfire, talking quietly. Then, Károly had gone quiet. He'd stirred the embers with a long stick, sending a cascade of sparks into the night.

"Why did you come here, Anton?"

"I'm a soldier. I follow the orders given to me."

"You're not a regular soldier. We all know that. You and your mates are different. You volunteered for this."

"I guess that's true. Our unit motto is 'Free the Oppressed.' That's part of it."

"What's the other part?"

"Adventure, maybe. Living on the edge."

"Like a game?"

"No, not after today." That day had been the first time Anton had seen someone die a violent death. That scene had made him realize this wasn't a game, no matter what Kipling had called it.

"Aren't you afraid to die out here? Far from your home?"

"Until today, no. I didn't think about it much, but I guess it comes with the territory."

"Not something they teach in school. And in the movies, the hero always lives. Is that what you want to be, Anton? A hero?"

"I don't want to be a hero. I just want to help."

"I'm not sure you can help. This is how it's always been for us. One bad ruler after another. The people suffer and die. If I die, I don't want to suffer. I don't want to be crying for my mother or begging for one last cigarette," Károly had said.

"That isn't death, it's lingering," Anton had replied.

"How would you know?"

"I don't know for sure, I've never been there. Dying sucks, sure, but I think how you handle it is what reflects your character."

"So, you want to die like a hero."

Anton hadn't said anything; he hadn't thought about death before.

Károly had still been staring into the flames. "I suppose some people think it can't happen to them. Others don't believe it happens or maybe they fear it. I just don't even consider it, not that I want to die or cheat death. What is that? Arrogance, denial, delusion, disinterest? I don't think any of those fit the bill in my case. What can you call it? Maybe I'm agnostic? Can you be agnostic about death?"

"Stoic?" said Anton.

"No, that's just not complaining about it. Agnostic is the word."

"And what about going to hell?"

"Nah, hell is a fairy tale. So is heaven. Because in the end — when it happens — the first permanent thing you're guaranteed is that you don't have to think about it. Go to sleep, Anton. Tomorrow, we have things to do."

———————

That was then, and now Anton was alone on the streets of Berlin with only his pistol to comfort him. Instead of Károly's home-made bullets, it was loaded with factory issue .22 caliber Long Rifle that came as hollow points, basically dum-dums. Yes, they were forbidden by the Hague and Geneva Conventions, but he wasn't anywhere near either of those two places. He pulled the HDM/S from his waistband and stuffed it vertically, barrel down, in his armpit, his left arm pinning it in place, and continued to walk. As he walked past an intersection, he saw it was a short street and turned into it abruptly. Then, he disappeared into a dark alcove and waited. It wasn't long before he heard footsteps and saw the man pass in a hurry, probably thinking his quarry had disappeared around the next corner.

Anton stepped out, drew his pistol, holding it down, and padded quietly after him until he caught up. More than two arm's length away, he pointed the gun at the man and clicked off the safety, a sound no one wants to hear from behind them. The man stopped dead — his hearing was good. Anton was relieved the man didn't try any of those jiu-jitsu moves they taught back at Bragg — the kind of tricks the secret agents all know.

"Who are you?" Anton said with all the *Berlinerisch* as he could muster.

The man turned slowly toward Anton, his hands at his sides in a neutral pose. "I was trying to catch you. I thought you were a friend." his German badly accented.

"You've followed me before. What do you want?"

"I said I thought you were a friend."

"You're not German. Or Russian. Are you?" said Anton, his ear picking up the nuances.

The man's hands went up in surrender. "I'm American. I was visiting my girlfriend."

"Horse shit," Anton said, this time in English. "and I'm not your friend. Why are you following me?" Anton came close and, watching the man's eyes closely, patted him down quickly.

"It's true, I saw you a couple of nights ago. Close to the church. I recognized you again tonight and wondered what you were up to."

"Now, I'm wondering what you're up to — an American following me around when you should be home in bed over across the way. Aren't you worried about getting caught over here?"

"Aren't you?"

"Who are you?"

"My name's Charlie."

"And I'm Harry. Tell me something I don't know, like who you work for," said Anton.

"You tell me why you have a gun pointed at me first."

"I don't think that's how it works, buddy. When I point a gun at you, you get to talk first."

"Okay, but if you don't put it down, someone may see it and call the cops."

"Who. Do. You. Work. For?" Anton said slowly.

"The Americans."

Anton loosened his grip on the gun, lowering it to waist level but still pointed at the man. "And you're working tonight?"

"More or less. I'm trying to go home now, but I saw you."

"And you just had to follow me."

"Yeah. It was late the last time too. I wondered if you might be up to something."

"Kinda like I'm wondering about you now. Let's walk. You lead and don't forget that my gun has real live bullets," said Anton.

He weighed sending "Charlie" away, but he might have backup. If he could walk this guy across the frontier, he could ask all the questions he wanted. And should "Charlie" bolt before he got there, well.... That's why he stashed the pistol back underneath his armpit, where he could pull it faster than not. He didn't worry about the East German police. They wouldn't expect he was carrying if they stopped him, because all the weapons had been confiscated after the war. That's what conquering powers and despots did, confiscate all the guns to eliminate the people's capability to rise and fight back. Besides, with three magazines of ammo, he was comfortable in his new role of guardian escort, if not an angel.

22

COLONEL STÖCKER STOOD at attention before the general's desk.

"How long have you been in charge of your section, Colonel?"

"For two years now, *Herr General.*"

"Relax, Colonel."

Stöcker went to the rest position, but he was still tense, standing in front of one of the most powerful men in the *Stasi.* Markus Wolf, chief of *Hauptverwaltung Aufklärung,* the Main Directorate for Foreign Intelligence, looked at the man in front of him and recognized him for what he was. Stöcker was a scared bureaucrat out of his element, working for the Ministry of State Security. A legacy recruitment, his father had been one of the first and eldest of the cadre to come back from Moscow and, as his trusted son, he was brought on board. Sometimes, bloodlines provided the best security, even if the officer was inept. That was why Wolf knew Stöcker was harmless. Still, he could be useful. Working in the foreign liaison department, Stöcker was privy to details about what their Soviet comrades were up to that he didn't always have.

"Normally, Department 10 reports to the Minister. Why did you decide to bring this to me?"

"The Minister knows all about it, but as it involves active measures in what is technically a foreign country, I thought you should be made aware of it. It may have major implications on your area of responsibility."

"But you didn't tell him that you were giving me this information?"

"No, sir."

"Then, it would be wise if you don't mention your speaking with me. It will remain between us alone. Thank you, Colonel. Your efforts to serve and protect the Party will be remembered."

"Thank you, General. I had better return to my office before anyone comes looking for me." Stöcker gave an approximated military salute and pivoted awkwardly on his heels and left.

Wolf sat back in his chair and pondered what exactly Stöcker had brought him. Colonel Androv was well known to him, primarily as someone he knew to be Moscow's troublemaker, a man who fomented problems for the West by supporting "anti-imperialist" liberation groups in faraway places like Africa, the Middle East, and Asia. What was he doing here? Between Androv and his own boss, Wollweber, there was the potential for something bad to happen.

Wolf sighed — the sigh of a man burdened by the weight of the world, even though he knew he had it better than almost everyone on the east side of the Wall. As he thought, he poured a cup of tea from his thermos and stirred in a teaspoonful of cranberry jam, a habit he picked up in Moscow during the war.

He returned to the debriefing of the American walk-in he had done several weeks ago. The Russians asked for help because they didn't have any linguists available, so he did the job himself. At least until they found their own English speaker. What had he learned? The Soviets had an American army officer walk into their headquarters. He wasn't native born and he would only speak English, but he was seriously upset about something and would only talk if the Russians would guarantee him safe haven. Yes, the Russians were very much in charge of things in Berlin, at least on this side of the Wall, something he didn't mention to Stöcker, but they were also about as subtle as a brick thrown through a window. He wanted very much to recruit that American for himself. He hadn't had many good sources since one of his senior staff defected to West Germany a year ago and thirty of his agents had been arrested because of the information the traitor took with him. An American officer would be a nice feather in his cap. The question was: was this American somehow tied up with Androv's *FEUERSCHMIED*? He didn't know how yet, but he needed to find out. He sipped his tea and closed his eyes, looking for ideas.

23

ANTON AND "CHARLIE" walked a long way across town to get to the frontier, meandering northwest in instead of straight west or south. Security was tighter in the city center bordering the British sector, and the rivers in the middle of the city channeled traffic to the bridges. They were all well controlled. That left the southern part of the American sector, which was too far, or the French sector. So, he decided it would be the French sector, thinking somehow that his French might help him if he needed to lie to the *Vopos*.

They were near the Wollankstraße S-Bahn station, north of where he'd crossed the other night. He would have gone back to the church if he didn't have "Charlie," or the pistol, and if it hadn't been a weekday. But here he was, peering across the tracks from inside a small tuft of overgrown scrub along the railway. The tracks were illuminated by a moon that turned them into lines of silver that cut through the city like a scar. It was fifty meters of open space to cross, but as long as a train didn't come and the police didn't see them, they would be okay. "Charlie" sat on the ground. Anton watched him play with a twig and then went back to looking up and down the dimly lit tracks for cops or soldiers. It was quiet.

"Where you come from, Harry?" said Charlie.

"What do you care?" Anton said. He wasn't ready to discuss anything with this guy.

"Well, I'm from Nebraska and I know a little bit about train tracks."

"You do, do you?" Anton said.

"I do. And you know what? This might look like an easy place to run across, but there's two sets of tracks, a whole bunch of old rails and junk strewn all over, and a lot of places to fall on your face. Besides, there might be a couple of *Vopos* on the train platform down there."

"The station is inside the French sector. No *Vopos* there, only on this side of the tracks. We'll be fine running across unless you have a better idea."

"That I do. I can show you a spot. May I lead?"

A moment of hesitation whether to trust the man, then, "Lead on, Charlie."

Charlie brushed off his pants as he stood and turned back into the tree line from where they had come. He turned north and walked away from the station paralleling the tracks. Soft light filtered through the trees from the occasional yellow pole light that marked the S-Bahn's right of way and was quickly absorbed by the dense brush on the other side of them. It was enough to see the ground and they made good time but only for about fifty meters. Charlie stopped and held up his hand signaling Anton. He crouched as Anton came alongside him and saw an overgrown path crossing in front of them.

"Where's it go?"

"To an old tunnel that goes underneath the tracks. There's a street that crosses ahead as well, but this path is rarely used except maybe by people like us. We can go if you're ready."

"Do it, you're still on point."

Anton waited as Charlie stepped forward onto the trail and turned toward the rail-line. Charlie hesitated a moment looking back at Anton who waved him on. Then he walked off. Anton followed with one last look behind him, his pistol held low at his side. He was fairly sure Charlie was okay. No one said they come from Nebraska unless they really did, and he sounded right. No German or Russian he knew of could talk like a mid-westerner. He saw the man disappear into the dark orifice of the tunnel behind a large bush and followed him. The tunnel was narrow, a tight fit for a big man and blacker than the night sky, but in the dim light coming from the small archway at the opposite end, he could see his "Charlie" bobbing ahead of him.

————————

They crashed out of through the brush on the other side and Anton had a better appreciation for being on the wrong side of the tracks. He felt the uplifting euphoria that came after doing something forbidden that could have ended badly but hadn't. And then it was gone.

"How did you know the tunnel was there?" Anton asked.

"My predecessor showed me."

"So, you and your predecessor do much business in the East?"

"Some. And you?"

"Some," Anton said.

"Okay, we're getting nowhere fast. Who do you work for?"

"The Americans."

"So, we have a guessing game. You army? Maybe military intelligence?" said Charlie.

"Army, yes. MI, no. That must mean you're not Army or MI. You a civilian?"

"Yes."

"Then you're a spy, right?"

"Close, but this isn't the best place to be discussing our jobs. Let's get out of here."

———————

There were always bars to be found open on the Ku'damm, but Charlie had a specific one in mind and, when they ended up at the Savoy Hotel on Fasanenstraße, he declared it as if he was unveiling Tutankhamun's treasure.

"Here we are. The 'Times Bar' and they have great booze and good Cuban cigars."

"At this time of night?"

"This is Berlin. Where you been anyway?"

Anton knew he had stepped into a different league when he saw the decor. He felt out of place because it was so obviously beyond his economic strata. His eyes took in the dark wood paneled walls with framed portraits of the famous, infamous, and just notorious, around to the oyster shell scalloped into the ceiling above the bar, fluted pendant lamps shining with a wine-red light, and then the walk-in humidor. The only other place he'd seen like this was "Arnaud's," a little place in New Orleans someone called "sumptuous" and just one more place he couldn't afford even if he did have his wallet.

Anton let Charlie order two double scotch whiskies, "Bowmore," he said, "neat." He spoke in English, which was just as well as the bar tender was Irish, making them a trio of displaced persons. The rest of the clientele were older men in suits, all horse traders and thieves to Anton's eyes. The few women present were also professionals, but of an even older business.

Drinks came and they found their way to an empty corner to overstuffed, leather armchairs and contemplated their surroundings, neither wishing to break the silence. Charlie pulled an identity card out of his pocket and laid it on the table. Anton picked it up and read from it, "Charles Palmer, U.S. Mission Berlin. So? What is it?"

"My inter-zonal pass. I can travel into the East and back without being hassled."

"You don't carry a weapon?"

"Why? It's not dangerous over there," Charlie said.

Anton shook his head. "You should think about protecting yourself over there. Those folks don't play by the same rules as we do."

"Really? How do you go over?" Charlie said.

"I don't think I can talk about it."

"How old are you, Harry?"

"Twenty-three, and you?" Anton said.

"Older than you. What are you a private or maybe a butter bar?"

That would have pissed Anton off if he was capable of being pissed off. Instead, he sized up the man in front of him and decided whoever or whatever Charlie thought himself to be, he — Anton Thibodeaux — was in spades.

"I'm a Staff Sergeant," Anton said.

"Well, Harry, you're a mystery to me, an enigma, a conundrum. Because I don't know of anyone besides us or maybe the MI guys who are supposed to be in the East. The Soviet zone is off limits to soldiers."

"Maybe for regular folk. But we're not regular folk," said Anton.

"Who the hell are you then?"

"I'm a soldier. That's all I can say."

"Okay, I'll leave it for now."

"You're a spy."

"You like to test my patience, don't you?"

Anton took a sip of his whisky and smiled. "Good stuff, this."

"It is. First off, your terminology is wrong. Spies are people who betray their country by stealing secrets. I'm not a spy. I'm an intelligence officer. I recruit spies. I'm kinda like a businessman — like them, I have to know people who can help me and those who cannot. Some people are just useless, I avoid them. There's one other difference, businessmen are in it for the dollars, the money. We're not a 'for profit' organization, our money is information, and the stakes are far greater, like national security."

"For God and Country, like it says in the Norman Rockwell painting?"

"I don't think I've seen a Norman Rockwell painting that says that."

"They all do in one way or another," said Anton. "You just have to look for it in the picture."

"That's profound," said Palmer.

"I am profound, yes. So that makes you a spook."

"In proper English slang, yes."

"You're trained to lie," Anton said.

"I don't lie. I tell people what they need to hear, what they want to hear."

"We call that bullshitting where I come from."

"Where I come from, we call it being expedient. Now that I've told you about me, why don't you tell me about you?"

"No. I don't know you from Adam," said Anton.

"I got you out of the Soviet zone!"

"I would have taken another route if you hadn't been tagging along. You did me no favors. Come back to me when you can prove who you are and why you need to know. How about that?"

"Not very grateful, are you?" Palmer drained half his glass and slammed it on to the bar. His whisky splashed up and only half what remained found its way back into the glass."

"Not yet, Charles Palmer. You should be grateful I didn't shoot you."

24

---◆---

JOZEF CIERNIK WAITED at the bottom of the back stairs in the old tenement house. He could see down a good length of the alley in either direction. When he saw Maja's shadow flit into his vision, he moved to the door and turned the handle. All he needed to do was pull it open when she got to the top of the stairs and let her in.

When she was inside, she took off her scarf and shook off the dampness of the cold, misty rain and looked up at Jozef.

"Go, up the stairs," he said, brusque, commanding. He locked the outside door and followed her. Only when they were inside the second floor apartment's foyer did they embrace tightly. He smelled her hair. He wasn't sure if it was the same scent he remembered, but it didn't matter. It was Maja.

"Come, sit. It's been too long since we've been close together, Maja."

"Yes, too long. It's been what, ten years now?"

"Twelve. But I think that will change now."

"Maybe, do you really believe you can help?"

"My people have promised me. I have one final thing to accomplish to make that happen."

"And you can't tell me about it?"

"No, I can't. It's better for you and Roman if you don't know. Has he given you what I asked for?"

"Only some of it. He promised to give me the rest when he returns from Dresden this week. What will happen after I give it all to you?"

"It hasn't been worked out in detail yet. Everything depends on the situation when I have all the information, and when my job is finished. Maybe in two weeks, I'll know better."

"It's not dangerous, is it? What you're doing."

"No, just some quid pro quo. I do this and they'll help me out. I should say, they'll help us out."

"Roman's contribution," she said. The maths working in her head, the conclusion obvious.

"That's part of it, yes, but not everything. Don't worry Maja. I have it figured out. But when can we meet after Roman gets back?"

"Maybe Sunday or Monday. Saturday's too soon. I will leave a message like you told me to do," Maja said.

"For Sunday you will mention 'cafe' and Monday is…?" Jozef said.

"Monday is the 'butcher.' Tuesday the 'store.' And the time will be the number I mention plus ten hours and fifteen minutes. Right?"

"Perfect," he said. A tinge of regret to his words. So few they were though, Maja didn't hear. She did sense them because, despite the long, absence from each other she was well tuned to Jozef.

"Not to worry, *mój drogi*," she said. She smiled up at her protector, her love. Not even Roman, her husband evoked the same feelings. "My dear, no worries. We'll be back together soon. But, for the moment, we need to play this game."

"Sometimes, I think you're better at this than I," he said.

———————

Ciernik let Maja leave the building before him and waited a long while to follow. It seemed longer than it was but then it always did when you were breaking contact and going back out onto the street. Going into a meet, you felt like stepping into a Venus Flytrap, just waiting for the jaw-like leaves to snap shut around its prey. Surviving the meeting without being rousted by the police or security, you went back out, aware that the wolves might be waiting somewhere out there on the hazy, dark edges to pounce on your treachery.

It was probably just minutes, but he slipped outside, thinking it was longer. With the door locked, he placed the key back in its hiding place and continued down the alley. On a whim, he headed in the opposite direction she had taken. It was quiet. The neighborhood was almost completely residential, no *Kneipen* to grab a beer, no restaurants for blocks. Just the emptiness of a wounded city, divided and framed at the same time by trauma and politics. It seemed the wind made the only sound, save the occasional, rheumatic coughing of a car trundling down the street or the crash of the trains coming from the Friedrichstraße station not so far away.

Head down, hands deep in the pockets of his long wool overcoat he was heading for the inter-city border. A funny thing this border, sometimes the East Germans patrolled it heavily, sometimes not. On the other side, the Allies didn't really care who came and went, no control whatsoever, except maybe a few West Berlin policeman to watch what was happening. The only military presence was from the former Allies, the Soviets sometimes crossing into West Berlin to show their face, and the three western powers doing the same in East Berlin. There were no German soldiers, from East or West, inside Berlin itself. That was the agreement. Only police, though some of them were heavily armed, but still police. *Of course, there was the Stasi — they had their own goons....*

The pavement was slick beneath his feet, he hadn't heard the rain. The street lights glistened, reflecting off small puddles turning the ground into a canvas of watery stars, the concrete black behind them.

Perhaps that was why he didn't see the two men approaching, his attention was captured by the lights. Or maybe because he was thinking about Maja and the disgust and fury he felt at having to use her in the way he was. Then, they were there, twenty feet in front of him. He knew from the uniform that they were neither police nor *Stasi*, they were *Kampfgruppen* — the ruling-party's factory militia. *Old men and Boy Scouts with guns*, he thought.

He knew them well, having read the intelligence assessments and spoken with people who had encountered them. He saw it in their faces, the arrogance, not because of competence, but because they wore a uniform that gave them power, authority, and false confidence. Stupid because of that, assuming all people without a uniform or rank were beneath them. That was always a mistake, but Ciernik didn't telegraph that he knew they were worthless.

"What have we here?" said the leader, a horizontal red stripe on his sleeve.

"Hey, *Opa*! What are you doing out so late?" Said the one with no stripe.

"I'm going home, gentlemen. Are you keeping your factory safe?" said Ciernik. No mood to deal with anyone. *Besides, Opa? These kids ought to show more respect to their elders.*

"We don't need a factory to be here. We're watching for smugglers and criminals," said "stripe," fingering his pistol holster.

"I am neither of those things. I have nothing to smuggle, no money, and I am a good citizen."

"Your accent is strange, comrade. Where are you from? Show your papers." The strap came off the holster flap.

Ciernik pulled out the empty wallet he carried and tossed it on the ground in front of the two. "My papers are in there. I'm from Poland, a guest of your government."

A sneer on his face, "stripe" said, "Pick up your papers, *Opa*. You show disrespect, making me do it."

"My sincerest apologies, comrade. I will retrieve them." Ciernik held his hand up in abject surrender and stepped closer, reaching in to pick up the wallet lying at the militiamen's feet. *This will hurt*, he thought and bent over.

The younger of the two, "No stripe," made the mistake of putting his hand on Ciernik's shoulder. Ciernik grabbed his wrist and jerked the man behind him as he stepped between the two and pivoted around. The man spun, off balance, and slammed into his partner before he flew headfirst into the fence railing. Ciernik stomped hard on the back of his neck, crushing "no stripe's" face into the concrete before turning to the leader who was trying hard to pull his rarely drawn pistol from the holster.

"If you don't use your weapon much, it sticks to the leather, you know," Ciernik said as he struck him hard in the solar plexus, batted his hands away from the pistol, and stepped around to put on a choke hold, his arms pinioning the man's head forward, chin on his chest. He knew he didn't have time to suffocate the man, so he pulled "stripe's" head back and twisted it to the side and forward again hard. Still alive, the man squeaked pitifully as he flailed at Ciernik's hands. Feet wide apart, Ciernik lifted the man and drove him hard onto the steel railing feeling the spikes impale the East German's body. "Stripe" jerked and quivered for a moment, then was still.

Ciernik checked his pockets quickly, finding a small identity wallet that he pocketed, and then flipped the body over the rail into the basement access well. "No stripe" was lying still on the ground. Fingers pressed to the neck. No pulse. Ciernik looked around to see if anyone had noticed the scuffle. They either had not noticed or refused to see it from behind their curtains. He picked the man up by his belt and jacket collar and dropped him over the edge into the stairwell with his partner. *No one will notice until morning*, he hoped. Whoever lived in the basement would have a surprise waiting for them when they opened the door.

Despite the cold, he was sweating heavily. Brushing himself off, Ciernik walked away, a little more respectful of his surroundings than he had been before. *Fascists*, he thought. He didn't feel bad about what he'd done. He had even less love for the communists than he did for the Nazis, and no one would keep him from completing his mission. Next time, he'd bring a knife.

25

PALMER HELD OUT a Headquarters Berlin telephone directory like he was presenting evidence in a courtroom. "The army is hiding things from us," he said, a declaration, accusation, and remonstration all in one.

"Hiding things from us or the world in general?" said St. John.

"Both. I mean, I can see why they might hide stuff from the Soviets, but from us? We need to know who is out there, doing secret stuff in our area of operations."

"What are you talking about?"

"I ran across a young guy in the Soviet sector last night. I saw him a week ago, the night I met B/1, he was near the church on Bernauerstraße that time."

"And?"

"When I saw him out again last night, I tried to catch up to him, he pulled a pistol on me. Then, I find out he's an American soldier in civilian clothing. But, and this is important, he's not MI."

"So?"

"So, no one but MI and us are supposed to be over there at night, right? Aren't we supposed to be briefed on cross-border operations run by the army. You haven't been briefed on anything going on over there, have you?"

"Recently? Only that Buchanan thing. You sure he's not with CIC? Why do we care?"

"I asked Myers, who said he isn't his. As to why we should care, I think it's a good idea to know who's playing around in our neck of the woods."

"Are you sure Myers wasn't lying?"

"I don't see it, he's not a manipulator. CIC doesn't do that."

"Counter-intelligence, that's an oxymoron if I've ever heard one — countering intelligence wherever they find it. So, what did this guy tell you?"

"Nothing, other than his first name, which may be Harry."

"Can you recontact him?"

"I don't know how. I'm trying to figure out in what unit he could be, but the directory is no help."

"Maybe they're unlisted. We aren't in there."

"Yes, we are. Just under cover."

"Right, State Department Pol-Mil section. Like that tells anyone anything. Maybe that's what you need to look for, any listing for a military unit that doesn't make sense."

"Like Pol-Mil?"

"Yes, like us."

It was a start. Look for listings similar to his own office's cover entry in the directory, an organizational name that said nothing with only a couple telephone numbers that connected to generic position titles. He quickly went through all the Headquarters staff, the State Department, and civilian listings and then, concentrated on the military units stationed in the city. Most he scratched off immediately, others were a bit mysterious like the ConDinFac, which he only determined was an abbreviation for the consolidated dining facility. He figured that out after seeing the Mess Officer's telephone under the heading. He looked closely at anything with "Special" in the title, but decided most of those were anything but, like "Special Services," the office responsible for handing out basketballs at the gym. After an hour, he had a short list of possibilities. One of them must be what he was looking for, the army's version of "Pol-Mil" aka Berlin Operations Base hiding in plain sight. Now he needed to do the gumshoe work.

26

"DID IT GO better this time?" Makinen asked from the chair behind his desk. "Top" Becker was sitting in his own GSO-approved, grey-upholstered, swivel chair across the room, looking on, waiting expectantly for a chance to throw in some time-honored leadership tidbits or down-home homilies if Anton sounded discouraged.

But Anton wasn't discouraged. He seemed almost energized. "It went fine. I made the drop and had no issues on my run in or out. Except maybe two," he said. He was tapping his pencil on a drawing he was making of the cache site, an improvement on the rudimentary sketch he been given to find it. It included the precise layout of the flagstones, each carefully shaded and hatched as he'd learned in art class, as well as the measurements from the designated tree and the wall that surrounded the site. He leaned back to regard his artwork and was pleased.

"And?" Makinen said.

"I picked up a tail on my way back. I guess he got on my nerves because I got behind him and confronted him."

"You didn't kill him, did you?"

"I could have. When I asked him what he wanted, he told me he'd seen me before. In bad German. Then, he told me he was an

American. Goes by the name of Charles Palmer. I think he's with the Agency."

"Why do you say that?" Becker said.

"He told me as much. We came back across the frontier together, he showed me a new crossing point, and then. we stopped for a drink at the Savoy."

"The Savoy? High class digs."

"His idea, he paid. Showed me his ID card and said he wanted to know who I was and what I was doing in the East."

"What did you tell him?"

"I told him to get lost."

"What did his ID card look like?" Makinen and Becker were playing off each other in their questioning, not hostile, just prodding. If it went much further, it would be wheedling, Anton thought.

"It was gray and printed in English, French, Russian, and German with about five ink stamps and four signatures. He called it an inter-zonal pass. It looked official and clearly said he was American," Anton said.

"It's what you carry when you can't handle a cover story," said Becker.

"Or don't want to bother with one. The difference is you don't go to jail if you get picked up by the *Vopos*," Makinen said.

"Maybe we should have those," said Anton. "as a last resort thing."

"No, the whole point of having a cover is so we can do our wartime mission. When the balloon goes up, those cards aren't going to be worth a damn," Becker said.

"Game over for them, then."

"Yes, when the war goes from hot to cold, they will be dead in the water and our mission will be just beginning." Becker swept his hand across the map like he was clearing a chess board.

"You said there were two things. What else happened?" said Makinen.

"I met a girl over there."

"Explain."

———————

After loading the cache, Anton said he had headed east, deeper into the communist zone, before starting back to make the run for home and sanctuary. He had been sure he wasn't being followed and, when he was in the Prenzlauer Berg neighborhood, he'd found himself being drawn to a familiar place. When a sign proclaiming the Kastanien-Eck appeared in front of him, Anton had wondered if he should go in. *Yes, but only for a moment.*

She had seen him walk in and by the time he'd reached the bar, she had begun to pull his beer. She had looked at the beer then at him, a slight nod. I see you, it said. He had stood silently as she went about her business of serving the other patrons, his beer took several pulls to get the proper seven-minute pour. He'd watched the glass fill and the bubbles slowly recede, she poured again. She watched him. He took a breath and looked at her.

"Katja," she said.

"What?"

"Katja, that's my name. What's yours?" She gave him a sideways glance as she watched the pour.

Caught off guard, Anton had stumbled. "Klaus." *Almost forgot who I'm supposed to be,* he thought. He stopped himself from giving his last name. It was his cover, but it was too much information for a first meet.

"Hello, Klaus." As she handed him the beer.

He'd seen her only briefly the last time when he'd been preoccupied with his internal self-critique. There must have been something that had snared him, brought him here again, enticing him in for a second encounter. He looked at her critically for the first time, brown hair cascaded over her shoulders, smooth skin with a prickle of perspiration on her nose. There was something there beyond her luminous, dark brown eyes and flashing smile that she seemed to hide sometimes. It was all a bit unsettling, and he couldn't quite think straight. For one, he knew he shouldn't be looking for a woman in the Soviet sector. Second, he needed to get home in one piece.

But just one beer. How could that hurt?

Katja was fully engaged with the customers anyway. He'd left his money on the counter and found a seat at his same isolated table so he could watch over the clientele. It was busier tonight, and he relaxed, sipping at the bitter beer, watching and reviewing the evening's activities. Nothing to worry about. Soon, his glass was empty. He looked about, but Katja was nowhere to be seen, an older man pouring beers in her place at the bar.

Just as well. He wouldn't have to say goodbye. He'd peeled himself out of his chair almost reluctantly this time. *When was the last time?* he thought as he stepped outside. He oriented himself before he stepped off, a slight angle, and around the corner. The same direction he gone before. *Consistency, just in case*, he thought with one chanced look behind him. When he looked back to the front, there she was. Just stepped out of the dark, cigarette in one hand, an arm wrapped tight across her breasts trying to stay warm.

"Leaving?" She'd said.

"Yeah, have to get home."

"To your wife?"

"I'm not married." He almost asked — didn't need to.

"Me either."

"Just have to get up early for work."

"You live close?"

"Not really. Pankow."

"That's not that far. I live nearby — *Hagenauer Straße* — a couple of blocks from here. Alone." Pointedly.

"No family?"

"Mom and a sister. They live in Mitte. Lost my dad."

"Sorry."

"It's okay. Are you coming back?"

"I think so. I was hoping to talk, but you were busy."

"It's like that sometimes. What work do you do?"

"I'm a machinist with Borsig."

"You work on the other side? That's nice, I think."

"You think? Not sure? It's okay. Maybe I'll get a better job with Zeiss. They're in Jena."

"I'd rather be working in the West. Rather live there too," she said.

"Why don't you leave?"

"Can't. They won't give me papers."

"Why?"

"Because of my dad. *17 Juni.* He was there, killed during the uprising. Now, they don't trust us. I can't even go to the *Uni.*"

The 17th of June. Anton understood. The 1953 uprising — brief, spectacular, and deadly. Maybe a thousand people gunned down or executed later by the Russians, a turning point in East

Germany and the communist world. Hungary had followed on its heels in 1956. Its uprising had failed as well — Anton knew well its cost to friends and family.

"They killed your father. That's why you want to leave."

"Yes. Don't you think this government is bad?"

Anton looked about nervously. No one on the street. Say what he felt or say what was expedient?

"I suppose. I mean, I haven't thought about the options much."

"Don't waffle, I know you've thought about it," she said. Her eyes, even in the dim light of the street lamps, were fiery in intensity. "You're not one of those *Lumpen* in there. Those low-lives. I can see it."

"I'd better go. It's getting late. They might wonder where you are."

"Don't worry about me, Klaus, I can take care of myself. You should worry about yourself."

"I do, Katja, believe me."

She'd stepped closer, laying her hand on his arm. "Don't get me wrong, I worry about you too. I would like to see you again. Just remember what's at stake here." She held up the West German 2-Mark piece he'd left on the bar. "Be careful. Someone might get the wrong idea."

———————

It was strange, he thought. He was attracted to her, but still didn't understand why. His experience with women was limited. He'd had no luck in high school — the female classmates he'd found interesting didn't return the favor. Once he joined the army, the only girls he met seemed to be waitresses or the euphemistically described working girls, both of which he had learned, generally too late, were the wrong type for him.

Katja could have played the defenseless woman in need of a protector, but she hadn't. She seemed to be strong, and she saw something in him. If she was to be believed, he wasn't one of the *Lumpen,* which he took as a compliment. She was different even if he knew absolutely nothing about her.

"What did you say her name was?" Makinen asked.

"Katja. Katja Peters."

"Not that we can check her out with the Russians or the Germans. She doesn't know anything about you?"

"Only a little of my cover story."

"You know this goes against every rule, Thibodeaux," said Becker. The only time he used Anton's family name was when he was serious.

"I know, Top."

Becker continued, "I'm just saying, you're probably the only unmarried guy in the outfit who doesn't have a girlfriend in the East, but no one else reports it. That reporting bit just causes problems. Most of the guys just go over there with nylons and chocolate every weekend and don't say a word. Now, you come along and tell us the whole story."

"Top, that's enough," Makinen broke in. "I suppose you want to see her again? Do you trust her?"

"Yes and yes, boss. She doesn't know who I really am yet and she's nice."

"Puppies are nice, but they grow up and bite. It could be dangerous for both of you, and I don't want you to screw up what we're trying to do here. So, don't do anything stupid until I talk to the colonel and see what he says. Then, you will follow his guidance. In the meantime, this is just between us three. And no war stories in the bars, *keine, nichts.*"

"Got it, boss. But what about that Palmer guy?"

"Top?" Makinen knew this was a name that Becker could run with.

"I'll have S-2 check him out; he's got connections."

Bill the S-2, the unit's intelligence officer, was the unit's conduit to Berlin's entire intelligence community, at least the western side of it. Bill was small, wiry, a bristly sort, prone to anger anytime he heard something he deemed stupid, which was often. The only people he was afraid of were the commander, sergeant major, or anyone who stood up to him. But Bill's Napoleonic complex wasn't so big that he didn't understand the better part of bravery required he sometimes run away. Becker wasn't threatening him, so he didn't slam the steel gate to his office and instead stepped out into the hallway.

Bill took the three-by-five card with the name that Becker handed him and stared at it a moment then looked up at Becker. "You want to contact him or you want to know who he is?"

"Just tell me if he's the real McCoy. After that, we can decide what to do with him."

"Well, be sure to dump the body in the French sector. That'll keep the police guessing,"

"Right, but there's one other thing. Anton's contact yesterday," Becker paused to make sure Bill was following.

"I got it. Over there, right?"

"Yeah. Well, he said something to Anton you might want to check out." He handed the S-2 another card. "What do you think?"

"I think I hate cryptology. I dunno. I'll pass it to our friends. Maybe they can make something out of it. I'll let you know." Bill said as he slammed the gate to his private sanctum.

27

———— ◆ ————

"I JUST HAD an interesting conversation with someone who said he knows you," St. John said.

"Who?" said Charlie Palmer.

"Not sure exactly, but we'll find out soon enough. He and a friend are coming over to talk to us. Your friend Myers was on the call and verified that they are on our side and we need to meet them."

"You actually spoke to Myers? I'm surprised."

"He snuck onto the call along with the Colonel Harris, the G-2. By the way, he's not on your list, is he?"

"Harris? No. He was at work or home with wifey and kids that night."

"Good to know. Anyway, they said someone met you and wanted to confirm you were on the up and up. Part of the home team. A good guy, so to speak."

"Am I?"

"You are. I confirmed it and Harris and Myers confirmed that these folks are on our side and need to meet you. Mentioned you specifically by name. So, they're coming over."

"Myers and Harris?"

"No, a major Brock and a Captain Mack-something from some army outfit."

"What unit?"

"They didn't say. It will all be explained when they come over."

"More secret stuff. This might be something to do with my encounter the other night."

"Wouldn't be surprised. They'll be over this afternoon, so don't do a late lunch or anything."

"Are you going to be in on the meeting?"

"I think I have to be. I'm chief and you're one of my people. I need to know what's going on."

Palmer thought that may have been the first time St. John had admitted he had a team, and he was part of it or, more precisely, in charge of it. Unusual in an agency where most officers tried their best to avoid associating with other personnel in case, they were tainted by something that might rub off. Unless it turned out to be a good thing, they hoped to be included in the honors list. He wasn't sure what St. John wanted. Maybe he was just protecting his turf.

The gate to the BOB's section of the compound was less formidable than the front gate. The main gate had a huge steel fence that was protected by the MPs in a building behind bullet-proof glass in a guardhouse and was the bastion of America's strength presented to the German public. Entering required waiting for the outer door to be unlocked only to be met with a second locked door and a tiny window where your identity card was passed to a soldier who checked your name against a list before permitting entry. If you worked there, a special ID streamlined the process. Around the corner on Saargemunder Straße, the alternate entrance was protected by one overweight and one meager German Labor Service guard, who together looked whimsical, kind of Laurel and Hardy-like wearing polished U.S. Army helmet liners, rather than representing any kind of deterrence.

Major Brock and Captain Makinen had parked a couple of blocks away hoping their car would remain at least somewhat anonymous and walked the final hundred yards under the tall oaks that lined the quiet street. They were thinking it was better not to make it too easy for hostile watchers, those people around the headquarters compound whose only job was to note which car or person entered the compound and report back to their masters in the East.

The Dahlem area with its huge trees had survived the war mostly intact, much like the Standard Oil building in Frankfurt remained untouched — perhaps designated as a "no-go" area by bomber command in anticipation of its use by the Americans in a post-war Germany, or so went the theory. The compound was surrounded by a three-meter-high stone wall topped with barbed wire and penetrated on this side only by an opaque metal vehicle gate with a pedestrian door to one side. And, had either Brock or Makinen seen "The Wizard of Oz" as children they might have been struck by their resemblance to Dorothy's attempts to enter the Emerald City. They pounded on the door and the thin guard stuck his head out the guardroom window. Similarities ended there as Brock flashed his ID and commanded the man in perfect German that he was to open the door. He'd been here before.

Finished with formalities at the gate, it was a short walk to the BOB's office in Building 6b, marked only with a sign announcing with German precision in blue on white porcelain that this was indeed Building 6b.

Entrance into 6b was a bit more rigorously controlled. Push a button, talk to a scratchy, metallic voice, step back, and wait for the inevitable scrutiny from someone peering through the spy hole. Then, the door opened and they were ushered inside by a women on the near side of thirty, attractive, long black hair, dark green eyes devoid of make-up and better looking for it, her finger nails unpolished, a wedding ring on the right hand. A clear American accent told them to follow her as she punched in the numbers on the vestibule's mechanical door lock. Once inside, she led them to a small, spartan interview room that contained a table and five chairs. Several photographs of the city taken from the air appeared on one wall, the opposite with a large city map of Berlin. A Thermos of coffee sat on the table, with four cups, saucers, and teaspoon. Sugar and cream naturally. Their visit was expected.

"Sit gentlemen, I'll tell the chief you're here," Maria said as the door closed behind her.

"Nice scenery," said Brock, looking at the pictures and meaning something else.

Makinen sat on the opposite side of the table from the map and wondered if it depicted anything different than the one in his team room and decided it didn't. Brock was about to join him when the door opened. The chief led the way.

"Ted St. John, I'm the chief here," he said, sticking out his hand and affecting his best homeyness. "And this is Charlie Palmer, the man you asked about. I understand you have all the proper clearances, is that not so?"

"It is. We're both cleared for TS" Brock remained standing as Makinen joined him. "I am Major Thomas Brock and this is Captain Mack Makinen," he said.

"Yes, my assistant told me. Welcome to Berlin Base. How can we help you?" St. John said without really meaning it. He was more curious about how they managed to find Palmer and what exactly their business in Berlin was, and so was Palmer.

"We're assigned to a new unit in Berlin. You may not have heard of it before. It's called Support Detachment Berlin. I am the executive officer, the number two, and Mack is an element leader."

"No, I don't think we have heard of your unit. That's the United States Army?"

"Of course, why do you ask?"

"Your accent, Major. You sound foreign."

"Foreign as in different, Mister St. John? Or foreign as in not citizens," said Makinen, his accent even more pronounced.

"Not Americans," said St. John, trying to waffle. Hiding behind the boss for once, Palmer winced imperceptibly.

"We're Americans, chief," said Brock. "Just latecomers. I was born in Germany, emigrated from there to the States before the war and became a citizen in 1942." His smile was accommodating, he'd met New Englanders before.

"And I'm Finnish. United States citizen since 1954," Makinen announced. He, on the other hand, was a bit miffed by St. John.

"And I'm from Nebraska," said Palmer stepping into the limelight. "Call me Charlie," he said with a smile and an extended hand to shake. The momentary heat passed, and everyone sat down at the table. Charlie had the feeling he was about to see a grudge match between the university football team and the debate squad. On one hand, St. John might be able to charm his assets — those who wanted to be charmed at least — with his fine diction and big words, while the two gentlemen sitting across the table looked like they might pull knives and have at him when they got tired of his mouth. *'Grizzled'* was a word he'd heard bandied about before. That was what he saw, two grizzled veterans. One looked as if he could have been a poster-boy for the *Waffen-SS* if his family has stayed in Germany, the other seemed more like a hardened mountain-man without a beard, kind of old for a captain, but he probably had a story. And both had ice-blue eyes, not menacing or cold, more like two predators casually sizing up their lunch. He wasn't sure of the circumstances of their *grizzledness*, but he knew it when he saw it. Some of his dad's friends had the same look in their eyes, the look of bored tigers who would just as soon chomp off a man's head as listen to him speak. St. John seemed not to have a clue.

Brock spoke. "We're here because of a near miss we had the other evening in the Soviet sector. Your man, Mister Palmer there, was following one of our operators who was conducting a task over there."

"Operator? Not soldier?"

"We prefer operator. He's a very skilled soldier and an operator."

"So why didn't you bring your operator along?" Turning to Charlie, St John said, "What did you say his name was?"

"He told me it was Harry, that's all."

"Yes, Harry. Why isn't he here?" said St. John.

"His name doesn't matter, but he has even less reason to be seen over here on the headquarters compound than we do," said Makinen.

St. John was about to speak, somewhat taken aback by the officers' tone, but didn't get the chance.

"We're here to let you know a little about our mission and, hopefully, deconflict our activities," said Brock.

———————

Makinen wasn't sure what he'd been expecting. The office didn't look special, nor did the people inside it. It appeared normal except there were no windows to look out or for anyone to look in. A coffee pot sat next to a bunch of filing cabinets with combination locks all marked "OPEN," but with the drawers closed. On the way in they had passed a big map of Berlin, another of the two Germanys, and another of Europe and the eastern half of the Soviet Union. The few people at work ignored them, papers were covered. Nothing to see here.

The BOB was in a seemingly run-of-the-mill building that looked like all the others on the compound, filled with the same GSA-supplied furniture they had in their building. He hadn't seen that they possessed anything secret like everyone had told him they did and none of them looked special. They looked normal. Except maybe for the one who sat across from him now, he'd run into guys like him before, those privileged, upper class types who thought they controlled things.

Mack had heard of the Agency when he went through training at Fort Bragg and one old guy spoke to them about parachuting into France, then into Norway. He said he was OSS, a Jedburgh, then Agency before he retired and taught classes about guerrilla warfare as a civilian. He listened to the man carefully, comparing his own experiences before he wrote up a paper that was their homework for the weekend. Unlike most of the other students, he didn't need to refer any reference books or manuals. Makinen wrote from memory and, despite the problems he had with the grammar, he thought it was pretty good. The Special Warfare School staff must have thought so too, because they told him it would be going into the center's reference library, albeit the classified one that no one could check anything out of.

After the Russians and Germans tore up their non-aggression pact in 1941, Finland fought with the Germans against the communists. It wasn't his idea to let Germany take control of the country and after the war, the new government in Helsinki decided he and his soldier comrades were somehow to blame — how was that fair? He hated bureaucrats and the man in front of him looked and smelled like one.

The other spook, this Charlie Palmer guy, looked different. He might actually be okay. They were all still spooks like Thibodeaux said. Makinen must have looked hostile because he caught Brock looking at him with a bemused expression. He smiled to show he wasn't about to kill anyone. Brock sighed and pulled a card out of his pocket, unfolded it and looked at the cryptic notes. He knew what he was going to say, he just didn't want to say too much.

"The Detachment's mission is to prepare for war and, if and when it comes, we will slow the Soviet advance through sabotage and guerrilla warfare."

"Really? That sounds ambitious. How do you expect to do that with a million Warsaw Pact soldiers all around us?" St. John said.

"Unconventional warfare. Get in and get out quickly and without being seen. We'll do our damnedest to make it hard for them to move forward. Destroy choke points, rail lines, petrol dumps. We need to give NATO in Western Europe and Germany at least seventy-two hours of breathing space so they can react."

"Sounds like a suicide mission," said Palmer.

"Maybe, but it beats waiting to be executed like the rest of the troops in the city," said Makinen. "You know Berlin is just a pre-planned prisoner of war camp, right?"

St. John attempted a course reversal, "So are you some kind of military intelligence unit? Why are you working in the East? We're supposed to know what's happening over there."

"I'm not sure why you haven't been told. Our instructions come from your War Plans Staff, that's part of the Coordinating and Planning Committee, right?" Said Brock.

St. John looked like he didn't have a good answer for what he didn't know, instead he said to Palmer, "Draft a message to Bonn. Ask them to find out what the heck's going on with WPS and what they're doing on my turf."

"Now?"

"No, when we're done here." He turned back to Brock, clearly, he bristled at the thought of having been left out of the loop, his mild expletive indicative of a Quaker upbringing.

"Well, this message should clear things up. I'm supposed to know everything that happens in my area." St. John said with an irritated look on his face.

"Everything? I'm not sure anyone knows anything about this place, much less everything. As to your other question, we're not MI. We're Special Forces; that information and the fact we're here in Berlin is classified Secret. Only the senior army staff knows," said Brock.

"Nice that the general didn't tell me. Something else I don't know," St. John huffed. "What are Special Forces anyway?"

"Like the Office of Strategic Services, chief? You were one of those, weren't you?" Palmer only used chief when visitors were present. "They're like them. You know, 'PhDs with guns.' I think that's what Wild Bill Donovan called them." What Palmer didn't mention was that St. John spent the war at the U.S. Embassy in Switzerland fighting paper cuts.

Makinen smiled. "Actually, what General Donovan said was: 'PhDs who could win a bar fight.' We're a bit different. We don't have PhDs, only guns, knives, and explosives," he said.

"And our wits," said Brock.

"I take that to mean you're not the normal kind of soldier. So, tell us why you're working in the East."

"Our mission requires preparation. We're taking advantage of being behind enemy lines before anything kicks off."

"Before the balloon goes up," added Palmer helpfully.

"Yes. A question if I may, your message traffic is all encrypted?"

"Of course, everything we do is classified," St. John said.

"Okay, when you send your message back to the WPS ask them about this special program," Brock wrote a word on a card and pushed it over to St. John. "We're not supposed to mention it out loud, but our commander said we could give you the name. Your folks should be able to clarify things that we can't talk about without permission from higher."

The word KIBITZ was written neatly in block letters. St. John passed it to Palmer. "You better send it to them TS/RH," he said.

"RH?" asked Brock.

"Restricted Handling. Our most secure channel, keeps it away from prying eyes."

"Speaking of, can we do some sort of coordination to keep our folks from running into yours over there?" Makinen said.

"No, that really wouldn't work. We don't ever tell people when we will be where. Compartmentation and all, you understand?" said St. John.

"Not really. So, I guess the best thing is just tell your people not to follow our folks. You travel with those inter-zonal 'Get Out of Jail Free' cards. We don't. I think that makes you feel invulnerable. We go over there under cover and can't risk having any attention brought to us when we're operational, hence the guns. Your boy there is lucky." Makinen nodded towards Palmer.

"We know we're not invulnerable, we are just realistic about what we can and can't do over there, but I've learned my lesson, captain," said Palmer. "On the plus side, I did show him a good crossing point."

"One point for you, but no points for the Scotch you bought while trying to interrogate him."

"If that's all, gentlemen," said St. John. "I have one final question. Who is your commander?"

"Colonel Ciernik. Great officer with a lot of experience." Brock said as he headed for the exit, Makinen in tow.

"Ciernik? I haven't heard of him before. He's a colonel?" asked Palmer guiding them out.

"Yeah, he's a full bird colonel, but you won't see his name anywhere. We're trying to keep our people out of the spotlight, just like you," said Brock.

28

———◆———

"NOW WHAT?" STEFAN asked as he set his glass down unsteadily, half on, half off the coaster, as he was, wobbling on his stool.

"What?" said Rolf.

"What's next?"

"Twenty questions."

"What's that supposed to mean?" said Stefan.

"You keep asking questions about things I don't know anything about. Drink your beer and shut up."

"That's not right. What do you say, Anton?"

"You do talk a lot, Steve."

"It's Stefan, not Steve."

The evening had started inauspiciously at "The Speak," the local watering hole for the "Det" as they had begun to call themselves. It wasn't as dismal as the bar Anton had visited in the East, but it certainly wasn't as upscale as "The Times" in the Savoy, either. For their purposes, it was fine. The Speak was not like the shared, communal, watering holes of the Serengeti, where predator and prey drank together. The only other GIs who came in were by invitation only — a few trusted friends and contacts, mostly. Others who stumbled in were quickly dissuaded from remaining very long. It didn't take much, a cold reception from the bar, slow service, and icy stares were a hint that they were not welcome.

Germans came in occasionally, some returned, most didn't. The Speak was a pub, not a *Kneipe* as the Germans usually called their bars. It was owned and run by a cantankerous old lady, a Brit whose husband had either defected, got himself shot down somewhere over Africa, or ran off with another woman, depending on who told the story and how late into the drinking it was. Nobody wanted to ask her about it. Her name was Bea, which could have been German or British, but after CIC checked her out, she was verified as a full-fledged citizen of the UK. She didn't like Germans much because they were cheap and obnoxious — the same for Brits, but everyone assumed there was more to that story — and the French stayed away because it was just too far to drive back to their *Quartier Napoléon* in the north of the city. The establishment was on the ground floor of an old apartment block in *Lichterfelde*, accessed by a short flight of steps, which often proved more of a challenge on exit than entry. Rumor had it that a Prussian cadet by the name of Richthofen had once lived upstairs, as did a lady called Marlene Dietrich before she came to her senses and bailed for America.

The façade was a crumbling gray stone on the outside, the inside was afflicted with the same dysphoria of most dive bars: beer advertisements and show posters applied with abandon, old calendars, photos of unknown places and persons tacked to the wall, and a cigarette machine by the front door. The clock above the bar tolls the correct time twice a day, while in a corner, the dartboard hung on a wall that registered as many hits off the board as on. No one had resorted to firearms to hit the bullseye. That would come years later.

Bea had proven somewhat reliable and her clientele reasonably trusted, so the Speak was determined to be free of eavesdroppers and a mostly safe place to communalize, although conversations stopped every time the bell over the door tinkled announcing a new arrival. It was here that the Det members felt free to blow off steam and tell wondrous tales, none of which had any relationship to reality. Stefan Wolpak was one of the primary purveyors of these stories, which, like his street name, was pure unadulterated fiction.

"Okay, Stefan, but you still talk too much."

"Maybe I like to talk."

"That's fine, but some people get tired of listening. You need to understand the difference," said Anton.

"Ich stimme zu," said Rolf. *I second that.*

"Whatever," said Stefan as he stood up and waddled off to the dartboard. "I'm going to toss some Bullseyes. Anybody wanna lose a game?" He was a bit overweight, gone to seed, it seemed. Too many years on the staff at Tölz and away from a team had taken their toll. Anton shook his head at the sight. He would have to get in shape soon or leave the city.

Rolf ignored him and turned to Anton. "Hilmar tells me your *Berlinerische* is coming along."

"That's good, 'cause he's killing me." Speaking too much German in the bar was frowned upon not only because English was supposed to be the common language or that some of the guys spoke another language like Serbo-Croat or Polish, they also didn't want to highlight the fact the unit was filled with linguists.

"Well, you must be doing well if he says so. I expect you've had some interesting encounters. Mine have all been fairly routine," said Rolf.

"Kind of interesting, challenging too. Makinen said I shouldn't talk about them." Anton said as he took a long pull from his half-liter glass.

"I know that. Just take it from me, be careful. Relationships over there can go bad for both people involved. Worse, they can be deadly for both of you."

"How did you figure that out?"

Rolf smiled. "What? That there might be a love interest over there? Because you stopped talking about women when you came in here."

A crash punctuated Rolf's sentence. They both turned to look. Stefan's glass lay in splinters as he rocked above it like an inflatable punch toy. Bea shook her head and started another glass. "Clean it up if you want another, damned if I'm going to. I will be adding the price of the glass to your tab," she yelled.

"He's an okay guy. Good demo man," said Rolf, turning back to Anton, "but his team sergeant has a plan that he probably won't like."

"What is it?"

"Not exactly sure, but Randallmann is calling it his 'Spartan' program."

"About time, Team Three has been spending way too much time in urban mode. All those cover stops at the *Konditorei* will do you no good," said Anton.

"Yeah, we're in much better shape than them, doing all these half liter curls," Rolf said as he raised his beer in salute and quaffed most of it.

29

THERE WERE MOSCOW Rules and then there were Langley Rules.

Langley's version was: Admit nothing, deny everything, and make counter-accusations. Allegedly. The Agency wouldn't admit it. When asked, the Public Affairs Office just said, "No comment."

That origin made sense to Charlie Palmer. He'd heard it often enough in the halls of the headquarters building, even at the Farm. Unofficially, of course.

When Bonn Station's answer to their KIBITZ cable came back, he thought of the rules as he read their response. *"The project is compartmented and BOB wasn't on the bigot list. Sorry. Terrible oversight, the fault of previous management, we'll get right on it."*

Nothing to answer the question of just what the hell KIBITZ was. He knew the drill, Bonn asks Headquarters for authorization to talk to the War Plans Staff in Paris about it and get their 'Okay' to request that Berlin be formally included on the distribution of plans and then, Bonn could go back and ask HQ for permission to make it happen. The whole convolution overlooking the fact that BOB should have been included from the beginning.

I thought we were supposed to be nimble — above all the bureaucracy. Obviously not.

St. John came into the bull-pen, back from a grueling lunch at the Officer's Club in the Harnack House across the street. It was the only place to get a good steak in town and the Martini's were good. That last bit, Charlie had to take on the word of his boss, who said Hemingway would approve. Then, St. John had learned the hard way not to order "Dry Martinis" in a German bar because he once ended up with three of them.

Today, he didn't smell too boozy. His eyes were clear and he was steady on his feet. All good signs that he was in control.

"Anything come up while I was out?"

"We got a non-answer cable from Bonn on KIBITZ. We're waiting while they ask the originator if it's okay to talk to us about it. I thought of something else after the two SDB guys left."

"What?" said St. John.

"They said their CO is a colonel. Colonel Ciernik."

"Yes, so?"

"His name wasn't on my list of colonels."

"I hope it is now."

"He is, I think he was the one name I was missing, boss."

"So Ciernik and… who was your other name?" said St. John.

"Brad Monroe, the NSA guy."

"Have you talked to Myers about them yet? That's his bailiwick, finding traitors."

"I just figured out who the second guy is. But how about this: wouldn't it be nice for us to find him first? Before Myers and his CIC?"

"I'll think about that. What about your other job? The plan to take down the killer?"

"I'm still working on that and figuring out who the traitor is will be key. Don't forget I have some real-live assets to handle too. I need to produce intelligence reports too."

"Work harder on all of them, you know the general gets on my back every time I see him."

Charlie said, "We don't even know if he is East German or Russian yet. Or maybe it's a them?"

"Doesn't matter. Find the traitor, he'll tell us who the murderer is, and then we can take care of him. Or them."

———————

Charlie was thinking that if he said anything to Myers, he might sacrifice a chance to nail a traitor, a penetration; something that would be good for BOB's balance sheet. He still had questions like: what was it that Myers hadn't told him? The CIC chief might just know something that would be worth some quid pro quo, something he could use for his Tar Baby.

He smelled her before he saw her eyes peeking over the cubicle wall, his own were fixed on the paper in front of him. She was watching him as he scribbled to outline a plan of action. She had a delicate scent, more fragrant than cloying, he hadn't noticed it before.

"How the meeting go?" She asked. "They were rather intimidating, one of them was pretty rough looking. Did you notice his ring? A wolf's head, I think."

"Fine. No, actually, it was good. The guy with the wolf is Finnish-American. And they gave me a lead on a colonel I didn't know before."

"That was nice of them."

"They don't know they did it. He's their commander."

"The commander of the Support Detachment?" Maria said.

"Yes, SDB they call it."

"I know, I figured that out all by my little self. And then I looked them up in the directory. They're located on Andrews Barracks, the old Prussian cadet school. You did want to find them, didn't you?"

"Yeah, and I forgot to ask them. I should go take a look. Where's it at?"

"*Lichterfelde* on *Kadettenweg*, about two miles away. Oddly enough, it's the old Prussian cadet school and during the war it was the headquarters for Hitler's SS Bodyguard Division."

"You've been there?" He said.

"Once, I went swimming. They've got a big indoor pool on the grounds."

"Show me."

"I can do that," Maria paused. "If you buy me dinner."

Seeing her lips curve up sensually into a smile, so did Charlie's.

"One question though, Maria, if I may?"

"Shoot."

"Why do you wear a wedding ring on your right hand?"

"Keeps the Germans away. They're all jerks."

"Wow, that's pretty harsh."

"I know, but most German women agree with me and don't want to marry them either."

"The good thing is that there's a shortage of German men, what with the war and all."

"That may have been the best thing the Allies have done for humanity," she said.

30

RICHARD BECKER SAT on the veranda of his third story apartment, tipped the beer bottle back and swallowed. "I'm glad you came over. Too much time all locked up by yourself is bad for you as is too much time out with the boys at night," he said when he came up for air.

"You assume that I don't have a girlfriend here? You're as bad as Rolf."

"You're right, ever since you mentioned the girl you met over there, I kinda assumed."

Anton knew he was right. Rolf probably also informed on him after their conversation at the Speak. That's what team members did in an outfit like the Det. They either watched out for teammates or told outrageous lies about them. It all depended on where you were on the scale of friendship. Shitheads didn't last long and they didn't get invited over to the Team Sergeant's home for *Cervelas à l'alsacienne.*

"What is it anyway?"

"More or less, it's fancy hotdogs and cheese wrapped in bacon," Becker said. "My favorite lunch when I was a kid. But we're not having that. Claire said hot dogs were too low class for guests. We're having cordon bleu instead."

"I'm pretty low class. That would have been perfect for me."

"Me too, but she keeps trying to make me upper class even though I told her I wasn't ever going to be an officer. It's too late for me anyway. This might be my last overseas tour."

"How did you get started in this anyway?"

"I got drafted in time for the war, served in France with the OSS. That's where I met Claire. I could talk to her because my family came from the Alsace. I had learned French and German at home. I brought her back to the States in '46, joined the reserves, got a job, then we had a boy, that's Kimball."

"He's what, nine?"

"Ten. Learning German at school. Already knows French. Claire made sure he knows her language because she doesn't want him to turn into *le Bosche*, or so she says."

"Why did you come back in?"

"Korea started and a lot of us got called back to active duty. I was lucky though. I had orders for Germany and when I reported into Fort Dix, I heard about this new thing called SF. I volunteered. That was 1952. That's how I ended up in Tölz."

"So, now I know why you ended up here, language, experience, but why me?"

"Why not? You may be young, but we see potential there. Besides, if we just went for experience there'd only be a bunch of old guys here. You do have some experience, the kind not many of us have. What you did in Hungary for example."

"I didn't do anything special."

"That's not what your team sergeant said."

"What'd he say?"

"Enough to get you here."

Claire appeared at the door. Diminutive, but pretty, all tucked into a flowered apron and looking like a happy housewife.

"I brought Kimball back from the park. He wants to meet you, Anton. Richard tells me you know French," speaking to him in the language.

"More or less. I speak Acadian. I'm from Louisiana," he said, letting his accent flavor his speech.

"You're Creole then."

"Cajun, not Creole, ma'am. We're from the po' side of N'orlans," breaking back into English, letting his accent slip in as well.

"You have a favorite food from there?"

"It'd have to be crawfish gumbo, ma'am."

A young Kimball Becker bounced onto the balcony holding a red, blue, and white FC Bayern Munich football tightly.

"Do you want to kick the ball with me?" he said, his childish energy spilling all over.

Claire smiled. "Please do, if you want, Anton. There's a small playground out back. Dinner will take another half hour."

Once Anton and the boy left the apartment, Becker hugged his wife tight and kissed her. "I'm glad I don't have to chase girls anymore. You're all I need."

"You mean, you don't want to put up with all the trouble of the hunt."

"Maybe, but you're still my best decision ever."

"Silly GI, you didn't make any decisions. I did." Claire said as she squiggled herself out of his hold.

Marginally frustrated, Becker followed his wife into the kitchen. "Kim's taken to Anton. Maybe we could ask him to babysit for us so we can go to dinner sometime?"

"Doesn't he have a girl to chase?"

"He does, but it's a bit complicated."

"I don't want to know."

"I wasn't going to tell you."

Claire looked at Becker hard, her eyes as mean as she could make them before her face softened. "Just try and keep him out of trouble. He's a nice kid."

31

———◆———

AS HE STEPPED out the door after dinner, he saw that the day was already dead. It was dark and a cool breeze out of the east told him to button the coat he was wearing. Looking around, he saw that he was alone in the brownstone's fore garden. The street beyond was empty, save the few parked cars at the curb. At the end of the street, a taxi passed through the intersection, it's roof light signaling it was free. He let it pass — he rarely took taxis. Even in West Berlin, their drivers were likely to report any strange passengers to the police. In East Berlin, it was a certainty.

Anton decided to walk. The Oskar-Helene-Heim U-Bahn station was near, but once he got up a head of steam he didn't want to stop. The line didn't go where he wanted to, anyway. His apartment wasn't far but the Speak was even closer. And it was Saturday. It was bound to be interesting and better than sitting around at home; he had nothing to read and with nobody to talk. He took off towards the bar like a homing pigeon heading for the roost, all his routes, walking or city transit, were imprinted on his brain. He rarely used a map and, even then, definitely not when he was on the street. That was bad form and distracted him from keeping an eye out for surveillance. *Except … there are always exceptions,* he thought.

Walking down *Kadettenweg* to *Finckensteinallee*, turning the corner, he saw the sign. It was indeed busy. Two of his comrades were standing on the front stoop, smoking, beers in their hands, as music spilled out the open door. Not too loud as the little old lady block wardens were sure to call the cops if it was too loud after eight p.m. Even then, the German police knew better than to show up by themselves. The MPs would also be there so a tense standoff was likely to ensue, the proprietor being warned while her patrons glared at the police and mused of taking the cops out.

Not tonight. It was relatively quiet, sedate almost.

As he climbed the steps, he glanced up into the sky. Crystal clear, he saw the nearly full moon through the bare branches of the oaks. He looked at his watch, not to know the time, but to mark a start point for later reckoning.

Murmuring greetings as he went inside, Anton saw the usual faces through the layers of smoke that formed their own weather patterns and drifted across the room. Most of the smoke came from Bea's cigarette. Stefan and Rolf, who should have been candidates for the most frequent drinker award, had such a thing existed, were sidled up to the bar on stools. As it was, they had monogramed drinking glasses which hung from hooks in a line along the wall when not in use. Stefan's glass mug had been replaced several times after the previous ones had been "killed in action" as he told the story. Bea had resorted to inscribing it with a grease pencil. Currently, Wolfpack's glass was fully engaged, fill, drain, repeat; faster than the others, Anton judged. And, for once, the Lodge Act guys, Kullek, Vuckovitch, Janke, and Rolf, outnumbered the American-born, he and Stefan. Not a single civilian Berliner and no women. Except Bea.

As he reached the bar, a *Becher* was slammed down onto its pewter top, foaming up and over the rim a bit. It was for him. Bea worked quickly when she decided someone was acceptable and there were ways around the usual regulation seven-minute pour for a Pils. He sat next to Rolf and drank only after he greeted his teammate with a toast of clinked glasses. Rolf's cheeks were emblazoned with a pale red glow, but his eyes were focused, a good sign. Stefan, in his street persona a couple of stools down the bar, was not in such good shape. He barely acknowledged Anton's arrival, head down staring into the glass as if it was a long-lost lover. Anton hoped that Randallmann would somehow pull Stefan back from the abyss.

"How was dinner at Becker's? Did you like those cheese and bacon sausages?"

"We had cutlets instead. Mizzus Becker said saucissons were low class."

"I'm offended. She fed me the sausages when I went there." Rolf stewed.

"Maybe that was a comment on your background?"

"I don't know. Maybe. Aren't people from Alsace half German?"

"Doubt it. She seems proud of her Froginess."

"That's what caused the war in the first place. Denial."

"What, you say the Alsatians don't like Germans? I think there was a bit more to it than that."

"Whatever. How's your friend doing?"

"Which friend?" Anton said.

"The one over there." Rolf indicated vaguely in an easterly direction with a tilt of his head. "Does she have a name?"

"I'm not supposed to talk about her, but it's Katja."

"So, how she doing?"

"Don't know. I haven't seen her in a while."

Rolf regarded Anton a moment before speaking. "What did the boss and Becker say to you?"

"Nothing much. Just not to talk about her and that he was going to talk with the colonel."

"Anything else?"

"Nope."

"Don't you think you should check up on her?"

"How? I can't call her."

"No one said you couldn't see her again, did they?"

"No, just not to do anything stupid."

"Is checking on a friend being stupid?"

"No, but listening to you might be," Anton said.

Despite the bar noise, the bell clearly announced more patrons. Everyone looked at the couple entering and then, a moment later, the raucous banter continued. Except for Anton who continued to stare.

"Somebody you know?" Rolf said.

"The guy from the East."

Charlie was accompanied by an attractive woman. Both were dressed for work. Charlie in a rough wool sport coat, its origin obscure, but not obviously American. The woman in a long camel-colored overcoat. Anton glanced at her legs, bare below the coat, and saw they ended in heels — not the best for walking long distances, he surmised.

Standing near the doorway, Charlie surveyed the place, passing over Anton without pausing the first time, looking at each person as if categorizing and cataloging each. The woman was very pretty but not in a look-at-me kind of way. She wore her good looks effortlessly without pretense or show. Definitely the most beautiful tonight, even if there were only two women in the bar. Her eyes, dark and intelligent, seemed to soak up the atmosphere of the place and judge it at the same time. Maybe not out of prejudice, but self-preservation. She seemed to take in the decor, the drinkers, and Bea, as if deciding how long she could stay in this dump. Educated and observant, Anton decided, and not too attached to Charlie emotionally because she remained apart from him, not close. More likely, she was professionally independent and didn't need his protection.

Charlie's eyes returned to Anton as he approached. "You look as though you could use another," he said eyeing Anton's glass.

"Maybe. What brings you here?"

"We were in the area. This is Maria, by the way. And Maria, this is the man I told you about. Harry, is it? That's your name, right? Can't remember quite rightly."

Rolf nudged Anton. "Who's this?"

"Charlie Palmer, the guy I ran into the other night. You remember? The one from the Savoy."

Rolf's eyes ran the length and width of Charlie and then the woman. Anton thought he was doing a personality assessment because his face remained passive. When he was finished Rolf said, "They look harmless. You need some space?"

"For a moment, yes." Anton said turning to Charlie. "Is there something I can do for you?" One thing Mama had taught Anton was to be polite, no matter what you thought of the person in front of you. He had nothing against Charlie except the grief he'd caused the other night inside the Soviet sector. Grief that could have gotten him arrested by the *Stasi* or worse. No, nothing much at all. He stepped away from the bar to a standing table near the front window that was free of clients.

Charlie spoke first. "I just wanted to find you. After your officers came to brief us, I managed to figure out where you were located. I should say we, because Maria helped. And then, we watched the front gate until you appeared."

"I would say bad tradecraft on my part, but we also know where you work and live."

"Hard feelings?" Charlie said.

"No, but just why are you always following me?" Anton looked at the bar where Rolf and Bea were busy keeping Maria engaged or interrogating her, one of the two. "Who's Maria?"

"A secretary at the office."

"She's not your girlfriend or another agent?"

"I told you, we're called officers and, no, she's neither."

"That's good because I think my friend is making a move on her."

Charlie looked over his shoulder casually, taking in the scene. "I don't think I have much to worry about. He's not her type."

"Who is?"

"Me."

"Arrogant bastard, aren't you?" *Anyone else would have said, 'She'll be fine.' Not Charlie, it's all about you, isn't it?* Anton thought. He was beginning to see Charlie as a slick operator who was playing the game on a completely different tier. Soldier spies like Anton tended to work at the grass roots level, common people trying to achieve things on a more personal scale, while spooks tried to subvert and suborn people on a higher level, government officials, diplomats, entire countries. Strategic versus tactical. The things he'd read in the new Fleming novel he picked up in London

Heathrow were beginning to gel in his mind as he watched Charlie Palmer. *Something's up, but be careful, nothing here is as it seems.* He smiled at Palmer, nevertheless. "And my name's not Harry," he continued. "I'm Anton. So why are you here?"

"I wanted to get to know a fellow traveler, since we both visit the same place."

"I wouldn't call it visiting and I doubt we mix with the same crowd."

"I was hoping we could talk about that," said Charlie.

"I think you heard from my boss all you're going to hear. Besides, this isn't the place to discuss it."

"Too bad you think that way. I think we could help each other out."

"Help each other out to do what? Don't answer that. I know what you're going to say won't make any sense."

"How so? You haven't heard my proposal."

"I don't need to hear it — I have my own stuff to do. You're about to step over the line."

"What line?"

"Trying to recruit an American."

"Recruit? I'm not recruiting, I was about to ask a favor, I can do that you know. Who told you about recruiting Americans anyway?"

"I learned that at school — National Security Act of 1947."

"That's pretty esoteric stuff for a school to teach, but it only applies inside CONUS and you can volunteer anytime."

Anton had enough and stood close, invading Charlie's space. "You ask too many questions. If I didn't know who you worked for, I'd report you to CI."

"Go right ahead. It won't hurt me."

"Actually, I can't figure you out. You're like the first string of the real deal team. What kind of help would you need from me? We're like back benchers compared to you guys."

"You don't have a good idea of what you bring to the game, do you, Anton?"

"Don't try to flatter me. You should probably leave before someone decides to throw you out."

"Who would do that?"

"The owner. She doesn't like people who annoy her guests."

Charlie looked worried for a moment — his composure cracked. He stole a glance and saw Bea staring back at him hard. Rolf and Maria were also. Then, he noticed the other conversations had quieted down as well.

"Good enough. I'll go, but we'll be seeing each other again, I'm sure."

"Hopefully not. Remember what almost happened last time."

That brought Charlie up short. He gave a bit of an indignant shrug, seemed to think about saying something more, but gave the idea up. Then he turned, collected Maria, and headed out the door.

Rolf walked over to the table where Anton was looking out the window, watching Charlie and the woman walk away on the sidewalk and set a new beer on the table for Anton.

"He seemed a bit put out. You don't like him much, do you?" Rolf tapped a cigarette out of a package that looked like a deck of cards. *Karo*, rank East German things from Dresden with no filter and reeked of burning weeds.

"Why do you smoke those things?"

"Reminds me of the Russian cigarettes we had on the Eastern Front — the only thing that kept us warm."

"I guess you're just happy you weren't captured," said Anton.

"Oh, but I was. I escaped though, a story for another time. Now, about your friend…."

"I'm not sure what to make of him. It seems like he's looking for a favor."

"Or a fall guy," said Rolf.

"Good point. I'm gonna talk with Top about him. In the meantime, I need a drink."

32

————◆————

BACK OUT ON the street, Charlie and Maria walked a couple of blocks to where their officially unofficial sedan was parked. Berlin plates registered to a business downtown that was somehow connected to a private travel company headquartered in Hamburg.

"He didn't seem very happy to see you," Maria said as she slid into the passenger seat.

"I thought that might happen, but I wasn't expecting he'd tell me to get lost. I thought he'd be interested in what we're doing. Like he said, we are the first string."

"Maybe that's the problem. You see it as being better than them. He might see you as a challenge to overcome, not join."

Charlie paused at his door, looking over the roof of the Opel. Maria's comment was not what he'd expected. Something she did often. Of course, he'd missed it. Who wouldn't want to work with an Agency officer? The answer was simple, the who was Anton and the rest of his band of brothers who didn't trust the Agency anymore than they trusted the regular army.

"That's it. Because he's involved in something that he thinks is just as important as what we do, only they do it at a disadvantage," he said, climbing behind the wheel.

"Exactly. Now, while you figure out how to approach him again, you can take me to the Savoy for a drink. That place was pretty bad."

"I imagine it serves its purpose; it's a safe haven where they can congregate, enjoy the company of their comrades, and not worry about intruders."

"Intruders like you. Don't forgot you're part of that equation too."

———————

The following day, St. John found Charlie before Charlie found him, as usual. St. John generally was trolling to find fodder for his almost daily reports back to the headquarters at Langley. He was never squeamish about spending the government's money on communications, despite the fact that each individual encrypted character of a message was charged and assessed against the budget, this time by the army who ran all the secure telecommunications out of Berlin. There were ways to cut costs, like sticking in a code-word that made it military-related rather than straight agency traffic, then he'd leave off all the defense department addresses so they wouldn't see what he was saying. The technicians in the comms center didn't care, they didn't even know what was in the message because it was all in code, but it saved his precious BOB money, which he could then use for things like representational whiskey.

"Palmer, anything new?" St. John said, his head over the cubicle wall. St. John normally used family names when addressing his minions, using given names was far too familiar.

"I found the kid I met in the East. His name is Anton, he's part of that SDB unit. They're over on Andrews Barracks. Maria helped me find them."

"So, Maria's a stalking horse now?"

"Not stalking. I went right up to him and re-introduced myself."

"Why?"

"My plan is starting to come together. I call it "Project Tar Baby."

"Finally, we getting somewhere. How's it going to work?"

"Generally, it goes like this… we use bait to get our target to show himself and then, when he does, we nail him."

"That's kind of what you said the first time. What's new, what's the bait, and who's the target?"

"I'm still working on that, but I've got ideas. Those SDB folks are doing things over in the East. What if we use them to help us?"

"You mean set them up as bait? I don't think the general would appreciate getting any more of his soldiers killed over there."

"Well, it's either that or we find the traitor and turn him."

"Yes, that's a more palatable solution. We still need someone to pull the trigger."

"Not me. I wasn't trained for that at the Farm."

"Nor I. Maybe, that's how you could use the SDB guys. They're trained for that kind of stuff, aren't they?"

"I think so, but what about their commander?"

"What about him?" said St. John.

"He's on my suspect list."

"This is getting complicated. Even if their commander is the traitor, they probably won't want to shoot him."

"No, but I think they'll be willing to take out his handler. That's who killed Buchanan. Then, they capture the traitor, whoever he is, bring him back here and he ends up in Leavenworth for forever and a day. Everyone's happy."

33

SHE HAD SAID Hagenauer Straße, which was good because it was a very short street, only a block long. Bad for the same reason. He couldn't just hang out there, hoping to see her. Some suspicious, spinster block warden would call him in for being a vagrant or worse. He didn't need that. So, Anton stayed close to the bar, where there was more traffic, people, activity and a specific point to watch the door. When her work was finished, she'd exit and head home. He could then bump her close to her home.

He'd found the street on the map at the office and used his pre-war *Baedeker* guide book of Berlin to plan a quick visit to see her. He'd wrap the visit around the work he had to do over there.

On the way in to the site, he did a quick recon of the area, an act which doubled to make sure he was clean of the hounds before he did what he was programmed to do. Place another message in a simple drop. A good location, well screened, never used before. He was in and out, with the load signal placed in a matter of minutes. Work finished, he made his way across town, back from way up in *Pankow* down to *Prenzlauer Berg*. Shortly after he arrived on scene, the last patrons filtered out, some quiet, a few still lustily singing or simply drunk making their way in different directions, their voices echoing down the streets, getting smaller and smaller, then disappearing altogether. The lights inside started to go out and then, when it was dark, two people, an older man and a younger woman came out. Katja with the man he'd seen behind the counter once before. They exchanged words that he couldn't hear and she turned away as the man locked the door and set off in the direction he had anticipated. He waited and watched to see where the man headed. The opposite direction. *Good, no issues with him.* Anton followed the woman down *Kastanienallee*, heading towards the U-Bahn station. It made sense, there were more lights there. Atthree in the morning, she'd probably rather risk walking that direction than through the dark streets. It wasn't far, first turn at the station, then the second street on the right. Just which house?

She walked with a determined step, probably anxious to get home and have a quiet night to herself. From eighty yards back, he tried to see what she carried. Not a purse, but a shoulder bag with what looked like a loaf of bread peeking out. She either had gone shopping or the owner didn't mind her taking home the leftovers from the bar.

He began to close the distance as she neared her street, not too close, he didn't want to frighten her. She turned and disappeared a moment until Anton could quick step and get around the corner. It was a dark canyon of a street, as if all the light had been sucked out of the space he entered. Maybe one out of five streetlights was feebly trying to illuminate the gloom. The bright lights from the station couldn't turn the corner or get over the tops of the brownstones. It was pitch black. He paused a moment, searching. There she was, about a third of the way down the block. He walked fast, then she began to climb the outside steps of one of the buildings. He was close enough that he could say her name and she would hear.

"Katja."

She paused, hand on the rail, and looked to the sound. It took a moment to find his figure in the dark. Anton stepped closer, almost at the stairs. She looked up and down the street before she said, "Come, quickly." Then she continued up, not waiting, and unlocked the entry door and stepped inside. He hurried to the door, taking the steps two at a time, and stepped in with her.

Her finger was on her lips. Universal sign.

Quietly, "Hello, Klaus. I thought someone was behind me. Took you long enough."

"Five days minus seven hours," he said. "Busy at work."

"You counted. I'm flattered. We should get inside," she turned and continued up, not bothering with the lights, probably because they didn't work, maybe because she didn't want to be seen. One floor, two, at the third, she paused. Hers was the left door off the landing.

"It's not much."

The door opened. He stepped inside. The doors closed and the light went on. It wasn't much — pre-war poverty, renovated to post-war austerity. A room with a tiny kitchenette in a small alcove, a couch and table with two chairs, an old armoire, and another door to possibly a bedroom or a bath. Or a closet.

The curtains were pulled tight. She stood in the middle and dropped her coat around the back of a chair before she unloaded the food from the bag into a tiny cool box about half the size of an army footlocker. The loaf of bread went on top.

"It's all I have. It's not bad. Far from all the trains and most of the smoke. Just some loud neighbors"

"It's something. You're alone here." He'd seen worse in the city and the Mississippi Delta back home. Hers was clean, neat, and smelled fresh. All good selling points in Mama's book.

"I am, which is good for now. Why did you come?"

"To see you."

"Beyond that, why?"

"You intrigued me. I wanted to know more."

"You're new at this, aren't you?"

"Are you?"

"That's the right question. I'm new too, but I'm also a convenient target at the bar."

"For the men?"

"Occasionally, the women too. Maybe because I ignore the men."

"Why?"

"They have no future. That's why I talked to you. You seem like you've got a plan; you're headed somewhere. You not from here, are you? I can hear it in your voice."

"I was raised on the border near Chemnitz, down south," he lied, he'd finally remembered the story he should have used with König. "My mother was from Hungary."

"That must be it. You don't have to go soon, do you?" Katja was less than a meter from Anton now. Eyes seductive. She'd moved in close and when he didn't back off, she came closer.

"No, I can stay for a while. At least until I need to go for work."

"I probably smell like the bar. I should clean up."

"Wait. You're fine." He reached and touched her forearm, then pulled back, not sure how she'd react. She looked down at his hand briefly then back into his eyes.

Katja took Anton's forearm and led him to the couch, pushing him down onto the cushions. "Stay," she said and opened the double doors of the armoire that concealed a Murphy bed.

"It's not a big place, but it has what I need. And right now..." Katja pulled the cord at the top of the wall and a bed descended softly into position. She returned to the couch and grabbed his hand firmly as she pulled him up deftly — she could handle a beer keg, after all — and steered him to a new position next to the mattress. The look in her eyes burned into his and said only one thing. Even if he had wanted to escape, he had no time to react when she leaned in and kissed him like only a lover could. Anton felt his heart racing and spine tingling with electricity. She pulled back and smiled, then pushed lightly and laid him out on the bed.

He was frustrated at first wrestling to unwrap himself from the clothing that somehow conspired to keep him in a cocoon. Katja didn't help, she was too busy stripping herself of everything she wore, which further slowed Anton as he watched distractedly. Free of her drab, full clothing, he saw she had distinct curves, not fleshy, but strong, smooth, rounded. He got back up when free of all the encumbering cloth and stood in front of her, reaching around, pulling her toward him, and kissed her. She kissed him back, hungrily, and deeply. This time, he pushed her softly and she sank onto the bed crossways, legs half on, half off. He followed, dropping onto his elbows, feeling her body with his and enjoying the warmth. He kissed her again and she wrapped her arms around his back pulling him into her tightly. Breathing heavily, moving together, sweat running between them, ears next to mouths, listening, the world dizzying, nerves racing, and then, release. Quiet returned like a slow wave. Relaxed. Coolness returning to the air around their bodies. He rolled over onto his back.

"Where did that come from?" he said.

"The dam broke. I couldn't wait"

His head on the pillow, he closed his eyes. He'd never wanted a girl like he did Katja. He smiled, but almost forgot she was there, watching him.

"What are you thinking about?" she said.

Why do women always ask that question after sex? he thought. Insecurity? Jealousy? Just plain curiosity?

"I'm thinking it would nice to be around you a lot more."

"What's keeping you from it?"

"Work. Travel back and forth. I'm always tired you know."

"Not the fact that I'm considered almost a non-person by the government?"

"No. Not that." He stroked her hair lightly, watching her eyes. Even though it the light was poor, he could see she was on the verge of tears.

"If they found out you were with me, they might keep you from your job."

"I don't think so. Besides, you didn't do anything. It was your father."

"That doesn't seem to make a difference."

"Well, it does to me. Maybe we should think about moving," he said. *A big step*, he thought.

"Please. Next time we'll talk more. Go to sleep, it's nearly morning."

It was still dark when he woke. He knew the sun wouldn't poke it's head up through the winter fog and smoke until nearly eight a.m., and, according to his watch, he had two hours to make it back across the frontier before it got really light. At least in the morning, going to work was as a strong a cover for action as anything and his documents were good. Next to him, the bed was empty. Groggily, he looked about. Light shone dimly from the alcove, where he could see Katja puttering about, a light robe thrown on. She must have sensed his eyes on her, she paused and looked back with a slight smile.

"Come on, sleepy head. Get some coffee. You have to go to work soon."

He swung his legs out of bed and pulled on his pants. He'd shower at the barracks after PT. He didn't want to waste any of Katja's precious hot water. Dressed, he stumbled into the living area where Katja met him coffee cup in hand. He took a sip, then a gulp.

"Not bad." He left out the "*for communist coffee*," and set the cup on the table. Wrapping his arms around her, he hugged, inhaling her scent, remembering the night.

"Thank you," he said.

She kissed him and pulled back a bit, her smile even bigger. "No, thank you."

"I better go."

"I know, but," she walked over to a small table near the door and pulled a key from the drawer. "Take this."

"What's it to?"

"This place, silly. Just in case you need it," Katja said.

"The neighbors will talk."

"They already talk about me. Just be careful out there. Two armed KG men were murdered not too far from here the other night and the cops are watching the streets pretty closely."

"Who would want to kill *Kampfgruppen?* They're pretty useless." Anton was concerned and curious. A murder of armed militia guards, even ones with minimal training, was not the sort of crime one expected on the streets of Berlin, East or West.

"I don't know, but the *Bullen* seem to like to pick on young men on the street, and that has given them more of an excuse."

"I'll do my best. I am an upright, law-abiding, German boy."

"Of course you are, my dear," Katja said it like Anton remembered his mom saying it, but she kissed him differently. Much differently. When they came up for air, she said, "Don't forget to think about what we discussed last night."

"About going over?"

"Yes."

"I am. How could I not? But I need to figure out how to make the move. Where to live and all that."

"I know that. Take your time. There is one more thing."

"What is it?"

"My little sister. I need to take her with us."

34

———————◆———————

"WE GOT SOME more info from headquarters on our new friends. SDB is an undercover special forces unit like they told us, but this KIBITZ thing they're doing seems to be a one-off. Not their usual job. They're helping the War Plans Staff to set up a resistance movement in the East, code-name STORCH, by placing supply dumps, caches, all over the Soviet sector and even some in the countryside. It's being directed by our very own WPS, who forgot to inform us of the operation. Apparently, many of the members of the group are part of the Young Jurist League."

St. John was ranting in his usual, low-key, patrician Yankee manner. Where other station chiefs would be bouncing off the walls, screaming at things, St. John relied on that cucumber-cool indignance so common with rich folk from New England. Either that, or he didn't give a damn, Charlie wasn't sure which.

"So where have WPS been getting all their dope on this movement? I certainly haven't heard of it."

"Apparently, Gehlen and his old boys have contacts over there." The *Org Gehlen*, the new German federal intelligence service, cobbled together by a bunch of former intel officers whose pensions had been cut off after they lost the last war.

"Langley must figure we can't be trusted with the information."

"That just changed. Apparently WPS took the 'need to know' thing a bit too far, so the seventh floor wants us to vet them."

"Vet whom? WPS or the resistance?"

"That might be a good place to start, but no, not WPS, the resistance, the Young Jurist people."

"Isn't that something you do before you start giving them stuff that goes bang?"

"All they've been given so far are radios. The other stuff stays in place until the group is activated."

"When the balloon goes up," said Charlie.

"Exactly. So now we have the names of the five cell leaders. That's all the Gehlen Organization has anyway. And then, only the leaders know their cell members, no one else."

"Besides Gehlen, WPS, and us, who has the five names?"

"SDB has been in contact with two of them. The other three names have not been passed."

"Will they be?"

"Not yet, if ever. Those two were just a contingency, so from here on out, SDB will just load the cache sites."

"Okay, I gotta ask, who trained them to do our kind of spook magic?"

"Interesting that you should ask. The message outlined that, along with all their other skills, they were trained by a group called Team Ten."

"Who are they?"

"They are us. Our very own traveling squad of tradecraft magicians."

"I didn't know we did that."

"For once, you admit you don't know everything."

"Right, boss," Charlie said. "Next question. What are the chances that War Planning will help us task SDB to help us with Tar Baby?"

"I think two — slim and none. Besides, I don't even want to ask. They don't need to know about our operations. But there is another way. We tell the general our plan and get him to task them."

"Will he do that?"

"You heard him, he's on a vendetta. I'm sure he would be happy to loan us his boys to take out a commie. He could use it as a point on his performance review. So, get our plan ready."

"Great, now all I need to do is finish it," Charlie said. *Now it's our plan, not your plan.*

"When do you meet B/1 again?'

"End of the week. Last time we met he told me he'd be out of town until Wednesday, some *Waffenbrüderschaft* get-together. So, we'll go for Friday night."

"*Waffenbrüderschaft?*" St. John said.

"Brothers in arms. All the Warsaw Pact intelligence officers meet and talk shop."

"Sounds like at least ten reports. One for each country."

"That would be eight, boss, but I will stretch it. I asked him to get the meeting's minutes and all the dinner menus."

"I can see it now, a report on the nutritional regime of Warsaw Pact senior intelligence officers. Unique approach, Palmer. I like it. While you're at it, get me a ground-truth report on his view of living conditions in Dresden."

"As if I didn't have anything else to do," Charlie said under his breath.

35

CIERNIK WAITED IN the dark. While he studied his surroundings, he smiled to himself. As a student, worker, then soldier, he'd often been left in the dark, waiting. It was part who he was and not much had changed, except now he knew exactly for what he was waiting. It had taken him years to get this far and, although many of the twists and turns he'd negotiated were difficult or unexpected, he was pleased to see his plans were coming to fruition. He'd managed to put most things in place, just a bit more waiting then.

Maja was showing a bit more confidence. *Growing into her role,* he thought. This time, she saw him before he moved. She'd probably spent more time in dark tonight, her eyes must be getting accustomed.

No words were spoken as she walked by. She led, only a short distance, to a spot where the path dipped through some trees. Even darker here and colder, the freezing waters of the lake cooled the air that slowly roiled through the undergrowth. Only the memories of a colder winter in 1944 near St. Vith kept his feet from complaining. Or as one of the men in the unit said, it's better than the Eastern Front.

Maja had stopped on the path and turned. They embraced.

"All is well? No problems."

"No, all is fine. Roman is back at home. He had a good trip."

"Did he give you the information?"

"He got what you asked for, but…," she said. Her voice caught, she stopped.

"But what?"

"He wants to see you in person."

"You've told him about me?"

"He's always known. It's not a problem, Jozef. He wants what I want, what we want."

The myriad of inescapable conclusions raced through his head, not one of them was without problems unless he just turned and walked. *No,* he thought. *I can't do that.*

"When?"

"Soon, he says it's important."

Ciernik thought for a moment. A readiness alert, deployment, anything could mess up his plans at any time, but he needed to make this happen.

"Fine. How about now?"

Maja was startled by his proposal and he certainly hadn't expected to say it, but it made sense. There would be no time for second thoughts, "I'll walk behind you," he said. "Don't look around and give me time to catch up when you're at your door."

Maja nodded and gave him the address. "We'll go in the back way. It'll be safer."

She had the good sense not to use the wide avenues built to commemorate Stalin's ideal of a city — soulless, wind-swept streets that were usually devoid of private cars because there were so few and only filled when the DDR's very own people's army, the NVA, paraded their olive-green tanks and personnel carriers down avenues between buildings hung with red party flags and portraits of the leaders, all old men, dead or alive.

Instead, she followed a quiet route through the neighborhoods and even took a meandering route through a park then a long apartment block's hidden courtyard. She was untrained, except by the necessity of surviving in a country that constantly scrutinized its population.

As they approached Maja's apartment through the courtyard, Ciernik sensed a change. He suspected they were close, didn't know it for sure, but when she stopped to adjust her shoe, he thought she was telling him something, a signal of sorts. He saw a few more cars moving on the streets, a few more people, and what looked to be an upgrade in the housing and the security. Not much, but noticeable. But in the back, it was quiet.

Maja stopped and fished out her keys before she climbed upward to the rear entrance of the building. He closed the gap and checked around him quickly to make sure he was unobserved before following her. He saw no one in the windows, no one on the path. Fairly sure, at least as sure as one can be at night in a place that could be hostile to him. She had the door open by the time he reached her and they stepped inside together. Dark, but the air was clean, not the usual staleness, laden with smells identifiable or unidentifiable, that attended most walk ups. The light stayed off. Maja grasped his sleeve and pulled him to the stairs and up. Not a word.

A door was reached and Maja tapped twice with her key before opening it and allowing Jozef to step inside. Only when she locked the door behind herself, did she turn and hug Jozef.

"Come, Roman should be inside," she said leading the way into a well-lighted front room. The apartment was a comfortable size for two people. Several pastorals adorned the walls, several wooden cabinets, and a couch upon which a young man sat, younger than Ciernik, about the same as Maja, perhaps thirty-two years under his belt. A curl of cigarette smoke snaked its way up from an ashtray and through the yellow light of a table lamp. He folded the newspaper he held and stood.

Extending his hand. "I am Roman," he said, speaking Polish. "And you are Jozef. We have much to discuss. Please sit. Maja, please, some tea." He looked to Maja, who nodded and went off to the kitchen where Ciernik could see an already prepared service.

"You were expecting me?" Jozef said.

"I suspected you would come when Maja told you."

"I assume it's safe here?"

"As safe as one can hope. Our people have checked the apartment out, nothing the Germans or Russians can use to listen or see us with. If anyone asks, I will say a colleague from the embassy visited."

"And nothing to worry about from *bezpieka*?" Józef said, using the colloquial for state security.

"No, and I would know because that's my job."

"You are still paranoid though?"

"Of course, always. But no signs and I am watching."

"Good. Now, what do you have to tell me and why?"

"First, I became suspicious when Maja began to ask me about my work. She finally told me you would be able to help us if I was able to provide some help. I could have reported you, but I would have lost two things: probably my job and, most importantly, Maja. Besides, I think Chicago is a place where I would like to live."

"That's a relief," Jozef said. "I would also hate to lose Maja." Jozef had many questions, not the least of which was why Roman permitted him into his home, but he assumed the man had his own agenda. He wasn't ready to question him or ask anything that might disrupt the relationship yet. Clarification would come later, there was time for that, hopefully.

"Good, then I will begin. So you are absolutely sure of who I am, my name is Major Roman Kossakowski. I am a First Directorate SB officer and a liaison to the Group of Soviet Forces in Germany, specifically the KGB at Karlshorst, but I work from our embassy," he handed over his SB identity book which Jozef flipped through and gave back.

"I know the SB. You're in the foreign intelligence section," said Ciernik as Maja poured tea for both of them. She gave Jozef a warm smile and said, "I will let you two to talk." Jozef watched her walk away, feeling awkward and happy at the same time.

"You mean a lot to her," Roman said. He sighed, head turned, also watching her. "She's wonderful, I understand you. But, like Maja said, I have important information and you don't have much time. The Russians are planning something big to force the Allies out of West Berlin."

"I know that, Major. But first, you tell me what you have."

36

AFTER A NEW Surveillance detection route that would end up costing him several hours sleep, Charlie was wide awake and ready for his asset, who had much more to lose than he. Another park on a different night.

B/1 appeared out of the darkness, the street lights and the stars were equally obscured by the mist that eddied about them in billowing wisps despite there being no wind.

"It's the effect between the cold canal water and the warmer air, the sudden temperature change." B/1 said as they watched a cloud float slowly past them, wispy, disappearing into the air.

"Are you a meteorologist?" said Charlie. A difficult word to get right in English, let alone German.

"A friend explained it to me once long ago. But I have other interesting things to tell you, my friend."

Charlie glowed a bit inside. It had taken him a while to gain B/1's confidence as a younger case officer, B/1 being much older. But he had and it all went back to those discussions he had with Wellington and Scott. Gain your asset's confidence and keep it.

"Tell me all about it," Charlie said.

"I've written a complete report, it's all here," B/1 said, handing Charlie a small package with several tiny Minox film cartridges. My written notes have all been destroyed."

"Thank you." He would have asked B/1 had he not said the evidence was gone.

"Dresden hasn't recovered from what the British bombers did to it, but we were not in the city. We stayed southwest of the city at a little place called Festung Königstein. If you like history, it's a nice place to visit."

"I don't think my folks would approve of me visiting Dresden, maybe later when this is all over."

"This, as you call it, will never be over. Nikita wants the Allies out of West Berlin and so does Ulbricht. The DDR is losing all its brain power though your sector."

"What are they going to do about it?"

"Nothing yet. Khrushchev is still waiting to see what the French decide about his ultimatum, but he won't risk war. Not yet. He's hoping you all pack up and leave peacefully. I've put it all in the report. The really big thing you need to see is my report on Ulbricht. You remember, I told you about their fight. Well, Ulbricht got the government to fire Wollweber. He's out. Retired to his dacha in the country."

"Why?"

"Because Wollweber was planning a takeover along with a couple of others."

"Who are the others?"

"The names are in my report. The important thing is that Erich Mielke is in charge of *Stasi* now."

"Who is he?"

"A thug. He fought in the streets against the Nazis in the Thirties, scampered off to Moscow when it got too hot, then came back when it was safe. I would compare him to Himmler but he isn't as smart, just a sly bastard. Dangerous."

"Will the change affect you?"

"No, I keep my personal relations private and my loyalties secret. Besides, I know things about him."

"Mielke?"

"Both of them, Mielke and Ulbricht."

"Is it in the report?"

"No, but I have some files on them that might interest your superiors. They're hidden."

"You waited until now to tell me?"

"I just got the papers from Wollweber before he left, it wasn't that long ago. His office hasn't even been cleaned out." B/1's said, his voice curt.

"Okay, okay. Anyway, this is great! Washington will be very pleased. Get me those files and I can get you an increase in your salary."

"That's all well and good, but I'm sure I'll never see it."

"Why? You think something's up?"

"Nothing special, but the counter-intelligence section is beginning to figure out who is giving away all our secrets. You know how that usually ends. A couple of guys are being questioned at *Hohenschönhausen*."

"Anything come up about you?"

"No, but you should be careful with your West German partners. *Die Gehlen-Organisation ist undicht.*" Gehlen's leaky.

"Always wary, my friend, aren't you?"

"You know I am. In this line of work, you can't afford not to be. Just beware."

"Get me all you can on Gehlen for next time."

Charlie didn't comment further on the unsettling news and pocketed the film while he went over the details for the next meeting with his asset. He tried for one week, but B/1 wanted to wait at least five. Too frequent was too dangerous, but it was B/1's skin, not his. Palmer would have to wait for the juicy details while fending off his chief's demands to meet sooner.

Palmer often wondered about his chosen profession, but the thought of staying in his boring hometown on the wide, windswept prairie of Nebraska made it easy to dismiss any whiff of regret. Still, he pondered why he had chosen this kind of stress. Headquarters' constant thirst for information — useless or not — that demanded he use any and all means necessary to extract it from his agents to meet those needs. Granted, B/1 was a volunteer, most spies were — the case officer is merely the guide who shepherds them with the promise of riches or maybe an eventual safe harbor for their small act of defiance whatever their motivation may be. Then, the CO takes charge of their life in return for giving them the illusion of helping them achieve their goal. A sword constantly hung over the agent's head, whether it be the fear of compromise or maybe the implicit threat the case officer held over him, the fear that if they didn't perform to expectation, they would be cut off from the protection and compensation the CO provided.

That Damoclean sword could pierce the CO as well. Pressure from headquarters and the station chief, the constant deception required, worrying about the opposition and on top of that, throw in the soul robbing aspect of lying to your agents and friends alike, took a toll. You had to believe it was for the greater good. Then again, he wouldn't have left Hastings if he wanted a normal life. Besides, it was fun sometimes. What he needed now was a drink.

"One last question," Charlie said, as he moved to break contact. "I need you to find everything you can about a journalist, an East German. His name is Michael Storm."

"I know Storm," B/1 said. "He was at the Nürnberg Trials, you know."

"Yes, that's the one. Who is he?"

"Storm's not his real name. His true name is Markus Wolf, he's the director of the HVA, our foreign intelligence service." B/1 tipped his hat and disappeared down the fog-shrouded path.

"*We found him,*" Charlie realized. *"The Man Without A Face."* Traipsing out of the park, he was filled with the giddy feeling of a good meet. He was already writing a batch of what he knew would be rated as outstanding intel reports. That lasted about a minute before he realized his thoughts of Langley's effusive cables telling him what he already knew — that he was great and maybe mentioning a step increase in pay — were distracting. He decided, instead, to concentrate on his route, fore and aft. Even if he did have a get-out-jail-free card, he couldn't risk being nailed by the *Vopos* with an incriminating film canister on his person. Carefully, but quickly, he put distance between the meet site and himself. He would wait until later in the morning to go into work, so any bad guy watching for unusual behavior on the compound, like lights on late or people coming in early, wouldn't figure out he had hot intel to pump out. Just another routine day. Besides, his reports would land in Langley at around three in the morning, which was way too early for the Director, whose coffee service wasn't even ready until six a.m. Despite his caution, the adrenaline rush hit him, and he couldn't wait to say it. *We finally know what he looks like. This will give BOB a couple of points on the scoreboard.*

He almost made it to ten o'clock. By nine, he was inching closer, sitting in the PX snack bar across from the Berlin Command compound. By nine thirty, he was burning off more time by walking the streets of the recently-constructed apartment blocks where the married American servicemen and their families lived. He was agitated, writing his reports in his head, not paying attention to his surroundings and all the soldiers and civilians wandering past him with a purpose. So much so that he almost walked in front of a Mercedes taxi whose driver presciently honked at him before he stepped off the curb. He checked his watch. Close enough, he thought. He knew the first five minutes in the office would be spent listening to St. John berate him for being late without an excuse. This time at least, his excuse was good.

The information on Wollweber's firing alone was worth a spot in the President's Daily Summary. Then, there was the info on Khrushchev and his threats. That was good for his ego, but being able to assign a face to Wolf was even better. Maybe he would get his GS-14 before long, that is if St. John didn't steal the glory to get his own promotion.

"Let's talk about your plan."

So, Charlie explained what he had, which still wasn't much. "The key to the plan is getting our traitor and his handler together so we can make something happen. The problem is, we don't know for sure who the traitor is, nor do we know how meetings are arranged. Without that, we can't set up a trap."

"Did you ask Myers?"

"Ask him what?"

"The small stuff like how they came upon this guy to begin? How did they know to surveil that house in the East? Stuff like that."

"I didn't think he would tell me because it's a counter-intelligence operation."

"You didn't try?"

Seeing where this was going, Charlie knew better than to give a straight answer, because despite the recent coup he'd pulled off with B/1's intel, he now saw that his promotion was directly tied to Tar Baby. He'd stuck himself into the trap and he had to find a way out.

"I'll deal with it," he said.

"You'd better. We don't want this traitor running amok with the HOG coming up soon."

The Heads of Government meeting. Charlie had forgotten about that and Ike's visit to Berlin.

"Boss, I have an idea that might give us a hand with the Buchanan thing."

"What is it?"

"I will talk to Meyers about the case, but what if we put surveillance on our two suspects? That might help us pinpoint which one is the bad guy."

"Where are we going to get the manpower to cover them. That would take at least four Remora teams," St. John said.

Remoras, the men and women trained to surveil sensitive targets. Named after the fish that trailed sharks like the pan-handlers who stuck to tourists in Tijuana, they were teams of old folk, young folk, pensioners who sometimes looked like drunks

— legend had it one spent a night in a trash bin to keep his eyes on one specific hare — other times they appeared to be schoolkids, although it was never clear how those were recruited. They could also have been called chameleons, since they blended in so well. Wherever they appeared, they belonged and, to the target, they were benign, accepted as part of the neighborhood, never threatening, just watching every movement, every contact, every detail. They might look harmless and you wouldn't notice them until you were bit in the ass.

"Langley might be willing to support the idea if we couple the op with finding out more about Wolf," Palmer said.

"By watching American military officers?"

"By watching an American who may be meeting with Wolf."

"Write it up and I'll think about it. When do you meet B/1 again?"

"Soon, but first I have a meeting scheduled for tonight with a developmental. B/1 will give me copies of the letters when I see him this week."

"What kind of developmental."

"An access agent. A construction engineer for the underground railway. He works in the U-Bahn train tunnels underneath the city, knows them like the back of his hand, and can get us plans for them."

"Exciting. Why would we ever need access to the underground?" St. John said as walked over to the coffee pot. Then, he bellowed, "Maria! Weren't you supposed to bring in the *Berliners* today?"

"You gave her the day off, boss."

"Somebody should have anticipated that," he said and steamed off to his office.

37

"SO, TELL ME how you found out about the safe-house. This Bornitz Straße 212 place."

Myers took off his glasses and rubbed his eyes, which Palmer had come to realize was a sign of irritation.

"I told you it's a CI matter and I can't discuss it with you or anyone else."

"Except the USCOB."

"Of course, he's the commander and it may be one of his people."

"You're no closer to finding out who?"

Silence. At least the glasses went back on.

"What if I told you I could help?" said Palmer.

"How?"

"I have two possibles of who the American colonel could be."

"Who said anything about a colonel?" Myers said.

"Supposition. A little bird told me. That and the 'C - O - L' in Buchanan's notes."

"Who are they then?"

"First, maybe you can give me something. Tell me how you found out about the meeting."

"I told you, a source gave us the info."

"But your guy didn't know who the participants were?"

"No, only that a meeting was happening, the place, and day."

"A meeting that involved an American?"

"Yes."

"Can he find out when the next meeting will be?"

"He? It could be a she." Myers said.

"You're really too paranoid. I don't care who it is, just when the meeting will happen."

"Okay, deal. I can do that. Now, who are they?"

"Only if you promise not to share it with anyone, including the general."

"What about my folks?"

"Not yet. I don't want anyone alerting them of our interest."

"You are saying I can't trust my people."

"What about Buchanan? Was it coincidence that they spotted and killed him?"

"Can't say." Myers paused only this time he tilted back in his chair. The glasses off again, he put his hand over his eyes, disappearing from the room a moment if only in spirit. "Agreed. I'll hold the names close."

"Until?"

"Until you tell me I can talk about them," Myers said.

"Fine. That will happen when we know who the traitor is and can nail him."

"Nail him, how?"

"Detain, arrest, jail. We'll need your help on the last two because we can't arrest nobody."

"Anybody. You can't arrest anybody."

"That's what I said. But you can."

"I can detain, the MPs or CID do the arresting. But we have to find the guy first and you still haven't told me the suspect's names or were you hoping I'd forget?"

"Colonel Ciernik and Lieutenant Colonel Brad Monroe. One is the commander of SDB, the other a staff officer at the *Teufelsberg* site."

"Kinda high-profile. I'll check out their backgrounds. That might help a bit."

"As long as they don't find out."

"No worries," Myers had put his glasses back on as he furiously scribbled notes. Noting Palmer's discomfit at his information being committed to paper he added, "It's water soluble, I'll eat it if I'm captured."

"Just be careful with it. Now, when you find out a meeting is going to take place, call me. Give me some pretext for meeting at the date and time and I'll understand."

"If I find out, you mean. But I can do that. I'll add one to everything — Tuesday will be Thursday, five o'clock will be six o'clock."

"And tonight will be tomorrow."

"You got it. You're a quick study."

"I'm a Nebraska graduate, where 'N' stands for knowledge," Charlie said.

"Bad joke, Palmer. Nebraska? Really? Did you study corn or cows?"

"International relations and journalism with a minor in German, actually. What's the matter? You look like you swallowed a worm."

"I'm just amazed by you guys. I get a J.D. from Columbia which got me nowhere, not a single bite from the big city law firms. Luckily, the Army needed guys like me who could talk the lingo, but this job is a ticket to nowhere."

"Why are you complaining? What don't you like about your job anyway?"

"Very simple. I'm the guy everyone is scared of, that everyone loathes. Everyone thinks I'm watching their every move. *Ich bin der Rattenfänger von Berlin.*"

"The rat catcher of Berlin. That's kind of ironic. Rats are what the Germans called your folk."

"The Nazis did, not the Germans. And, yeah, it was ironic. Many of the lawyers at Nurnberg were Jewish guys just like me. They turned the tables on the Nazis, but after all was said and done, most of them were smart and moved on, back to the civilian sector. Maybe I should try applying to the Agency, because if you guys can get hired, I'm pretty sure I can. Certainly, my degree and fluent Hebrew, Yiddish, and German count for something. But then maybe they're just as much a white shoe firm as everywhere else I've applied and I have bills to pay." He shook his head despondently. "Nine years in and I'm still a major. All the other guys in my intake are lieutenant colonels by now."

Palmer watched as Meyers finished his water-sol note and folded it carefully into a triangle which then put in his leather wallet to find later when he needed it.

"This will get me started. I'm going to check their records out and if I find anything interesting, I'll get it to you as soon as."

Palmer knew the records in question were held by the Command's S-1, the place that handled administrative stuff, processed promotions, shuffled people to and from assignments, or made sure all the paperwork was lost and had to be resubmitted at least twice. It also handled detailed personnel records, which would be Myers starting point. Then, he'd walk the names back and find out whether there were any gaping holes in their files. Easy enough. If he found derogatory, then he could begin to dissect the reasons. The hard part would be if either one was squeaky clean. Then, the crumb following work would begin. It was not a place an Agency person could get into.

"I'm counting on you. Whatever you do, don't put surveillance on them," Palmer said.

"Why not?"

"It's going to be taken care of. Don't ask."

"I didn't know you guys could do that," Myers said.

"Put surveillance on Americans? If it falls into the category of national security overseas, I'm pretty sure the Director will agree."

38

ON ANY OTHER day, Rose Range was a quiet, idyllic spot. Old growth trees, dark green and tall. Walking paths strewn with pea gravel, a dirt access road with a gate controlled by two guards as likely to be snoozing as not, a perfect spot for a picnic except that it was a police shooting facility.

Once inside, there were several rustic wood huts that looked straight out of the National Park Service building guide except that this was Germany. Dark wood siding over heavy framing. Green tin roofs that kept everything inside high and dry even if the noise during a rainstorm was unbearable. Neat and tidy, everything in its place with a range manager who patrolled the grounds looking for infractions. Not today. He knew better and stayed inside in his office when the "wild men" as he called them came to visit. He didn't like them because they refused to follow the rules that he had clearly painted on the warning boards posted about, as well as on the sign-in sheets that were never filled out and signed. When he complained, he was told to suck it up. Regulations didn't apply in this case.

They parked the vans in front of the range for convenience. The No Parking signs, if they had feelings, might have objected but no one else did. The front of the range was under wood cover, again looking like an old hunting lodge with tables for equipment and loading platforms, along with racks for weapons. Each firing lane was separated from the next with an old brick wall also sheathed in wood and, at the far end, a sand berm with reinforced earth served as a bullet trap. There were several fifty-meter ranges, but today was a simple recalibration of skills day, so the twenty-five-meter lane was suitable.

The men clustered about the tables, getting ready to fire several hundred rounds at targets that approximated man-size and thus, were almost suitable substitutes for the enemy. Their drawbacks included that they did not replicate a real enemy by moving around and shooting back, but that might have made it more difficult to achieve the initial training goals.

Three tables for six men, Rolf and Anton were busy at theirs, several boxes of 9mm Luger ammunition in varying stages of fullness or emptiness depending on your personal outlook on life were strewn about, alongside their submachine guns. Pistols were on their hips, one weapon always within quick grasp.

"Do you ever get the feeling that we're just a cover for the real guys?"

"Whadda you mean?" said Rolf, fingering cartridges into the magazine of his P-38. He had five mags loaded already and two more to go, that was the basic pistol load. His MP was already loaded, four mags in the pouch and a free one next to the weapon on the table.

"Maybe the only reason we're here is to distract the Russkies and the *Ossies* so the super-secret guys can do what they need to do," Anton said.

"You think we're being used as bait?"

"Yeah, something like that."

"After the run-ins you've had with that guy Charlie, you think they're better than us?"

"Maybe they're not better, just more secret."

"And you think, they could handle our mission? Come on, *Junge*. Let me tell you something. You've heard of the SS, right? Hitler's chosen ones. *Meine Ehre heißt Treue* and all that crap. They thought they were better than everyone — supermen. Total, BS. They were loyal, sure. They were fanatics, that's all. They died just as easily as everyone else and were no better at it when they did. Übermenschen, *mein Arsch.*"

"So, you think Charlie and those guys aren't any more special than us?" said Anton.

"They may get paid better, but no, they're just as exposed as we are and probably only half as competent when the chips are down."

Becker walked up to the two at the table, pistol holstered, looking ready for bear. "You two done chattering? We got some cardboard to kill."

Anton launched into a pet peeve, "Top, when are we going to get some new weapons? The pistols are all way old, some are starting to break, and the submachine guns…. Well, not one is newer than 1944."

"There's a reason why they're so old. They're German and Germany hasn't made any new weapons since the 8th Air Force closed their production lines. Secondly, it's what we got. If you have any ideas, let me know. Maybe we can get something else that's not made in America."

"I'll work on it."

"Now, everyone to the firing line. Load when everyone's lined up."

Four of the team stood at the seven-meter line, Rolf, Anton, Gavin Stone, and Harry Brown.

"I'm not sure I like you two behind us with those loaded guns," said Harry.

"Tell you what," said Becker. "I won't shoot you if you don't shoot me."

Makinen floated behind, only half watching the training, thinking about what the colonel had told him, so distracted that when the first volley went off, he flinched.

"Why the sudden emphasis on quick kill shooting, Top?" said Gavin, being the ever-analytical medic as usual. Never satisfied to follow an order without knowing why it was issued and necessary for him.

"The colonel wants us to make it real. No more static, slow aimed fire. We're going to make it real, step by step. Okay, this time, eight rounds, two shots in each bull's-eye. You'll have seven seconds, start on my word and stop on the whistle. Focus!"

Becker held the police whistle up and waited. Each target had four bull's-eyes. If this worked out, they would do a couple more runs and then move to multiple targets, then move and shoot.

A loud crack sounded on an adjacent range. Two seconds. Another.

"Snipers are at it on the three hundred," murmured Rolf.

"Fire!" said Becker.

Pistols slid from their holster and into each shooters eye-line with the target. Two rounds, crisp trigger pulls, no jerks, next bull, two more, next, next. The quiet settled back in, the acrid smoke drifted up and away. Two more cracks from across the way.

"Clear and holster your weapons. Check your targets." Becker turned when everyone had ensured they were safe and moved forward. Mack was standing to rear, arms folded, now observing intently. They both turned walked up range, away from the firing line.

"They'll be squared away soon. Everyone's rusty from spending too much time on the urban tradecraft stuff, but they're coming back. After the next round, I'm going to have Thibodeaux take over, he's the weapons sergeant after all."

"Good, because I think we're going to put these skills into action soon."

"What's up, boss?"

Makinen looked over his shoulder briefly, "The colonel told me we will probably be tasked with something in the East."

"Any details?"

"Nothing specific. Maybe a snatch mission."

"Is that why the snipers are out today?"

Makinen just looked at Becker. "He just said it would require a full combat load."

"That would explain a lot. So, a hundred fifty rounds for the MP and fifty-six for the P-38s."

"Not the 38s, TT-33s. We'll be carrying Soviet weapons."

For Becker, that meant only one thing, deniability.

"When do we tell the men?"

"Not before Ciernik gives me the go. One other thing, it'll only be the single guys. You won't be going."

Becker stopped dead in his tracks. "What? That's why I'm here, boss. For missions like this. I'm going to talk to him."

"SGM said you'd say that, but it's the CO's decision. First, the team can't afford to lose both of us and second, you might have to help get us out if things go to shit. Besides, we'll need you for when the balloon really goes up, which might be shortly after our little escapade goes down. If it goes down."

"You're going then."

"Of course. My team, my decision. I'm not married."

"How about if I got a divorce?"

39

ONE THING THAT Charlie Palmer could count on was that the office would be quiet during the weekend. He thought it the best time to catch up on the boring administrative stuff that followed all his exciting spy stuff. He sighed and leaned back in his chair. No, that wasn't quite true. His spy stuff wasn't really exciting. Frightening maybe, sometimes, for a brief moment. Then, he had to go write intel about what he'd learned, if anything, fill in his expense vouchers, accounting for everything down to the last *pfenning* and calculate the exchange rate. Then, he'd write reports that described his meetings and whether or not he thought his agents were on the up and up or just flatulating for money.

At least, it had been quiet.

He could hear St. John come in because he was talking to himself, all agitated. That must have meant he'd gotten a call to come in. Maybe a Night Action message had arrived, and the commo guy had ruined the boss's morning coffee. No one else but Charlie would come in unless St. John was already here. Dedication was in short supply these days.

Charlie thought he'd get the jump on the Chief for once and walked quietly over to St. John's office.

"Morning, Boss. What's up?"

Startled, St. John jumped back from the safe he'd been fruitlessly trying to open.

"What are you doing here? It's the weekend."

"Ain't no Sundays west of Omaha," said Charlie. "I'm catching up on admin stuff and planning."

"Homey saying, but we're east of Omaha."

"I suppose unless you're traveling west and then…"

"I get it, Palmer, but I have some priority work to do here. What have we got on new travel restrictions in the East? Langley wants to update POTUS."

"B/1 said nothing was currently being planned, just that Khrushchev waiting to see what the French would decide."

"So, nothing new. Well, ask B/1 for an update next time you see him. When is that?"

"Soon, tomorrow night and I will ask. But right now, I'm thinking of a plan to smoke out our traitor."

"This ought to be good. How do plan on doing this when we don't know who he is or how he talks to his handler or anything like that?"

"Did you not read my earlier IR from B/1 and what he said about the Gehlen Organization?"

"The part where he thinks Gehlen has been penetrated? That's probably an understatement, but what of it?"

"He doesn't just think it's compromised — he knows it is. At my last meet, he gave us a lead on who it is. So, what if we seed Gehlen with some disinformation that their asset will pick up and pass to the *Stasi*? Then they'll think our traitor is actually a double?"

"How? We don't know what he's discussed with them, what his code name is, or anything we can use to pinpoint who he is?"

"Remember the Battle of Midway? June 1942."

"Yes, what about it?"

"They told us a story at the Farm on how they figured out where the Japanese were going to attack. Hasn't been declassified yet, but the idea applies here, I think."

"Tell me."

"The navy were pretty sure the target was Midway, but they needed to confirm it, so to find out for sure, they sent a message in the clear that said Midway's water purification system was broken. The Japs intercepted that message and sent out their own that mentioned the water problem and used the code word for the island. It was the same code word for their attack target. That confirmed the navy's assessment and they were able to intercept the Japanese fleet. We can do something similar. Mention that our double met his handler at Bornitz Straße on that day."

"What would that do?"

"For one, we wouldn't have to sit on our hands waiting. I suspect they will call for a meeting. Myers said his asset will let him know when that happened and he'll tell us. Then, we put close surveillance our suspects and get ready to launch Operation Tar Baby," said Charlie.

"Then, the how to do it is the last question. What you're saying is that we need to have our Gehlen liaison slip operational details into a report and then accidentally pass it to the Germans on purpose."

"That's my plan. We'll need Bonn to help us do it. Then, hopefully, it will get to the right *schmuck*."

"*Schmuck?*"

"In Yiddish, it means — well, it means something like worthless. I've being talking with Myers too much."

"Whatever. But, yes, the right traitor has to read it and pass it to his handler."

"Hopefully."

"And then, what do you hope this will get us?'

"Two things. I'm thinking his handler should call a meeting and we can follow our suspect and he'll take us to Br'er Rabbit. That will confirm our guy is a traitor and lead us to whoever killed Buchanan."

"Just so I have this right, the handler is Br'er Rabbit and our guy is the Tar Baby?"

"Exactly."

"What if they don't take the bait? Maybe they'll just abandon him?"

"Why would they do that?"

"Simple, to protect their penetration of Gehlen. Or they might just see it as a ruse or a provocation, in which case they could just wait for confirmation."

"I don't think they have time to wait. If we do it right, they'll see it as a mistake on our part and they'll want to make sure one way or the other. Maybe they'll want to run him as a triple, feed him garbage to pass back to us. Disinformation. They don't like being played with."

"This whole thing is still very much like Alice's Wonderland. Confusing."

"Welcome to the wilderness of mirrors," said Charlie.

"I'm getting old, Palmer. Things aren't like they used to be." St. John headed back to his office.

40

————— ◆ —————

ANTON WATCHED PENSIVELY from the safe side of the Spree. Venturing over the river meant entering the dragon's lair and he'd taken to doing a visual reconnaissance at a distance before he committed. For long minutes, he searched the far side, watching the occasional vehicles' headlights playing on the ruined buildings, flashing across the river to catch the mist rising. A small cargo barge passed below him heading north, its red and green running lights reflecting in the black water. Behind him was the U-Bahn station *Schlesisches Tor* or, as Hilmar taught him, just *Schlesi.* He wouldn't use the bridge here, it was too busy. Further down the river were the bridges he preferred for this evening's excursion. Further from Katja's but safer and he was tired of going all the way up to the French sector to begin his crossing. Two bridges there, one for vehicles, one for the S-Bahn, the elevated train. First, he had to cross another, smaller one across the Landwehr canal. That would put him on the Soviet side but in an area that was almost always quiet and dark. "*Except for the Ost-Hafen boatyard on the other side. Details, details…,*" he thought.

As he turned south, he thought he sensed something. He stopped and looked behind. He had to know. If he was being followed, he'd just go home. Maybe stop for a beer near his apartment and try tomorrow. But there was no one. A couple walking the other direction. A long way away. He turned back. The bridge wasn't long, maybe seventy-five meters. It was better than using the big one behind him but still exposed, even if briefly.

Head down, long, wool coat wrapped tightly, he strode across the bridge, cold, cold air whipping down the open waterway that sluiced through the city. More canals than Amsterdam, his *Baedeker* had told him. Also, Berlin had more guys with guns. Then, he was over and in the darkness of Treptower Park. He paused, pulling out a pack of Lucky Strikes. A lighter in hand, unlighted cigarette between his lips, he waited, listening to the wind, the quiet, scanning from near to far, slowly, back and forth, all around. Satisfied, he put the cigarette back in the pack. He wasn't intending to light it — it just gave him a reason to stop. Besides, he might need to barter for something or have it ready as an offering. Luckies were the equivalent of gold on the street.

The apartment was about eight klicks away, five miles, more or less as the crow flies if it were tipsy. A pretty long walk in a hostile part of town, but he had little to do besides think of Katja and he'd rather do it on the street than on his couch. He'd been doing a lot of that. He was new at this game of love, he wasn't even sure what it meant. He was infatuated, that he knew. He liked Katja, but did he love her? What was the difference? A car passed by. Black. Almost all the cars were black here. A few were rust colored, but most were black. It turned the corner. Before it was gone from sight, he noticed a dent in its right rear fender. He'd watch for that and the plate number to see if it reappeared. He passed a few people on the way, some on his sidewalk. He peered down the streets he crossed watching for the usual things, repeats, things that didn't make sense, and police of course. If he saw them in time, he could divert around, otherwise he put on his best cover face and smiled or just nodded solemnly, eyes down, like most *Ossies* did. *Unterwürfig*. Another word Hilmar had thrown out. Obsequious. A people beaten down did not openly rebel against authority. They lived with it, humble, compliant, waiting. *Waiting for what?*

"We'll know it when we see it," they'd say.

"*I hope so*," he thought. *Onward, onward, half a league onward, into the valley of death*. He walked to the rhythm, but hopefully not the same end. Then, to his front, Hagenauer Straße. He checked his watch. One hour and forty minutes had elapsed since the second bridge. Fast enough, he thought. No one behind him was the important thing. He hadn't answered the question of Katja, but that wouldn't change anything right now. His skin grew warm, his senses tingled, just thinking of her closeness.

The rear entrance was also becoming familiar. Unlocking the door, he slipped in quietly and climbed the stairs, without tripping the timer for the lights to her door. The key slipped into place and turned easily, twice around before the bolt fully retracted. It was dark inside, as he expected. Katja was still at work and it would be an hour or so before she returned. He moved slowly, his small, red-filtered flashlight playing on the things he remembered. He found his way to the couch and sat a moment before he pulled an envelope from his coat pocket, its brown color nearly the same as the table he set it on. He thought about it a moment, it was all there for her. *Dear Katja,* The note would explain everything. *I am in love with you.* Then

again, maybe not everything. *There is something I have to do....*
It told her enough. She would know what to do.

Then he let himself out and disappeared into the city.

41

IT BEGAN EARLIER in the day with one of those "St. John blocking the way" moments because he was about to deliver a directive that Charlie couldn't ignore.

"We're going to a party tonight. Well, maybe not a party, it's a reception." said St. John.

"Where?" Palmer said. He didn't like the kind of parties his boss went and a reception would probably be worse.

"Villa von Stauss, the commandant's residence."

"Do I have too? I hate receptions."

"The Russians will be there. Their commandant, maybe a bunch of staff officers, probably some KGB guys too."

"Chamov will be there? What's the occasion?"

"Not sure. The RSVP just says it's a reception. It's at four p.m. Wear your best Sunday-go-to-meeting clothes and bring Maria. She'll distract everybody while you recruit someone."

Now, standing in front of the residence on Pacelliallee, he realized how far he would have to climb to rate a place like the commandant's. The house was North German Baroque from the early 1900s. He only knew that because Maria had looked it up — it was one of the many magnificent villas seized by the Allied forces for their occupation of Germany. While many others still sat empty, waiting forlornly for their owners to return from places like Treblinka and Auschwitz, the ones owned by committed Nazis were subject to immediate confiscation and repurposing when the Allies arrived in 1945. This one, owned by a bank director whose business ties had been a little too close to the party, was just another casualty of the war. At least, until the Americans moved in. Now, affiliations forgotten, it was the home to arguably the most powerful man in the city and tonight, the second most would also be present, although he might disagree with that placement.

Maria was tugging at his sleeve. "You're staring, Charlie. It's not even his real home."

Her evening wear consisted of two simple components, a black evening gown he'd seen just before she put on a long black, wool overcoat, and a contrasting string of pearls around her neck that turned her from businesslike into what his mom might call beautiful, his father, comely, and he, resplendent or even attractive. He'd never quite noticed the glow she gave off when she smiled and had already begun to think of her as more than an office mate or assistant, but now an unfamiliar feeling surged up through his nervous system. He shivered.

"Righto, people to meet, deals to close, and questions to get answered." That was the best Charlie Palmer could do when he was confused by a woman and about to go into the arena to wrestle a bear or three. "Keep your eyes open for good candidates."

They were doing the case officer version of "Good Cop, Bad Cop" or maybe just a tag-team match. One of them would quickly chat up as many people as possible and identify the interesting ones, while the other worked the crowd slowly. The last thing a CO wants to do is expend energy on worthless targets, but also not come off as a salesman looking to sell his wares to everyone.

Frank Barnes, the general's chief of staff, was waiting when they entered the grand foyer and directed Maria and Charlie to the improvised cloak room with an abrupt jerk of his thumb. After depositing their coats, Palmer saw Barnes lift the coat off another woman standing next to a British colonel with a huge mustache and a swagger stick. Obviously protocol and Frank's hurt feelings dictated that Agency civilians remove their own coats. Palmer didn't have time for Barnes's "mine is bigger than yours" games, so he turned to Maria and said, "I'm going in." And flung himself into the affair.

The main room was almost full already, the Brits in evidence, the French less so. The English came for the American abundance of food and liquor, the Frogs usually stayed away because of it. There were the inevitable American civilians, distinguished by a different cut to their civilian clothing than the Germans, and uniforms everywhere — none of them German as the West German army, like the East German, as those forbidden inside the city proper. The Russians had troops in the east and their commander hadn't yet arrived at the party; they never traveled alone and no one upstaged their Commandant, so they always showed up late and together. Most importantly, none of them would have the chance to defect.

The tinkling of glasses and sound of voices filled the room, mostly English he heard. A smattering of German. *The French who are here must be miffed, but then they probably don't give a damn.* He inspected the room as if he was a home buyer. Woven

Belgian rugs on the floor, heavy draperies tied back around the windows, and dark wood paneling made it feel like he was in a small castle. The fireplace at the end of the room was almost big enough to stand in but for the small fire burning in its maw. He could almost feel the warmth from twenty feet away, but people still congregated close to the dancing yellow and orange flames. Coal was still in short-supply or guarded jealously by those who had it either in anticipation of a cold winter or another blockade. The cutting of trees was officially discouraged now as the city government tried to return some green to the parks. But the Americans always had a solution to shortages, that much had been proven during the Airbridge of '49.

He focused on the people, trying to decide if there was anyone who might be an interesting target. He scratched off all the Allies, he had no interest in them, which left the Germans, and he knew that would be a chore. He thought he glimpsed Mayor Willy Brandt talking to the commandant. Another non-target. The Germans present were mostly members of the Senate — he saw little value in any of them. He needed a communist scalp, but East Germans wouldn't be anywhere near here, so the Russians were the only choice and the likelihood of getting one of theirs was near zero in a controlled fishbowl like this one.

Maria trotted past him with a scowl on her face. With an imperceptible shake of the head, she signed her frustration at finding anyone suitable. *Some days are like that — no joy in Mudville.*

A determined looking man approached and spoke, "You're a journalist, aren't you?" A gritty lilt of Scotland in his voice.

"No, I'm with the American Mission," said Charlie.

"Oh, I see," he said, disappointment evident.

"Why do you ask?"

"I was trying to confirm something and journalists are the best people to confirm rumors."

"And we Mission people aren't?"

"I know you folks only give the official line. The truth as it is handed down from on high, so to speak."

"I like rumors. Are you with the British contingent?"

"Yes, as a matter of fact, I am. With the Public Information Office, what I gather you Americans call Public Affairs."

Journalists and intelligence officers have much in common and rumors — either finding out about them or starting them — were things they both dabbled in. And the PIO was one of those places that seemed to harbor both kinds of people, some that actually dealt in public information, and the others who needed a cover job so they could ask the right questions.

"So, what have you heard?"

"Nothing really definitive, just that the East Germans are getting ready to restrict travel of their population to West Berlin."

"I hadn't heard. How would that happen?"

"Haven't the foggiest, but maybe they'll require more paperwork. Oh, well, I'll just have to keep looking."

"You should ask the Soviets when they show up. I'm sure they will know."

Looking over Charlie's shoulder, the man said, "I should, they have just arrived. But I don't think they'll tell me. If it gets out, it'll cause panic. By the way, I'm Casper Peacock. Off I go."

Charlie watched him walk towards the Russians, thinking Peacock was not a good name for a spook, he had to be a journalist. He doubted that Peacock would get the words out of his mouth before they turned away. Leading the entourage was the big man himself, Major General Andrei Chamov, followed by an eight-man contingent of gofers and heavies. Palmer noticed another general among them, probably Chamov's deputy, the rest being colonels and a rough-looking civilian with a red CPSU party pin prominently pinned to his lapel. Shown in by LTC Barnes, Chamov made a beeline for the USCOB, scattering the lesser guests as he led his entourage into the room.

What followed must have been well choreographed because as soon as Chamov shook hands with his equal, several waiters came out of nowhere with trays of vodka shots for the guests. The waiter's tray for General Barksdale held two glasses. Barksdale picked up both shots gingerly and handed one to Chamov before offering up a toast to peaceful co-existence, neither of the two men believing in any such thing, before they both tossed them down. There was a reason why Charlie had grabbed several hors d'oeuvres before, but now he was looking for more, anything to get some absorbent matter into his stomach before he put away more of the firewater. While he was searching, he saw Peacock make an approach on the Russian civilian, a heavy-set guy who looked more hitman than administrator. Peacock spoke and the civilian seemed to sneer an answer before the Brit turned to make a hasty retreat. Peacock was probably not an intel type, Palmer decided or, if he was, he was of the milquetoast variety. Charlie moved into the gap and noticed the civilian was staying close to one of the Russian colonels. He also had a suspicious bulge under his left arm. Definitely not a recruitment target, rather a guy you didn't want to notice you existed. *Maybe Peacock realized that too late.* Charlie backed off and found Maria at the back of the crowd.

"Worthless," she said.

"Who?"

"The lot of them. There's nobody you want to talk to except maybe one of the Sovs."

"I don't think I want to talk with any of them either. Is there a photographer working this thing?"

"There always is."

"Find him and get him to take pictures of the Russians, especially the guy in civilian clothing and the colonel he's attached to, okay?"

"KGB, you think?"

"Maybe, but the civilian is trouble, a bodyguard, but not the run of the mill variety."

"I'm on it."

"Good girl."

"Charlie."

"What?"

"I'm not your good girl." Maria wasn't smiling this time and her eyes turned frosty. Then, she disappeared back into the crowd.

Touchy woman, he thought as he made his way to the front door hoping to escape for a bit.

"Where are you going?" St. John interrupted his forward progress. From behind. He knew the voice too well.

"I need some fresh air. These aren't my kind of people."

"is the air too thin for you up here? But your new friends have arrived."

"My friends? Not the Russians, they're not my friends and I saw them already."

"Not them. One of the guys who came over to the office. What's his name? With his boss, I think."

"Which one? Brock or Mak-something?"

"Brock, that's the one. The ice-cube cool, blonde guy and their colonel, Ciernik."

"Where are they?"

"Over by Chamov. I think they're eavesdropping on the Russkies."

Palmer had to see that for himself and from the edge of the crowd, he saw the two Americans close to the Russians. They were talking to each other and neither were wearing name tags. He recognized Brock, but could only assume the older man wearing eagles on his epaulets was Ciernik. The colonel stood with his back to the Soviets while talking, Brock nodding his head as if he was taking mental notes of everything Ciernik said.

The Russians were crowded around their boss in a scrum as if they were ready for a kidnap attempt. Which was silly, but then the Russians had always been paranoid. Charlie looked around the crowd just to make sure no more of Ciernik's men were nearby. It was all clear. Chamov, the Russian, was talking amiably with Barksdale, the American, backed up with heavies from both sides. It was true, he thought, Americans like Brock, Makinen, and the guys he met in the bar the other night were capable of much violence, much more violence than effete academics like Ted could muster, that was sure. Or for that matter, Frank Barnes who stood harmlessly behind the general waiting to receive his next instruction. Another American colonel stood nearby scanning the crowd, seemingly relaxed as if he could care less about such a high-powered meet.

Palmer retreated back further until he found Maria in the foyer also about ready to give up the hunt.

"Who is that colonel with Barksdale?"

"Which one? They are dime a dozen here."

"The American standing next to Barnes."

"Not sure I saw him. Wait here," she said, slipping away to the door of the reception room. He could see her staring toward the fireplace a moment then doing a survey of the whole room, as if she wanted to be certain no new, potentially worthwhile targets had appeared in her absence.

"I think his name is Kader. He's with the POTUS visit advance team, one of Ike's military aides."

"Damn. I don't have him on my list. Why isn't he on the TDY roster?"

"How should I know? It must be an army thing."

"Well, that messes my calculations all up. Now I have a third guy to check out."

"You mean as our potential bad guy?" saying this in a quiet voice to make sure no one could listen in.

"Yes."

"Do you really believe that Myers person?"

"About what? The bad guy being a colonel? That wasn't Myers' idea, that was mine."

"Maybe you're wrong. 'Am Col' could mean anything like 'ambush' and 'collusion' or even 'colleague.' It might be the ambassador's colleague."

Charlie just stared at Maria wondering why he'd told this person the details of his guess. Finally, he decided he could speak.

"Because it's the most straightforward and logical answer."

"That doesn't mean you're right. You should be open to other ideas."

"Okay, give me one."

"I just did."

"Well, first off, we don't have an ambassador in Berlin."

"I said the ambassador's colleague. Maybe that's who travelled here."

"You want to check that out, go right ahead. But I don't know where you'd start."

"Once your guess doesn't pan out, maybe I will." Her disagreement with Charlie evident.

"Oh ye of little faith," he said with no enthusiasm. Come to think of it, 'pan out' was a good way to put it. Palmer was looking for gold, but the odds of finding it were slim.

42

—— • ◆ • ——

WOLF DECIDED HE needed to test the waters. If this *FEUERSCHMIED* thing was what Stöcker said it was, he needed to know the implications for his own operations.

The walk from *Haus 15* to *Haus 1* was always good for his thinking. Anyone in the quadrangle who saw him steered away. It wasn't out of fear, it was just known that the Master did not appreciate intrusions into his space. Of course, there was the occasional clueless wanderer who bumbled in, but Wolf was mostly gracious and ignored them without having the person later executed. At the "Snoop and Spy Company," as the Ministry of State Security was known on the street, rumors abounded, including the one about the guillotine in the basement of *Haus 24*.

Actually, that one isn't a rumor, he thought. Nor was the furnace not entirely fueled by coal.

He entered the main building, passing by the bronze shield insignia of the MfS that hung on the wall of the foyer. It depicted the organization as the sword and shield of the party, which it was, for both good and bad, he knew. Some allowance for the bad had to be made because the enemy of his country was stronger than ever. He loped up the staircase to the first floor. The twenty or so times he climbed them each day served as his exercise regime.

He knew Mielke was in his office because secretaries who work with senior officers have a signal system they use. His own was very experienced in pinpointing targets when he wanted to walk in on them unannounced, and Mielke's secretary knew better than to try and stop him. A smile was all she needed to know that it was time to go get coffee and a pastry from the cafeteria.

The door was mostly closed, Wolf glimpsed the general peering through piles of paper, a bank of telephones next to him, two black, three grey, and a red one. He pushed the door open and slipped in to stand at the corner of the desk, not in front because that would make it appear he was reporting to the man. An oblique angle put Mielke at a slight disadvantage and made him change his point of view. More comrade to comrade rather than colonel general to lieutenant general.

"Comrade Minister," Wolf said. "I have a concern that deserves your attention."

Mielke looked up, annoyed that someone had entered his realm without knocking and then saw it was Wolf, the head of the *HVA,* which he knew to be the bread and butter of his *MfS.* While he was in charge of the security apparatus that protected the government from its ungrateful citizens, Wolf provided the vital information that kept it safe from those capitalist countries which threatened its very existence.

"Comrade Wolf, how might I help you."

Knowing he had a limited number of cards to play in this game, Wolf came to the point. "You know that our partners from Karlshorst are planning a major operation in the western sector called *FEUERSCHMIED.* I need to understand the timing as it will most likely affect our foreign operations significantly."

Mielke stared at Wolf a moment, shaken. "How do you know about *FEUERSCHMIED*?"

"I understand the security involved with the project, but Wollweber briefed me on Colonel Androv's operation before he departed." *Probably the only favor you've done for me, Wollweber, was to give me a good excuse to drop your name.*

"Wollweber," Mielke said, his face reddened at the mention of the man's name. "He was a megalomaniac. He would have destroyed all we have worked for."

"He's gone now, comrade minister. We can proceed and the operation is still on."

"Yes, it's about to kick off. Androv is waiting for a specific bit of information from the western sector."

"Androv should have consulted my section, as we have very capable sources and would be able to provide what he needs. As it is, I think our brothers in the KGB won't hesitate to sacrifice us to achieve their ends."

"Their ends are our ends, Comrade."

"Mostly I agree, Comrade Minister, but we may pay a heavy price for what they are about to do. Our Germany will be a war zone again if it fails. I just want to make sure it is successful" *Just what will that success be, Comrade Eric? I've used up all my chips and my hand is weak.*

"Don't be so melodramatic, Markus. You know very well that it will look like one of their own assassinated that American bastard. Then, we will move in to protect lives and preserve civil order, before their police can even react."

"Our *Wachbataillon* will be deployed? What are the plans for the French and British sectors?"

"Yes, and the English and French commanders are also scheduled attend the Marble Gallery event. They should all be dead. When it happens, the special tasks company will go in first to secure key locations and seize the American *RIAS* station followed by the rest of the battalion and *Vopo* elements."

"Yes, so it was explained to me. It will indeed be a devastating blow, Comrade. The heads of the Hydra will be removed with just one cut," Wolf said. "I will signal my assets to provide up to date reporting on the occupation forces readiness and locations, I'm sure their alert status will be elevated for a VIP visit. I'll have the analysts provide timely reports on the situation beforehand."

"But don't tip anyone off. Not even the Council of Ministers is aware of this plan. Only Ulbricht and I — now I guess you — know."

"Me only because Wollweber thought the HVA could provide the intelligence needed to ensure its success. I hope you will emphasize that to Androv should you see him, Comrade."

Mielke peered at Wolf for a moment. Wolf stared back, a passive expression he thought wouldn't reveal his true thoughts. *Eric, with that bulldog face only a half-blind mother could love,* he thought.

Disquieted, the minister turned back to his papers. "Yes, yes. Anything else?"

"Nothing, Comrade Minister. Thank you for your time." He gave a casual salute and disappeared from the office as quietly as he'd entered. His head was spinning with the thought of the chaos that assassinating a head of state would bring about.

43

CHARLIE WAS BEGINNING to see coming into the office as a respite from work. At least, he could sit at his desk and calmly compose his thoughts while writing the necessary cables and reports. There was a rhythm involved and some sections seemed to write themselves. In others, he felt like he was translating a very complex story out of ancient Greek into something that explained his asset's demeanor or the information he'd provided. He was very choosy in his writing not to invent things or jump to conclusions when his agent had merely alluded to something. There was a fine art to reporting that defined a good journalist or a hack — it was the same with the Agency. Everyone wanted a scoop, but when it backfired and came back as bullshit, you got a bad reputation real quick.

St. John showed up in his cubicle as ever, waiting to ambush him in the hope that Charlie would get his reporting numbers up. Charlie was ready, having written everything in his head while lying in his bed last night. Charlie pushed back from the desk, took a sip from his still warm coffee, and relaxed a moment before answering his boss's query. He held up his other hand, five fingers extended. "At least five IRs. This is what I have so far. I'm doing the intel about the documents on Mielke and Ulbricht separately.

Both are damning. My biggest concern is this Fire Smith thing. B/1's doing his best to find out what it is, but he was nearby when the brief happened and said Mielke was excited, like the Russians have something really big planned and he's happy to be part of the gang. B/1's gonna talk with Wollweber if he can get close because apparently the Soviets briefed him before he got booted. This is my CR for the meet." Charlie handed St. John the message, who took it without a word and started reading.

SUBJECT:
CONTACT REPORT WITH CGBLACKGUARD/1 (B/1)

1. BOB Case Officer called for a non-sched Personal Meeting with B/1 to continue discussions on leadership issues within AEFLAG as well as possible CI / security issues within CAZIPPER.

2. Of immediate concern, B/1 noted that senior officer AEKICK officer (details SEPTEL) briefed the new head of AEFLAG alone on a plan known only as Operation *FEUERSCHMIED* (Trans: FIRE-SMITH). B/1 does not have specifics of the operation, other than it was to take place soon and is intended to force the Allies from WEST BERLIN. He stated that C/AEFLAG was visibly shaken after the meeting and refused to elaborate on the subject of the briefing. C/AEFLAG departed immediately thereafter to meet with H/AEPARAGON. C/O asked B/1 to follow up with details ASAP by fastest method possible.

3. B/1's information on CAZIPPER will be sent in restricted channels.

4. B/1 was in place and on time for PM at Site DOMINO. Meeting lasted eight minutes and C/O experienced no security issues. B/1 stated he was satisfied with his personal security and has no CI concerns. He provided concealed microfilm and paper copies of personal correspondence on both CHIEF/AEFLAG and AEPARAGON which detail both individuals cooperation with previous regime that would be extremely detrimental to them and their government if exposed. Copies of the correspondence will be pouched to HQs.

5. Based on increased production and quality of his reporting, request B/1'S monthly salary be increased to US$2000 (two thousand) with immediate effect. Payment mechanism remains unchanged.

6. All B/1 supplied documents have been forwarded to HQS via DIPLOMATIC COURIER.

    END MESSAGE

St. John was tapping his head with his favorite Mont Blanc. He paused when he finished reading. He looked up as he twisted off the cap and ticked his initials onto the page.

"CAZIPPER?"

"The Gehlen organization."

"They keep changing the crypts." Charlie knew they hadn't, St. John just couldn't remember.

"Maybe they're paranoid."

"With good reason. obviously. Okay, give it to commo for encoding and transmission, but who's the guy that briefed Mielke?"

"A KGB colonel named Androv. I asked for immediate traces from Moscow and Russia House. I sent that one already."

"I didn't see it."

"You weren't here yet and I thought it best to find out what we can on him ASAP. I held the other because of its implications."

St. John just nodded his head, reading the message closely. "Okay, get this one out immediately. The intel too."

"Not Flash?"

"No, not Flash. We don't have any specifics on imminence of hostilities, but copy everything to Paris Station, they may want to brief POTUS when he arrives. I think they just touched down somewhere."

"Reykjavík. They had to refuel. They're scheduled for an early arrival in Paris tomorrow. Apparently, he's stopping in London today for a meeting with the PM before they travel to France. I'm following the EUCOM chatter."

"Good. Keep me updated and keep the pressure on B/1 for details. Oh, what is in the correspondence?"

"Files that Wollweber was keeping hidden for a rainy day apparently. Mielke murdered two Berlin cops in the 1930s, and — you'll love this — although he was a member of the KPD, a full-fledged commie, he was also taking orders from the Nazis. He did the hit for the Nazis so that they would have an excuse to bust some balls. Got paid for it and they let him leave town. Ulbricht was also a stoolie."

"I thought Ulbricht was a hard core Red? Hypocrites, all of them."

"It's all about survival, I guess. But it means we could burn both of them if we wanted. Show the people of East Germany just what kind of leaders they have."

"Maybe, but to be replaced by whom? You never know who you might end up with. And when you get those messages done, let me see them, and then write up a Flash message in preparation for whatever this Fireworks thing is. Just say it's underway, details to follow. And put it in the hold queue for immediate release if and when the balloon goes up."

When Charlie said, "You mean Fire Smith, Boss," Ted's face contorted; he hated being corrected.

44

CIERNIK CLOSED THE door to his quarters and walked down the path to the street. It was a residential neighborhood in Dahlem, old houses with a few new ones mixed in to fill the craters, residuals of bombs dropped from the many USAAF Fortress or RAF Lancaster runs over the city in 1944 and 1945. Most of the bombs went into the eastern part of the city, but the strays that fell too early or late had made suburban living dicey here. Once peace had settled back in, houses left standing were quickly reoccupied, with a baker's dozen or so going to the senior officers of the American occupation force. A full colonel with a family rated a big house, but he, even as a colonel, had to make do with a three-bedroom apartment in a modern quadruplex since he was a bachelor. There was parking out back, but he left the car and legged into the dark.

The city government's budget balancing had ensured Dahlem would be dark; funds went instead to paying for lights in the high traffic and money-earning Kurfürstendamm downtown. It gave Ciernik a bit of an advantage in watching for surveillance. It was habit, but he knew it was also a plus for anyone else out there, whether they were the fox to him as the hare or just plain criminals.

By the time he got to the U-Bahn, he was sure someone was behind him. If they had waited for him on the edge of the neighborhood instead of committing as soon as he walked out his door, he might have missed them. But they did and he didn't.

It took several crossovers from one train line to another before he had identified most of them, and a switch from train to foot and then back into the underground by the Zoo station capped it. They were still on him, but fairly disheveled and strung out. When he exited for the last time at the *Gesundbrunnen* train station, he put in some more moves to make it clear that he didn't want company. He wanted to cross the frontier with no trackers in trail because he expected a new set might appear once he was in the East. It was quiet compared to the West. Not as many people on the streets, not as much light, and the noise dropped as if he had stepped into a graveyard. *The contrasts of capitalism and communism,* he thought. *Soon, my job will be done here. Tonight, no meeting at Maja's apartment. The risk is too great.*

He was in a graveyard now. "It's ironic," he thought, standing so close to the dead and one so famous. Hegel's grave loomed before him as he thought of the great man's comment on Napoleon, "he reaches out over the world and masters it." *That will be me,* he thought.

Lost in thought, Maja almost startled him.

"What are you thinking?" she said, glancing at the inscription. Name, born, died, nothing more. A simple burial for a complex man.

"Nothing important. It's good to see you. I wanted to tell you that my time here is almost finished, and I am finishing the planning on how to get you...." he paused. "How to get you and Roman out of Berlin."

"When, my dear?"

"Soon, maybe in a week if you're ready. Did he give you the materials?"

"A week is quick. We'll be ready, I think. Roman is excited, but he's trying not to show it. He doesn't want to alert his people at work." She handed him a bulky packet. "He said everything is there and to be careful, they might be able to trace it back to him."

"Tell him not to worry. It will go to the right people and you'll both be protected. You're not worried about leaving?"

"No, why should I be. The family in Poland is gone. So's Roman's. We're alone. Being in America would be better. And he understands about you."

"I hoped that's what you'd say." He handed her a packet of his own. "There's some more money in there. For things you might need to take care of."

"What do we have to take care of?"

"I don't know. Rent, pay the staff, bills, anything."

"You worry too much, Jozef. We'll be fine. When do we meet again?"

"Call the number in one week like before. We'll use of one of the words for the day and give a time to which you add ten hours and fifteen minutes. You remember?"

"Of course. I can't possibly forget something so important. I mean, I could, but I won't. Don't worry." She stretched up to kiss Jozef who embraced her in a bear hug. Just tight enough to tell her what he felt. "I love you," he said as she walked away.

45

"HOW'S YOUR PETER Rabbit thing going?" St. John was standing in an imperious way at the entrance to the cubicle. His favorite manager interrogation pose.

"Br'er Rabbit, Peter Rabbit was Beatrix Potter's creation. Peter's not half as clever as my brother rabbit," said Charlie.

"Whatever. What's happening?"

"I think I'm down to one candidate, Monroe, the NSA guy is almost off my list. The Remora teams have reported that he is pretty much a couch potato. Goes to work comes home, does nothing, and that's it, but Ciernik's another story."

"What's he up to?"

"First thing is that Myers came up with some good poop on him from the records."

"Give it to me."

"After the surrender, Ciernik was stationed in Berlin with General Gavin and the 82nd Airborne. He speaks Polish and Russian and because of that he was assigned to be a liaison with the Soviets."

"So, he could have been turned back then?"

"Maybe, but there's one other thing. He made a trip to Poland in the fall of '45, ostensibly to see relatives, but he said he was detained by the Russians and interrogated."

"How long was he in their hands?"

"Almost a week, he said. But they released him and he came back to Berlin. CIC interviewed him when he got back to Berlin, but the report said he was hostile to questioning. He ended up walking out. Nothing conclusive except for this. About the same time, two other American military officers from the Embassy in Warsaw went out into the countryside and they never returned. So, why did they let Ciernik go?" It was a rhetorical question. Palmer knew why, but he also knew St. John would want to make the discovery himself.

"That's obvious. Because he's been recruited," said St. John. "What was the other thing?"

"He went out last night and headed downtown on the U-Bahn. Got out at Nollendorf Platz and promptly lost the Remoras. They tried to pick him up again, but he was gone. Disappeared like a ghost. He showed back up at his quarters about one thirty in the morning. They said he seemed to be making damn sure that nobody could follow him."

"Those are pretty good indicators," St. John said.

46

"SO, HOW DO we do this?" St. John was no more capable of choreographing an operation than he was of planning a birthday party. That was to say, he knew what was required, but he had no idea of how to plan a snatch. Charlie stepped up to the plate as he knew he would have to.

"We know the meet will take place at 212 Börnitz. Our traitor will show up there for the meet. The handler should have already shown up, at least that seems to be the pattern according to Buchanan's notes. Our SDB friends will be covering the place from the outside and will take the handler before he goes inside. If they can, they will try to snatch the traitor and bring them both back."

"But if the traitor is Ciernik, he'll know and would warn his handler."

"You're right, boss. So, we should divert Ciernik and maybe send in one of the SDB guys in disguise?"

"What if someone realizes the substitute is not their man?"

In the ensuing silence, the wall clock continued to tick away, metallic clicks sounding each long second across the room. Charlie thought he had the answer.

"Then he should arrive at the same time as the handler and SDB can take them both at once. There won't be time to react"

"That might work. I'm still worried that whoever the handler is might already think it's a set-up," said St. John.

"Because he might not trust the info from CAZIPPER?"

"CAZIPPER? You mean Gehlen, right? Yes, because he doesn't trust the Gehlen source, or he's figured out that we've identified a leak."

"We ought to be able to see that by the number of security folks around the safe house."

"Maybe. There are still too many permutations to this plan. I don't like it. If one of the SDB guys goes in and the *Stasi* or KGB know the meet is bad, he'll be arrested and probably won't come back."

"Then we send in someone with diplomatic immunity and a U.S. Mission card. Me, for example. I'll dress up like Ciernik did in the photo and go in. The SDB will cover me and snatch the handler. If I get arrested, we have witnesses and they'll toss me back like so much bad fish."

"Not you, I need you for B/1 and all your other cases, especially that new train engineer." St. John smiled at what he thought was a great joke. "No, I don't think there's anyone I can let go in there, it's too dangerous, except maybe myself."

"Really, boss? You're kidding?" Charlie saw St. John's move as nothing more than grandstanding. "You can't go in. You know too much about our operations."

"Palmer, I know you believe I hold the keys to the kingdom, but do you really think I can't forget everything? I can't betray what I don't know."

"You can try, I'm sure, but I'm sure they have ways to make you remember."

"Perish the thought, son. They will treat me as a fellow traveler and return me untouched."

"Just like they did Buchanan."

"Buchanan wasn't carrying his Mission card."

"And that will make all the difference?"

"Of course. Besides, they don't know who Ted St. John really is."

This wasn't grandstanding, this was Ted's death-wish. All because he wanted to be cited for bravery. *No doubt, he will ask Maria to write up an award citation before this thing takes place. 'Just in case,' he'll say.*

Shaking his head, Palmer decided not to say the obvious.

"Okay, boss. Then the only question is when do we feed the information to Gehlen?"

"I'll brief the USCOB and if he approves the plan, we'll get SDB ready and then have Bonn pass the misinformation."

"What about headquarters?"

"What about them? We're smoking out a traitor. I'm not planning on telling them what the army's up to."

"Or the fact that you're going to walk into a *Stasi* safe house?"

"I think that will be something that I mention on the day of, not before. If we ask permission, they'll shut us down and we'd lose our chance."

For glory, Palmer finished St. John's sentence silently.

47

"BARKSDALE HAS GIVEN us the green light for the operation. Now, the easy part. We just need to plan it and carry it out," Makinen announced grimly.

"A hit on a Russian inside East Berlin? And it's not even in wartime? I don't imagine we could see the signed order?" Rolf said.

"It's a snatch, not a hit and it was VOCO," said Makinen.

"VOCO? What's that?" Rolf said.

"Verbal Order of the Commanding Officer. VOCO." said Becker.

"That means no paperwork to follow us around," Stefan said, looking at the others, each in turn, seeking approval of his insightful wisdom.

"And no proof he gave us the order," said Rolf, who tended to be more critical of officers.

"Stop nit-picking, Rolf."

"I don't pick no nits."

"Rolf, that's not quite how it's translated," said Becker.

"We do what is ordered of us." Makinen was standing, speaking with his hands behind his back, a sign he was serious, so everyone shut up. "We've been tasked to take out a Russian. The question is what's our plan."

"Kill him or kidnap him?" said Anton.

"Kidnap is the first priority, kill him if that won't work, but make it look like an accident."

"How about suicide?"

"Maybe if he's alone. Otherwise, we going to have some push back from his colleagues," said Mack.

"The meeting will happen in a residential area? Wonderful. I'm reminded me of a little ditty we used to sing in the *Jagdverband*" And Rolf broke out in song,

"Riding down the road, in a black Mercedes Benz,
Killing commie toads, saving all our friends,
Ratatat, ratatat, mow those bastards down,
Oh, what fun it is, to have the bad boys back in town."

"So, that's my plan. We just drive by and kill everyone there." Rolf said, obviously pleased with himself.

The team's response: *Silence.*

"I imagine you'd have us all carrying Thompsons," Mack said.

"Either that or our Schmeissers. Whatever can put the most bullets down range fastest," said Rolf. "Except for our driver, of course."

"I'm surprised you didn't end up at Nurnberg," said Stefan.

"*Du Kannst mich mal,* Wolpak. I almost ended up in Siberia as it was. That would have been worse, there weren't any lawyers in the Russian camps. Besides, I wasn't like those guys that stood in the lights at Nurnberg. We were professionals, not murderers. We hunted Tito's *Partizans* and they hunted us back." One look at Rolf's face told Stefan he was needed elsewhere.

Once the terrain and scenario were analyzed the plan came together. No '30s style drive-by shooting — this time at least. A bit more intricacy and subtleness would be required.

"Okay, then. Equipment. We go in light. Three walkie-talkies, one with the boss and a spare, one with the overwatch team. Rolf, you've checked them out?"

"Roger, Boss. I tested them on the network, they're good, but we'll be on the margin for strength and readability. Each has a spare battery."

"We'll do the best we can. Our weapons will be the TT and the PPs-43, except for Stefan with his long gun."

"I hate both of them," said Anton.

"Don't bitch. They work, don't they?"

"Most of the time. You saw how cranky they are on the range."

"Practice your immediate action drills and carry a big knife then."

"Gavin. You're the only one carrying anything else. Your medical kit. You good to go?"

"Yeah, Top. I'm carrying a small, but complete first aid bag. Bits and pieces I've picked up here and there, some East German. Their kit is pretty good, much better than the Soviet junk which is pretty scary. The important meds are from the West, like the plasma expander which I wanted to be clean. No American stuff."

"Where did you find it?"

"Black market, trade, and some stuff I acquired from the policlinic where I volunteer. They think I'm a nurse."

"What clinic?"

"Klinik Kollwitz in the East."

"And they let you work?"

"I've got a perfectly good diploma, I know the lingo, and they need the help.

"Diploma? I wouldn't let you work on me," said Becker.

"That's fine, Top. I'll just work on someone who appreciates my expertise."

"Next subject. The target. Stefan and Rolf, you have the photo of our primary. Code name is ZORRO for radio comms. He is said to be the enemy we are supposed to bring back."

"Said to be? We're not sure?"

"If he shows up, he is the man. If another guy shows up, we'll make a decision. The boss will give the final go or no go. Got it?"

Everyone nodded.

"And he's supposed to be the East German master spy?"

"That's what we've been told. His name is Markus Wolf."

Stefan pulled a rifle cartridge out of his pocket and held it up, so everyone's attention turned to it. "I'm going to write his name on this one," he said. "Then I'll deliver it to him personally." He pressed the bullet to his lips, put the cartridge back in his pocket, and patted it gently.

"Only if we don't grab him, Stefan. Don't kill him before the boss says so. And don't look so sad. There'll probably be plenty of commies to shoot after this little party is over."

"Now, I don't know whether to be happy or very scared, Top. What kind of back-up do we have."

"I have this one," Mack said. "Teams Three and Five will be deployed on our exit route. They'll be in small groups of two or three and can provide some cover on our way out if needed, not much, but enough to hinder and delay if necessary. The COB wasn't happy about that part of the plan, but the colonel said he wouldn't send us in unless he was sure he could get us out."

"There goes deniability," said Gavin.

Top took centerstage again, "We'll get back at this tomorrow morning. Everyone get out of here and be back at zero nine. Do PT on your own beforehand and I'll know if you slough it off." Beckner waited until almost everyone was gone before he spoke. "Stefan, wait a sec." Makinen looked up from his notes, took it all, and went back to scribbling on the paper effectively removing himself from the conversation.

"You ready for this, Wolpak?"

"Yeah, Top." Sheepish.

"Because, sorry to be blunt, some of the guys have said you've been hitting the juice pretty hard."

"I know, but Randallmann has been working me hard. I should say he's been kicking my butt, but it's helped. I only get tanked on Fridays now," Stefan said, a grin took over his face.

"I hope so, because part of this plan relies on your dead-eye aim. It's critical."

"Top, two days ago, I test fired the rifle again. Ten rounds into a five inch bull at two hundred fifty meters. Rapid fire. I think I'll be okay. I won't drink that day."

"I know you won't because we'll be in isolation. Now, get outta here."

Just Becker and Makinen were left in the room. "You better go home, boss. Morning's coming early and we move downtown tomorrow."

"Soon, Top. You happy with the plan?"

"It's good enough for government work. We're not going to make it better by agonizing."

"And Wolpak?"

"He's steady. I talked to Randallmann, he agrees." Now that everyone was gone, he pulled a cigarette out of a pack on his desk. "Want one?"

"Yeah." Becker threw him the pack. Mack fished one out and let Becker light it before he turned to his own.

"And the guys?" Makinen regarded the burning Camel in his hand.

"They're good. There's no one I'd replace."

"Then, we're as ready as we'll ever be."

He took a puff and blew the smoke out slowly, watching it climb toward the ceiling.

"Funny, I think this is a first. I've never had so much time to plan a mission. Usually, we had maybe a couple of hours. This is a luxury to have days to get ready," Makinen said.

"It is strange. To be so close to home and able sleep with your family. I just hope it doesn't come back to haunt us and them."

"That's why we have to get this right. If it doesn't work, the consequences will be ugly."

48

ONE LAST CONSULTING session, as Ted called it. He said it like it was going to be a corporate board meeting to discuss something like new advertising. Except it wasn't. Makinen came into the conference room inside the BOB with an intensity St. John and Charlie hadn't quite seen before. Becker and Thibodeaux followed, finally Maria, who closed the door.

"Is she involved?" Mack asked. He wasn't questioning her abilities — he'd worked with enough women in combat to understand their value. He just didn't want to brief anyone who didn't need to know.

"She is. She'll be driving us down to *Tiergarten* where we'll launch on our foot route. Then she'll wait at the pick-up point," Charlie said.

"Which is where?"

"Near the Oberbaumbrücke, about three miles by foot from Bornitz."

"Any of you armed?" Mack said.

"Just me," said Charlie.

"We'll be in place before you arrive at the safe house. Ted, you need to be outside just before the meet is set to go down. Hopefully, the handler will arrive at the same time. Three of us will grab him. When you see that happen, just get the hell out of there."

"What if the handler doesn't show up?" said St. John.

"Break it off and get the hell out of there. Charlie, what are you doing?"

"I'll shadow the chief in and out."

"Good, but you're just his personal protection. If there is any confrontation, you need to get him out of the line of fire. We'll handle it from there. We'll have a long gun providing overwatch. Try not to get in our way."

"What's a long gun," said Maria.

"It's a sniper rifle."

"Is this how you plan all your trips into the East?" said St. John.

"Some, not all. Depends on a lot of things. This one requires a bit more care."

"And when you service the STORCH people?"

"I seem to remember you believed in compartmentation," said Mack.

"Yeah, but those folks won't last long in a war. Who cares?"

"I hope that's not what you say about your assets."

"Like you said, it depends. Some are worth it, some not so much," St. John said.

Appalled would be a kind word for what everyone was thinking.

"I'd hate to be one of your assets," said Mack.

Charlie jumped in, "He's kidding," knowing Ted wasn't. "All our assets are valuable."

49

THE SAFE HOUSE was on the almost top floor of a derelict, pre-war walk-up. Pre-war meant that the building had been erected before the Great War, around 1905. It had somehow escaped the bombs and shells of the second and in 1945 had stood alone, surrounded by piles of rock, stone, and concrete where its neighbors had once been. But derelict, it was ugly, not nice to look at. In 1957, the building was the odd stepchild. Then, the neighborhood began to rebuild, cheaper, with more modern designs. This building had missed all the beauty treatments. Inside and out. The room they were in had also been forgotten. Drab, dusty, and filled with cheap, utilitarian furniture, some of it older than the persons sitting in the chairs. Safe houses were like that. The Agency sets them up according to the budget and then forgets about them until they are needed. Without a keeper, things went bad — the heat didn't come on because the landlord was too cheap or the pipes rusted shut. The electricity might be spotty because the rats had chewed the wires, or someone had screwed up the wiring trying to fix it. You just had to deal with it. An anonymous person paid the rent and, if you were lucky, you only had to stay there one or two nights, sleeping in an army-issue sleeping bag laid out on top of a dusty bed or a couch.

There were six of them, seven if you counted Charlie, but he was sleeping elsewhere. The six were from Makinen's Team 6. There was Mack of course, the boss. Becker, who kept things in running order, both the men and the mission. And the remainder were the specialists — Anton was weapons, Rolf was intel and could communicate with anyone anywhere by means of the six different radios he had access to, Gavin, the medic, more a doctor without a diploma, and Stefan, the "demo-man," the engineer who actually was on Randallmann's team, but as the best sniper in the unit, he needed to be here.

Because the mission plan was finished, approved and in the can, the men were ready. With no paperwork to be signed, there was a calm in the apartment. Waiting was the thing that soldiers practiced most — they spent countless hours training to wait. It was the hardest thing they did. Except maybe that split second before someone said "Go" or the first bullet of an engagement snapped over your head.

Mack was in the kitchen, kicking the stove and trying to make coffee while Becker watched. In the front room, Stefan was inspecting his rifle, a vintage Mosin-Nagant with a 4x scope that he'd last fired only a couple of days before. On the outside, it was battered, too long, and he preferred his own M1D any day, but it was mechanically, ballistically, and optically sound. It was also perfect for this little job — the weapon of choice of Soviet snipers. If it was found after the mission was complete, it could be traced back to one issued to the 79th Naval Infantry in Sevastopol in 1941. How it came to be in Stefan's hands was another story. He pushed a brass button behind the trigger guard and slid the wood buttstock off the custom rail that the armorer had added. In two pieces, the rifle would be easier to sneak over the frontier under his greatcoat.

Rolf sat on the floor next to him polishing the lenses of a set of old Zeiss 7x20 binoculars He would be acting as Stefan's spotter when it came time to pull the trigger. The binos were marked with the word *Kriegsmarine* which meant they previously belonged to someone in the German Navy, probably a surface ship captain as most of Hitler's submarines were on eternal cruises, never to return to home port. Rolf wasn't thinking of that. He was going over reticle lines, ranges, and the ballistics of the cartridges Stefan was using so he could give him accurate range, windage, and elevation guidance when it was needed for the shot.

All the while, Gavin kept himself busy, watching the street below through the gauzy lace curtains. They were still in the American sector, but there was a small possibility that some busy-body war-widow might call the cops because six military aged men were hanging out in this dump. "They might be criminals," she would have said and that would result in them explaining things to the *Polizei* and Becker have to flash his credentials unnecessarily. Little old ladies were always problematic.

Charlie and Anton were sitting in the bedroom, locked in conversation, still trying to figure out who the person sitting next to them was. It could be that they were jealous of each other. Or not. They hadn't decided.

For one, Charlie was intrigued by Anton, a young soldier who seemed like he'd seen more in two years than Charlie had in his entire life. He wanted to hear all his stories. Anton, on the other hand, just wondered how Charlie, a county-boy from Nebraska, could be involved in the kind of stuff he'd read about in a Fleming novel. Imagination always seemed to run wild in the minds of young men who don't know they're out to prove something but really are.

"Do you worry about death? In your line of work, it must be a continual concern, no?" said Charlie.

"Hasn't been one so far. It's something you can't worry about. Don't you worry about it? Oh, wait a minute, you don't have to worry because you have those 'Get Out of Jail Free' cards. It's all a game to you. I think we look at things a bit more seriously than you do because it is a about life and death," Anton said.

"We're serious, we don't want a war."

"Of course, you don't because that would mean you couldn't play your spy games. War zones aren't conducive to that."

"I'll give you that. I don't want to get caught up in a war."

"Well, that's where we're different. War is what we're all about. Being ready for war. And I guess that means being ready for all that comes with it, including death. You have a job to do and if it happens, it happens, I expect," Anton said.

———

For a brief moment, Anton relived the open door he'd stepped out of months before. Into the roaring slipstream, out into the unknown at five hundred feet over a denied area with no idea what awaited below, except what the ops and intel guys had optimistically told you. A blind drop on an unmarked Drop Zone, relying on the skill of a pilot flying by dead reckoning. Then, after hiding their parachutes, they had moved overland to contact the underground fighters or, just as easily, the security service if you'd been compromised. The parachute snapped open and you went from a hundred knots to five in a flash of pain as the harness bit with a sharp jerk and you hoped your jewels were well protected. You'd look up to verify that the chute was fully open, but could only see a black shadow cast against the even blacker sky. Then, you only had seconds to orient yourself under canopy before you hit the unseen ground with a hundred pounds of equipment dangling below on a drop line, the night as black as black could be.

———————

I didn't think about death then. Only about finding the drop zone and not breaking my legs. Everything else was gravy.

"Nope, I'm not worried," Anton said, as much to reassure himself as Charlie. "I know it's there, but not going to let it affect how I accomplish the mission."

"That's it?"

"I suppose. Death is just a phase change. It's how you get there that matters."

"Waxing philosophic?"

"I suppose. Death will just put me to bed a bit early."

"With no waking up in the morning," said Charlie.

"Pretty much," said Anton. He decided that his trips to the East were no more a threat to him than Hungary had been and he had resolved to take each new operation as it came. He was ready. He leaned back against the headboard and closed his eyes. Time was crawling.

———————

The phone rang.

One thing you could count on in Germany were the phones. The *Bundespost* kept everything to do with efficient communications up to snuff, especially in the western sectors. Mail got through and so did telephone calls. Of course, it may have helped to have one of the Postmasters recruited as an access agent who ensured your telephone was hooked up, not tapped, and made sure the bill went elsewhere.

Charlie picked it up. *"Fritz hier."* He listened a moment, nodding his head, then hung up. He turned to Mack who had suddenly appeared in the doorway, waiting for news.

"The meeting time is confirmed. It goes tonight. 2317 hours," Charlie said.

"Damn Russkies. They always pick weird times," said Makinen.

The piping for the old cast iron radiator under the window chose this moment to clang and bang several times, arrhythmically, but in seeming agreement with the captain. In actuality, it was just signaling that it was also about to fail.

———

"Eighteen hundred hours, time to move." Everyone shifted, breaking the stasis that locked them in boredom so long. Equipment was gathered, actions checked almost for the last time. A final look in the mirror, at each other. Finally, they were ready to launch.

"Top, you close up the apartment and wait for us at the RV. We'll come to you, not the other way around. Don't follow us in. Where will you be, Mister Palmer?"

"I'll meet up with the chief and Maria, then we two will go over on foot like you guys, but using a different route. We get there about thirty minutes after you. Our imposter, Ted, will go in to make the meet exactly on time."

"And what happens if the real traitor shows up?" Becker asked.

"He won't. We have him under control."

"The King's Bishop," Anton said from behind everyone.

"What did you say?" said Charlie.

"I just realized. The King's Bishop is the traitor. The King's Bishop is who you should have."

"How did you know about that? It's in restricted channels."

Anton's hand went to his temple in a flash of realization. "Because I was the one who reported it. The Grandmaster told me. The bishop's bad."

"Of course he's bad, he's the traitor." Charlie said.

"Who is he?" Anton said.

"I can't tell you."

"Why not?"

"Because you're going into hostile territory and might get captured."

"That's weak," Anton said. "You'll be in there too."

Makinen reached and grabbed Charlie's shoulder. "This mission isn't about the traitor, if you already have him under wraps. This is about retribution."

"You knew that's what the general wants. We're following his orders. Just don't shoot my boss when it goes down."

Stefan piped in, "No worries, man. I only shoot bad guys."

Charlie paused a moment then said, "St. John isn't that bad of a guy."

Mack shook his head. "I'm liking this op less and less, but let's get it done, men. Your commo is good right?" The last comment was directed at Charlie.

"Maria and I both have comms. She has a rig in the car that she can talk to headquarters with and will relay everything to us. We tested it and it's all good."

"Good, then you get out of here. As planned, we'll go in two groups — Rolf and Stefan as the sniper team will move into position first, Gavin, Anton, and I will follow. We'll set up as planned in the alley next to 212 just before it goes down. Clear?"

Together everyone confirmed. "Then go for it and good luck."

People moved to the stairwell and started down quietly.

Becker stood at the door as they all filed out, reaching out to shake his captain's hand. "*Sisu*, boss."

Sisu — strength — a word he learned from another crazy Finn down at Bad Tölz.

50

---♦---

CIERNIK STEWED LIKE a frog in a pot that realized the water would soon be boiling. His men were on the streets — he should be there with them, not providing updates every time the general asked. There was only so much he could do with the VHF radio that connected him to the team. For one thing, Makinen's walkie-talkie didn't have that much power. Where he was, a good six or seven miles away, was on the far side of good reception in a concrete urban environment, even with the big receiving antenna on the headquarters' roof. Mostly what he got was static. Luckily, the code words were short and easily repeated. *How much time did Makinen really want to spend on the radio while he was in the East?* The Germans were good at radio direction finding on either side of the frontier.

"I'm wasting my time here, Barnes. My XO could be doing this job."

"He could have indeed, sir. In fact, I recommended that, knowing you'd probably want to be with your men. But he insisted, doesn't trust anyone else." Barnes had done nothing of the kind. In fact, he had no clue what was going on other than he didn't want to piss off the obviously agitated colonel in front of him, nor did he want to confront the general.

Ciernik glared at Barnes, but decided nothing would be gained by kicking the hapless man out of the office. He could see a useless REMF from a long way away and Barnes was clearly a dyed-in-the-wool rear-echelon mother.

Shaun Myers deflected Ciernik's ire by walking into the office. "Heard anything, colonel?"

"No." He wasn't going to waste his time on the spook either. Then, he realized something.

"Barnes, where's Kader? He should be here too," said Ciernik.

"I don't know. He told the general he was not feeling well and left."

"Not feeling well? You get to go home if you're not feeling well? Even in the middle of a god-damned operation? Maybe I should try that."

"Who's Kader?" asked Myers.

"Colonel Joseph Kader, one of the President's aides," said Barnes obligingly. "He's in charge of the military side of the visit."

"Kader's first name is Joseph?" Ciernik said.

"Yes, sir." Barnes said confidently for once.

"Damnation."

"What?" said Myers.

"You're not going to believe this," Ciernik said.

"Try me."

"A Warsaw Pact intel officer told me the KGB is planning a major incident to force us out of here. They call it Objective OSIP."

"Us? Who do you mean by us?"

"Us, the Allies. You and me and the other twelve thousand troops in the city."

"Wait. You admit that you're meeting a hostile intel service officer? And what the heck does OSIP have to do with anything?"

"OSIP means Joseph in Russian."

"Right, you're Joseph."

"Yes, my name is Jozef, but I'm not spying for a HOIS officer. I'm trying to get one to defect."

"But you've been meeting at a *Stasi* safe house in Bornitz Straße…"

"What are you talking about? My contact is a Polish SB officer who lives in Pankow near their embassy. Bornitz is in Lichtenberg, completely different district."

"I think you're going to have to answer a lot of questions, Ciernik. You're a traitor. The Russians got to you because of your family, right? What did it take? Money? Promises to keep your relatives out of the Gulag?"

Really the wrong thing to say to man who had lived with bad jokes and hatred most of his life.

"Don't push it, Myers. You're not listening to me, so I'll say this again. In Russian, OSIP means Joseph. Barnes just said Kader's name is Joseph."

"So is yours," said Myers.

"But I'm not your traitor. Where's Kader? POTUS is coming soon, isn't he? Don't you see?"

"See what? I saw your CIC files from 1945. You were recruited by the Soviets."

"I am not a damn traitor," Ciernik thundered as the cold realization hit him. "That's why they wouldn't show me the final report. You CIC bastards are all full of it." Ciernik drew himself up to full height and put his hands on his hips, not like Patton, but a man determined.

"Barnes, take a walkie-talkie and find Kader. Tell him to get his ass back here now. Tell him the general wants to see him ASAP."

"But…" Barnes was backed up to the wall, looking as helpless as he was.

"No buts. Go! Now!" Barnes ran for the door like a flushed pheasant.

Once he was gone, Ciernik turned to Myers and said, "I have some questions for you, Major. My people are in the Soviet sector right now waiting for what? Did you set them up?"

"Your meeting is scheduled for tonight. With the man who killed Agent Buchanan. Your people are going to kidnap him. And what's this story about getting someone to defect? Why haven't you reported this contact?"

"I don't have a meeting tonight, you ass. As far as my defector, I have been getting information on the Polish service from a SB officer. I now have enough to guarantee them being allowed transit to the States."

"*Their* transit? How many are they?"

"Two. A man and his wife."

"You're playing a dangerous game, Colonel."

"And you're not? You thought I was the guy meeting Buchanan's killer, whoever he is?"

"Yes."

"If I was, then I would have told him, don't you think?"

"That's why we brought you here. To make sure you couldn't warn him."

"That might work if I was your traitor, but I'm not, and now it means we're up a creek and my folks have no paddles."

"I wouldn't worry, the meeting site changed. I just got a message from my source," said Myers.

"My people are waiting for it to happen at Bornitz Straße right now. When were you going to tell us it has been changed? Where's the new meeting supposed to be?

"I just got the message, but I can't tell you. I'll tell your team, but not you."

"Wrong answer, Myers. The only way to tell them is through me." Ciernik took a step toward the much smaller man who backed up to the wall just as Barnes had done.

"The Russians are going to meet their man one hour later at the *Gaswerk* in Prenzlauer Berg," Myers said choosing the easy way out.

"Russians. Damn it. If any of my people get hurt because of you, I suggest you find a quick exit because I will end your career and maybe your life."

Ciernik picked up his walkie-talkie. "Pack Leader, Pack Leader, this is Big Dog. Over."

Myers picked up the phone while Ciernik was talking on the radio and spoke several words, his back turned, the handset shielded to cover his voice. He hung up and turned to see Ciernik looming.

"Who were you speaking with?"

"My secretary. I asked her to pull some files for me."

"Files? Whose files?"

CIC files generally dealt with people, not operations.

"Yours. And whatever we have on Kader."

Ciernik wasn't sure what that meant and left it for later.

"What else did your source say?" he said.

"That the target is the *Marmorgalerie*."

"What's the *Marmorgalerie?*" Ciernik said.

"The Marble Hall. Our ceremonial conference room in Building 1."

"That's where the meeting with Ike is supposed to happen in the morning."

"Was," Myers stated.

"What do you mean 'was?'"

"As long as Kader is on the loose, Barksdale will cancel it," said Myers.

"So, I convinced you, did I? How does Barksdale know?"

"My secretary is going to wake him up. I just called an audible."

"On the phone? You just called an audible for what?"

"Security Condition Red."

"Who knows that?" Ciernik said.

"The USCOB, me, my secretary, and you."

"Not Kader?"

"How would he know?"

"Never mind, where's this marble hall"

"It's in the main building." Myers pointed vaguely in the direction.

"Show me."

51

MAKINEN LISTENED TO the transmission and took a second to absorb it.

"Big Dog, Pack Leader. Understand Abort. Please confirm, over." Mack released the transmit key.

"Pack Leader. Roger, abort your mission. The location has changed and there is no time to re-set. Break it off. Over."

"Big Dog, understood. We are to abort and return to base. Over."

"Pack Leader, that is good, copy. Report when you are clear. I need you back here to help protect Providence. Out."

Radio by his ear, he waited to see if there would be anything else. Nothing. A three count, holding his breath, then he keyed the mike, "Archer, this is Pack Leader. Abort. I say again, abort. Confirm, over."

Rolf listened to the transmission and looked at Stefan. "You hear? Abort. He said abort."

Stefan reluctantly took his finger from the trigger and snapped the safety on. He gave one last look through the scope. "Damn, from here, I could have had all of them."

"The man said abort. Break it down and let's get out of here." Rolf keyed the radio. "Pack Leader, Archer. We copy abort. We are pulling out and will meet at Romeo Victor, over."

"Something must have gone bad," Stefan said.

"I think that's pretty obvious." Rolf led the way out of the hide, his submachine gun sweeping back and forth across their front as they picked their way through the rubble. Stefan followed, his rifle at the ready. *Not the best weapon for close combat*, he thought.

Makinen dropped the radio to his side. The look on his face said that this wasn't ending where he wanted it.

"It's all over, we're going home. Boss said break it off, the meeting's not happening here."

"Where is it happening? Shouldn't we try to cover the meet? What if Palmer's guys have the wrong man and the real traitor shows up?" said Anton.

"You heard, we don't have time to re-set in a place on short notice."

"Where?"

"He didn't say."

"Ask him."

"He said abort. I can't ask him now."

"I can. Let me have the spare radio."

Makinen hesitated.

"Let me ask, boss."

Anton took the spare, clicked it on, and spoke, "Big Dog, this is Cajun. What's the new meet location, over."

"Prenzlauer Berg. The Gasworks. Same time, plus one hour. But I said abort, over."

"Roger, Big Dog, out." He clicked the radio off. No chance for a recall now. He looked to the west and then back at Makinen. "I know where the meet is, it's no more than five clicks from here. We can get there in maybe thirty-five minutes."

"No. The commander said abort, so we abort." Mack stood stock still, eying Anton. "It's too dangerous, we could be walking into an ambush."

"Something isn't right here. I plan on finding out what's going on."

"On your own?"

"If need be. When have you ever not taken a chance?

"If it was just me, I might, but I have a team to worry about."

"Well, in that case, tell the colonel you gave the abort, but I said I'd make it to the RV on my own." Anton slung his weapon under his coat and took off down the street.

Mack didn't try to stop him, just said, "*Sisu toveri.*"

Anton paused a moment and turned to look back at Makinen. "*Sisu*, boss."

You're going to need that strength yourself, mate, Makinen thought.

A movement caught his eye across the street. St. John. Even wearing an overcoat and a hat, Makinen recognized him. He was about to yell when a black car raced in, the doors already opening. The brakes squealed as some rather large men jumped out on all sides of the Agency man and took him down with one punch to the head.

Mack was frozen, there was nothing he could do. Gavin was already gone. He saw Anton down the street, watching St. John get dragged into the safe house, then, he too was gone.

He didn't get the abort signal. Damn, bud, you're on your own now.

52

————•◆•————

DESPITE BEING WEIGHED down with his gear, Anton made good time, run-walking where he could through the empty streets.

He was thinking about two things, what he remembered of the *Gaswerk* layout and Ted St. John. The first was easy, three huge tanks of natural gas in the middle of a train yard, some small buildings, and only one easy way in off Dimitroffstraße. The second was a bit nebulous, but from what he had seen and heard, his faith in St. John was not strong.

That was enough to make him stop a moment at a corner phone. He put a ten *Pfenning* coin into the slot and dialed the number he had memorized. The line crackled with electronic static and he wondered if it was tapped. *No matter, this would be a one-time shot.* Four rings, and then the jostling of a handset picked up out of the cradle. A rustle of clothing as it was brought to an ear. Then a gruff, "*Ulbrecht hier.*"

He was surprised she didn't yell at him for calling so early in the morning. He spoke slowly in his best *Hochdeutsch.* He wanted the message to come through precisely.

"Good morning, Madam Ulbrecht. This is Klaus, I'm a friend of Rudolf. I'm sorry to call at this time and disturb you, but it is an emergency. I have an important message that he needs to get immediately. Would you please give it to him?" He gave her the message and asked her to repeat it back to him. Then, satisfied, he repeated, "Please give it to him immediately. Thank you." There wasn't a question. *"Alles Klar,"* was all she said."

Hanging up the phone, he hung his head for a brief moment and breathed deeply. He turned away from the phone and looked across the street. An apartment building with many windows. So many dark windows. *Where would the cameras be?* If they spotted him now, it wouldn't matter. He looked at the center mass of the building and mouthed the words, *"Du kannst mich mal"* and smiled wickedly.

Shoving his hands in his pockets to keep them warm and to stabilize the weapon at his side, he hurried on toward Dimitroffstraße, not bothering to check for anyone behind him. His mind wasn't on the streets anymore. He became part of the cold, gray stone and concrete that was inhospitable during the day, hostile at night. There was no reason for that other than the fact that East Berlin represented everything opposite to what he believed or had come to believe, even if he now felt at home there.

Now, he focused on the gas works ahead of him. He could see the first tank in the distance, five stories clad in an ugly shade of faded and weathered yellow brick with a crown of steel girders. There would be a small rail yard where the coal was brought in and several furnace buildings where the solid was turned to gas and pumped into the three huge tanks. Then, there was what remained, the coke, chemicals, pitch, and trash. A perfect place to meet in the dead of the night. Even at night he could see thick smoke belching from the chimneys. This was the place that kept the East warm at night and choking during the day.

Dimitroffstraße was suddenly there in front of him, a cross street that ran along the edge of the plant. He pitied for a moment the people who lived in the apartment buildings nearby, but he had no time for them. He hoped to be inside the facility before the appointed time, knowing the Soviets liked to keep their meetings short and get away before anyone noticed. He glanced at his watch. It was close, three minutes past midnight, fourteen to go. A brick watch building stood astride the main entry, its lights glowing in the dark. There was no gate, no fence, no security to speak of around the facility. Pondering that for a moment, Anton decided there was no reason for anyone who didn't work there to enter the place. No riches to steal and certainly the fire and brimstone that happened inside was enough to keep all but the most intent out. *That left the traitor, the handler, and me. The title for my book*, he thought.

It was easy enough to get around the hut, skirting the administrative building. Once past the entry to the facility he prowled in the darkness. The men he saw, certainly no women at night, were intent on their destination, either their place of work or their home. He looked for vehicles and saw only one. He was certain one man would come on foot, the other by car, as before. The handler was on his own turf, he could afford to drive or be driven.

He listened to the plant, heard the rolling roar of flames cooking the coal, the conveyors moving it, and somewhere a locomotive, it's bell sounding as it rolled on the track. The road ended in a parking lot. Beyond that no private cars could access further inside. He'd wait here. His watch indicated ten minutes past midnight. He shed his overcoat and left it at the base of tree. It wasn't that cold and he needed the freedom of movement. He'd pick it up on the way out.

He just finished checking gear, the stock on his weapon extended, four spare magazines and a pistol stuffed inside his pants, knife on a belt hanger. He pulled the radio from his belt and keyed the mike. "Big Dog, Big Dog, this is Cajun, over." He waited a couple of seconds and then said the words again.

"Cajun, Big Dog here. Are you clear of the target? Over."

"Negative, Big Dog, I'm at the new site. Do you have any new info on the players? Over." The was silence. He could imagine Ciernik cursing under his breath. He waited.

"Cajun, you're going to be up to your ass in Russians in a second. Get your butt out of there. Copy?"

"Big Dog, copy, but I got something to do here. If I see the target, I'm going to take my chances. Out."

He clicked off the radio again and dropped it on to his coat — there'd be no one to talk to anyway — and checked his pockets. Everything was accounted for. As he looked up, headlights swept into the entry way and a big, black sedan, rolled past the guard. It's Soviet occupation force plates cleared the way everywhere. He took a deep breath trying to relax and smelled the acrid stench for the first time, at least the first time he noticed. The unsubtle smell of the gasification process. There would be no smoking here tonight.

The car had stopped. Lights out, the doors opened. Three men got out. Two were average height, although one was stocky, his hands in his pockets and seemingly in charge as he was giving short commands in Russian to the others. The thin one carried a submachine gun to boot. "Crap. Number one threat," he said to himself. The third man was just big. Tall, he looked like a linebacker he knew from high school who was the biggest reason he'd decided football was not for him. That one carried a fat briefcase.

"Number one target," Anton whispered. The men moved off, stepping over a low fence that separated the parking from a lone, small gauge rail-line. They followed the line away from him into the dark.

Anton waited until they had almost disappeared before following, making sure he couldn't be seen from the car in case someone remained inside. Fifty yards behind, he was still walking carefully, avoiding kicking the cinders that bedded the track, watching where his feet were going, and trying to step on the steel cross ties without making a sound. So far, so good. In front of him, the stocky guy was having trouble navigating the tracks in the dark. He stumbled. His companion reached out to help, but he was sworn off. Another stumble. The guy with the weapon stayed back a step or two, but was constantly searching to the front, swinging with his head and the barrel, back and forth. Big guy was spending more time keeping eyes on his boss. None of them were looking for Anton.

Suddenly, the scene changed.

The three stopped as a fourth man stepped out of the shadows. A hat shielded his face from what little light there was. He stepped into the track bed and stood in front of his opposites. Anton moved forward, hoping to catch some of the words exchanged. He was unclear of what would happen next and suddenly realized he didn't have a plan other than trying to capture four men on his own. The briefcase was passed from the line-backer to the new man. Some words were spoken, none that he could hear. The man set the case down and took his hat off to wipe his brow.

I've seen that face…, Anton thought.

He noticed the noise that had surrounded him suddenly quieted, a rush in his ears drowned all else out and he felt his body react to the anticipation of what he needed to do. The anger that welled up as he realized he was watching an American betray his country. He remembered a night in Budapest, and the frustration of abandoning the mission because someone in Washington said his comrades were not worth the pain and effort. That kind of thinking wouldn't interfere here.

"Halt!" A voice rang out from behind Anton. Shouted loud enough that Anton's quarries turned to look, as did Anton. A lone figure stood behind him, a pistol held by one arm outstretched, awkwardly. *The driver*, thought Anton. He hadn't been as invisible as he thought. But the driver hesitated — Anton didn't. He couldn't afford to hesitate with four men behind him. Anton was already pointing the weapon at the driver, a natural occurrence for him, the barrel points where the eyes looked. The safety clicked off as the index finger went to the trigger, everything smoothly.

The first burst was from the hip, weapon low but extended somewhat. He brought it up to his shoulder and fired a second, unnecessary, but finishing burst, and saw the man twist and fall to the ground. He took two steps to the side and turned back to the group. The man with the submachine gun had planted himself firmly in the middle of the track and was coming around with his own weapon. Anton registered that first, then saw the big man turn as well. The briefcase was gone, he was pulling a pistol from a shoulder holster. The fourth man had disappeared into the shadows in the background. Anton fired a burst and saw dirt and stones kick up and felt the bolt go forward on an empty chamber. The answer came with a short burst, wildly aimed, no doubt the man's aim disturbed by Anton's incoming. Anton ducked to the side, jettisoned the empty magazine, and stuffed a new one into the well, pulling back the bolt, cursing the wasted seconds, and fired again into the quickly separating group in front of him. The stocky man took the brunt of it. His arms flew skyward, his overcoat billowed out, and he fell backward in a crumpled pile.

Driver and Boss-man down, but still two out there. Was there a limit on how many Russians you could bag in a day? And then there was the runner with the briefcase. He'd worry about him later.

Anton heard curses, and another burst from the submachine gun, a crack from the big man's pistol. He pulled the trigger again. Nothing. He moved, at least he remembered to move, jacking the bolt back, half turned, half running for his life, but still calm, time slowing and fired again. Nothing. He felt a sharp pain in his side, heard the single crack after. And ran on. He looked at the gun and saw a bit of brass winking up at him defiantly. "Fucking Russian weapons," he said not caring who heard. They knew where he was. He ran into the alleyway between some big buildings just off the tracks. He stopped and spun around, no one yet.

They must be moving slowly, carefully. But he knew they would come, he turned back and tried to run, but the pain hit him. He bent over, breathing hard, his heart racing, but the rush was gone. Then, he ran into the smaller alley.

53

CIERNIK SPRINTED FROM Building 3 on *Kronprinzenallee*, across the courtyard toward the main building, his hand on Myers back pushing him to move faster. The guard didn't have time to badge them as they busted through the entrance doors and ran up the main staircase. Luckily, Myers was a scrappy, little guy who'd played stick ball in his younger days and had run sprints, generally, away from chasing policemen when he'd been into street larceny. He cleaned up his act after his mom called him out on it. He wasn't in bad shape and, although law school stole some of his conditioning, he could out distance most. Except for Ciernik, who was right on top of him all the way.

The second-floor gallery was indeed impressive, even in the dark. The compound's security lights streamed in through the twenty feet tall windows on one end. The greenish-brown marble shimmered as the oak trees shifted in the breeze outside.

A long table split the room, with at least twenty chairs on each side, and one at each end.

"OSIP," Ciernik said as he took in the room.

"What about it?"

"This is Operation OSIP. It's to kill Eisenhower. Just like *Valkerie*."

"*Valkerie?*"

"When they tried to kill Hitler at the Wolf's Lair with a bomb."

"You think Kader is going to try to assassinate Ike?"

"What else would it be?"

"Why? That's what I want to know?" Myers said.

"You can ask him when he shows up. We're going to wait here." Ciernik drew his 1911 from the holster, checked the magazine, and made sure that there was a round in the chamber. Satisfied that it was safe, he placed it on the table and sat down.

"Make yourself comfortable, it might be a while."

"Shouldn't we alert the MPs so he can't get in?"

"No, they might spook him. We'll wait here. He has to bring the bomb here. Let him come on up. I want to see the look on his face."

"I'm going to get some coffee. I'll be right back."

"Make sure you do, major, otherwise, I'll be looking for you too. Oh, and black, no sugar is fine for me."

After Myers left, Ciernik unloaded his pistol and racked the slide several times. Once cleared, he held it up in the light. He liked the old warhorse better than the German pistols the unit used. The P-1 didn't compare either in construction or power and its nine millimetres was no match for the .45 ACP cartridge with its fat copper-jacketed slug. Much better because its slow-moving mass knocked things down while the 9mm just punched a hole. He marveled at the Colt's construction, solid steel, not prone to stress fractures like the Walther's alloy frame. He slid the magazine back into its well and pulled the slide back, letting it fly home with a satisfying noise. He engaged the thumb safety with a click and set it back on table. He liked American gear. Everything except the M-1 Carbine they tended to give airborne officers during the war. Nice and light but it was a useless peashooter as far as he was concerned. He ditched his for a Thompson. It just felt better, and it put out bullets that would actually kill something if your aim was true. But the 1911 was his real friend.

Myers came back bearing two ceramic mugs in hand. "The duty officer is set up with some decent coffee."

Ciernik said, "You have decided to trust me then."

"Why do you say that?"

"You came back."

"Oh, I had to see this. One of you is guilty. If Kader shows up here, then we'll know for sure." Myers blew on his steaming cup and took a sip of the coffee. "Good stuff."

Ciernik took a gulp from his cup and said, "I already know who. I want to know why."

Then they waited.

———————

When the door finally opened, it was almost morning. The sky in the west was still dark, but the tops of the trees in the courtyard were turning from black to green with the coming dawn.

A man came in, long overcoat, no hat. The face was not visible in the dark, but his fat briefcase was. He set in on the table, hand lingering over the handle to make sure it remained upright. Then, he took off his coat and turned, seemingly looking at the room's layout. He started to move, maybe to the light switch, who knew. Right then, the lights came on, three cut-glass hanging chandeliers seemed to slowly ignite, grower brighter as did the big wall sconces along the walls of the room.

If he was startled, the man didn't show it. He looked first to the entry doors he had come through, then to the side entrance where Myers stood.

"What are you doing here, Myers?"

"I could ask you the same question. I thought you were ill?"

"I'm feeling better. I couldn't miss today's events, could I?"

"No, I imagine you couldn't. But aren't you afraid you might pass something to the president?"

"I doubt it, it was a stomach thing. I'm okay."

Myers stepped forward. "What's in the briefcase? It seems heavy."

"Enough with the familiarity, Major. You should call me by my rank or say, sir."

"You didn't answer my question, Colonel, sir."

"It's none of your business. Now, I have things to attend to and you aren't supposed to be in this room before the event anyway."

"I suppose that applies to me, as well," Ciernik said as he stood up from the shadows. "Jozef Ciernik, we've met."

Kader swung back to the opposite side of the room. Seeing Ciernik, he said, "Yes, we have. At General Barksdale's reception."

"Well, Joe, what's in the briefcase? Major Myers and I are both interested."

Kader took a protective step towards the case. "You might not want to move, Kader." Ciernik's pistol was now pointing directly at Kader's chest.

"What's that for? What's this all about?" Kader said.

"I think you know. Major Myers has some questions for you, and I would like to see what you have brought us in that case."

"It's none of your business and you should point that thing somewhere else. Someone might get hurt."

"It is our business, Kader. Because you're a traitor and that thing has something bad in it."

Kader looked at the case then back at Myers and Ciernik, "You're insane."

"I don't think so. Why don't you sit in one of those chairs, Joe." Kader moved toward the chair closest to the briefcase. "Not that one, this one here, away from the case." He motioned with the gun barrel.

Kader stepped away, but not much. "You trust that pistol? You know they're prone to jamming."

Ciernik barked a short laugh. "That's an old wives' tale, Joe. I trust Mister Browning knew what he was doing when he designed it. Besides, they only jam if you've got a limp wrist. Do you have a limp wrist, Joe? Besides, at this range the first round will take you down really quick. Now sit."

What happened next would be later interpreted differently by the two witnesses, but essentially Kader moved — in the wrong direction. The .45 fired as John Browning intended. Two heavy slugs hit Kader in the upper left side of his chest, turned him sideways, threw him back into a chair, and then over it onto the floor. Dust floured down from the ceiling and rafters where it had accumulated over the years. Ciernik looked at his pistol.

"See, Major. It didn't jam. It's all in the grip. A good solid grip, a locked wrist, and you never have a problem with this weapon." He kicked Kader's leg. "He's dead. Asshole. I hate traitors."

Myers was a bit dazed and maybe harder of hearing than before. "So, I see," he said. "We should call EOD to get rid of this. It looks like a bomb, and I don't want to try to defuse it."

Ciernik peered into the case as well. Wires, a timer, silver metallic balls, and long, thin, paper-wrapped packages stained with some kind of oil stared back. "I think you're right, Myers." He put his pistol down on the table. "Perhaps we should call CID, as well. They might need to do an investigation."

Myers picked up the pistol and looked at it closely, "I fired one of these once in training. Could never hit a thing."

Ciernik smiled for once. "Of course, shooting someone at five feet is easier than shooting a twenty-five-yard target, you know."

"I'll take your word on that, sir. By the way, I think I need to burn some files after this."

"Really? Why?" said Ciernik.

"I think yours needs some revisions to reflect recent events"

"I may have been a bit rash in my judgement of you, Myers. You might make it in this world after all."

The main entry doors swung open and a phalanx of MPs entered, pistols drawn. "Put the weapon on the table and raise your hands, both of you," said the MP lieutenant.

Myers complied and they both raised their hands.

"Lieutenant, Major Myers is a hero. He just neutralized a deranged officer who threatened to blow up headquarters. He saved many lives today," Ciernik said.

Myers started to speak, but Ciernik cut him off, "Don't say anything, Major. The investigation will back you up. Kader was a traitor and you figured that out. Now, Lieutenant, you need to get EOD up here to defuse this thing," Ciernik said pointing at the case.

The lieutenant looked from Myers to Ciernik to the briefcase on the table to the body on the floor and turned to the sergeant next to him. "Do what the colonel said." The sergeant started to use his radio. "No, away from here. You might set the damn thing off." The sergeant scuttled from the room and the MP turned back to Ciernik and Myers. He picked up the pistol and moved it to the end of the table.

"Gentlemen, put your arms down. Now, Colonel, would you please tell me what the hell happened here?

54

ANTON CRAWLED TO the wall and lay against it as best he could, half sitting up. He set the submachine gun on the ground, it was still jammed, a ruptured cartridge gumming up the works. *It's what got me shot in the first place,* he thought. He was not in such good shape that he could clear the jam without a tool. He pulled the Tokarev out of his belt and checked the magazine. Full minus one down the spout. He set the pistol on the ground and found the two spare magazines in his jacket pocket. A total of twenty-four rounds. Enough for two squads of attackers, as long as he could aim and shoot fast enough and they couldn't. He smiled at the thought before the pain under his ribs punched him back to reality. His breathing was measured, a short inhale before the pain stopped him. Gloom gathered around the edges of his vision as blood leaked out of him, he focused hard. He pulled a wound dressing from another pocket, thanking God that he'd brought one and cracked the paper cover open. The bandage unfolded like a flower in the dark and he pressed it tight over the entry, he didn't think there was an exit. The lead was inside him, in there somewhere having done its damage before coming to a rest. Not in the lung, he thought. He'd be coughing up blood if it had. But he wasn't, just deep pain. Probably took out a rib on its way in, he thought. It was that sharp, the hurt.

Anton closed his eyes a moment and thought of Katja. *What had that been about?* He asked himself. He had met a girl, a woman who longed for something else, a change, a different world, a different love, of freedom. He wasn't sure. Now, he thought that chance was gone, maybe for her, certainly for him. What Charlie had said rang in his head like a bell now. Death. He had talked of death. The risk of it and the act of dying. No one mentioned living, even if living meant dying in the end. Living always meant to aspire to something, maybe only to fail, but more important, to aspire to something greater whether you get there or not. He had tried to get there. Tried to get somewhere, an unknown place, the end spot, somewhere he hadn't been before. An experience he hadn't known he could have and now he felt he was nearly there. Nearly there.

Anton closed his eyes for a moment, focusing his thoughts on his breathing. He tried not to think. Just breathe. The pain eased a bit, but he wasn't thinking about it. Nothing. He opened his eyes. A minute? Two? Ten? He didn't know, but he felt stronger. And calm.

He felt better despite the pain. He was sure he had taken out the senior Russian with the second burst from his weapon. That was a good thing. Too bad about the fourth man, but the door would close on him as well soon enough. Of that, Anton was certain. But he knew the game was not yet finished.

The sound of movement at the end of the alley. Scratching noises, maybe a mischief of rats or a conspiracy of bad guys scurrying about. Same thing, filthy animals. *Come on then.*

He found himself looking up at the high parapets of the huge gas tanks and beyond, into the heavens. A clear night for once, bright stars shimmering. *Clear sky, it'll be cold tomorrow.* Shook his head to focus, looked both ways down the canyon of structures and decided they could only come from one direction. Smart, they don't want to kill their own people; they want to flush him out like some grouse.

They must not know I'm hurt or they're not sure. Just trapped. Someone will be waiting for me down at the other end. If I could move, I wouldn't go that way. Too far, too straight to run. Would just die with another bullet in my back.

Anton waited, wanting to know. Slowly, they came into view over the trash piles, first one, the thin one. One more followed, the big man. He knew that one. He heard the voices, the first man stopped and turned. The stocky one Anton had heard being called Sergei came forward. More talk, whispers really. They were being careful, cautious even. The full-back retreated a bit, even more cautious, didn't want to be the first one shot. *Don't count on it,* Anton said to him under his breath.

He had one last trick which he pulled out of an inside pocket. Hard and knobby, its ring jingled quietly against the spoon. He held it up and looked closely, its surface cut with squares like a pineapple. An old Soviet F-1 from the special stocks.

My last resort, he thought, as he inhaled, long and slow. He remembered a line from a book he read in high school, "War's a bitch."

He straightened the pin and slid it out slowly, placing the ring over his thumb before he carefully shifted the grenade from his right to left hand, fingers pressing the handle down tightly. He could throw the grenade with either arm, but he shot better with his right. Satisfied, he picked up the Tokarev and waited.

55

HE WAS STANDING at the end of the bridge when Maria pulled up. She got out of the car and walked swiftly to where he was, handing him the buff-colored envelope.

"Why are you here, Charlie?" she said. Her eyes were wide. He thought she looked frightened.

"You haven't heard, have you?"

She shook her head. "What happened?"

"Anton didn't come back, Maria. We may have lost him and I'm not going to lose anyone else. I owe it to Anton to get Ted back."

"This is suicide if they blame you for what happened!"

Charlie chose to ignore her. It was no longer a game.

"You found the papers, great. So, what did Wolf sound like?"

"Surprised, but pleasant enough." she said. "He asked me how we found his phone number. I told him we bought one of their phonebooks from a housekeeper."

Charlie chuckled. "Good thinking. Did you have a hard time convincing him to come?"

"No, I think he was expecting the call. He said he'd bring Ted as you asked."

"He called him Ted?"

"No, I call him Ted. He said Mister St. John. Formal. Said he would have had to toss him back anyway because of his ID card."

"He's lucky. Hear anything about Anton?"

"Nothing. I hope…" her voice trailed off.

"Me too." A sigh.

They walked forward and waited.

A big black car pulled up at the other end of the bridge. The east end. Three men got out, but only two walked forward. One stayed by the car, his great coat open and flapping in the wind. Charlie thought he saw the outline of weapon. Security. But not so much at fifty yards.

One of the two walked forward and paused, waiting for the other who walked stiffly.

"They've beaten him," Maria said.

"I imagine so."

"He's got you to thank for getting him out, you know."

"I wasn't going to leave him there."

"He should have never gone," she said.

"Did you write up the award request?"

"Just like you asked me to."

"Don't tell him we're going to send it. Anyway, I may want to add to it later."

"He'll be going home now, won't he?"

"Yes, he's compromised here, and he'll be suffering from shell shock after this. At least, that's what the report will say. He'll get a nice job on the sixth or seventh floor and retire gently in a couple of years."

He saw the two men were almost at the mid-point. "That's good," he said so they'd hear. Charlie stole a glance at Maria, who was standing next to him, a .38 caliber Colt Detective revolver half out of her coat pocket.

"Aren't you full of surprises? Where'd you get that?" he said.

"The office safe. Ted has me inventory all the toys, so I adopted this one. After all, I'm not going to lose both you and Anton in one day."

"Okay, but stand over to the side a couple of paces just in case."

"Don't be scared. My dad taught me how to shoot a guy's nuts off at ten paces."

"With one round or two?"

"Depends on the angle."

"You scare me, woman."

"Ah, when you're scared, I'm no longer a girl. I think you finally understand, Charlie."

The early evening streets of East Berlin were growing darker, cloaked with an air of dark uncertainty, the tension made even more palpable by the threatening clouds that hung overhead as the three men faced off squarely against each other.

"I have brought your man. Have you brought what you promised?"

"I did. I'll come to you."

Wolf stood with his arms down at his sides, hands spread open showing he had no weapon. Palmer holstered his own pistol and mirrored Wolf's gesture with his hands then moved forward slowly, looking closely at St. John. His head was down. "Ted, look at me." He did. His face was haggard, a bit bruised but none too worse for wear. Charlie turned to the other man and shifted to German. "It's a pleasure Herr Storm, or should I say Herr Wolf."

"Either will do, Herr?"

"Jorgensen. Frank Jorgensen. American Mission." Charlie would be someone else for the moment.

"CIA?"

"Whatever. I have the documents for you as promised. I think you will find them interesting." He pulled the envelope from his pocket and gave it to Wolf, who opened it and slid the papers out, thumbing through them quickly.

His eyes opened a bit as he read. "Mielke does not surprise me, but Ulbrich? That's indeed very interesting. Thank you. Where did you find them?"

Charlie went back to English, where the words were easier to find. "They were stored in our Berlin Document Center. It's where we archive all the captured documents from the previous regime."

"Indeed, a lucky find. I'm sure these are the only copies?" said Wolf.

"Of course they are. We have no use for them."

"Of course you don't." Wolf smiled. "You can take your man now. A fair trade I think."

"Thank you. Yes, fair enough. Ted, walk to the lady. She'll take you to the car."

They both watched Ted limp away, his arm held by Maria.

"My people may have been a bit enthusiastic when they grabbed him. My apologies."

"At least he's walking. He'll get over it." Charlie was still upset that Ted ignored him when he said to abort. *It's his own damn fault.*

"How did you find out about your traitor?"

"A fluke, he gave himself away," Charlie lied. "We've been watching him constantly."

Wolf nodded. "Spies and traitors often do reveal themselves. Over confidence or carelessness."

"I suppose. My experience with traitors is limited."

Wolf had his hands in his pockets. He turned and waved at the man by his car. "I just told him that I'm safe. I'm in no hurry to go back to work."

"You could always come visit us for a while. Stay if you like."

"That's a generous offer, young man, but I'm fine over here. It's not perfect, but tell me what country is? Other than that, my wife and a few other people would be upset with me. Was that the woman who called me? I'm sorry I didn't get to meet her. She sounded very attractive on the telephone and looks better in person. Her German is impeccable, you know." Wolf was looking beyond Charlie, maybe hoping to see Maria again. "You heard the shooting, yes?"

"Of course. How could I miss it?" said Charlie.

"Complete with artillery," said Wolf.

"Not quite artillery. That would have been much louder. A grenade maybe."

"You've heard them before?"

"No, but I'm pretty sure it was a grenade," Charlie said.

"So, the war isn't starting."

"I don't think so. Small unit action, chance contact."

"Hardly a chance contact," Wolf said, looking away toward where the noise had come from. Now it was quiet. Even the bleating of the sirens was gone. "I think the story will be something like a gang of fascist profiteers ambushed a valiant Soviet officer. There was a desperate firefight, and he vanquished the criminals, but perished in the fight."

"Why not the true story? That he was killed by a crazed American?"

"I don't think that would serve either of our purposes," said Wolf.

"Our purposes? What are those?"

"That the true story would ruffle a few feathers and maybe cause bigger problems. I think perhaps it's a good idea to have a rational mind on each side of the border. You over there, me over here, for example. We may be enemies Mister Frank Jorgensen, but neither of us want another world war."

"You're right. An officer was killed?"

"A Soviet colonel and three of his men. No great loss compared to what might have happened. What now?" Wolf, his attention back on Charlie.

Charlie wasn't sure what else to ask. All but one man had been accounted for and he was hesitant to ask. "Why was the meeting changed at the last second?"

"I warned the Russians and they changed the meeting site. I told them the safe house had been compromised."

"Won't they blame you?"

"Why? It was your traitor, their pet American spy who killed them, right?" said Wolf.

"Right now, I don't know who killed who. But you knew the traitor hadn't been informing us about his meetings. How?"

"The message you passed to Gehlen said your traitor met with a *Stasi* officer. He didn't know I was *Stasi* and all the others were KGB. It was a small mistake, but enough for me. But I'm not so sure now. It's all a bit confusing."

Charlie scratched his head, putting together several answers that had been missing.

"You just confirmed you have a source inside Pullach."

"And you confirmed that you know he is there. So that makes us even."

"You know, my folks have backed off but they're still watching us. We had orders to kill you because of what happened to Buchanan." He wondered if Wolf knew he was lying.

"Buchanan was the man killed near the border?" said Wolf.

"Yes."

"That was the KGB."

"So, it was Androv who killed Buchanan?" Charlie asked.

"Kudos, young Mister Jorgensen. You figured out who the Russian colonel was. But, no, it wasn't Androv, it was his SMERSH bodyguard. I didn't find out what happened to your man Buchanan until later."

"That he was murdered?"

"Yes, and now Androv is dead," said Wolf. "We're square now, as you Americans say."

"If you say so, but were you there when Buchanan was murdered?" said Charlie.

"No, I didn't know your Buchanan was even there. I was at the safe house and translated for the meeting with Kader. He didn't speak Russian and his German was bad. The Russians needed help communicating with him. I spoke to him in English then I left when they found one of their own."

"And that's how you knew he planned to kill our president."

"Not then. I found that out later that the Russians were going to give him the means. Then I found out why."

"Why? Tell me why he wanted to kill Eisenhower?" Charlie said.

"Because his family was Palestinian. He blamed your president for the creation of Israel. Many of his relatives were killed in the 1948 Deir Yassin massacre."

"He said he was Lebanese."

"He also said his family was Maronite Christian, did he not?" said Wolf.

"Did he?"

"He did and he lied."

Charlie shook his head. "He must have been a fanatic. Recognizing the state of Israel wasn't Eisenhower's doing, it was Truman's. Anyway, it wouldn't have mattered. Eisenhower would have been replaced by someone else and the Palestinians would bear the cost of his murder. Why are you telling me this?"

"You did me one good turn with the documents, so to speak. And there is one other thing," Wolf paused a moment. "One area where I disagree with Moscow and our very own leadership, including Mielke, is that they want trouble in the Middle East, I don't."

"Why don't you agree with them?"

Wolf looked down for a moment and then stole a glance at the breaking morning twilight in the east. Charlie thought he might be deciding which story to tell or maybe the truth.

"I am Jewish," he said.

Palmer waited and decided Wolf had shared his secret truth, not the lie. The weight of Wolf's words said a lot about the man. He reached into his pocket and pulled out a crumpled pack of cigarettes. With a flick of his wrist, he offered one to his adversary. Wolf accepted, a gesture of camaraderie between two men, one older at thirty-four, one slightly younger, both with souls already well-scarred by the business.

"*Papirosa?*" Wolf said.

"No, better. Lucky Strike."

"American as apple pie," said Wolf, sticking the cigarette in his mouth with a smirk.

Palmer snapped his Zippo open with a metallic clink and flicked the flint into a flame. He held it like a candle, his hand protecting the flame, extending out so he could light Wolf's smoke before he lighted his own.

"Also American," he said. "Here." He flipped the Zippo closed and tossed it to Wolf. The spymaster caught it with his offhand. He looked at the lighter with its military inscription.

"My father's from World War Two. Keep it."

Your accent, Mister Jorgensen, it is from the western part of your country? Maybe Dakota?"

"That's the Midwest, but you're close. I'm from Wisconsin," said Charlie, adding to his impromptu cover.

"From the cheese-country, yes. That makes sense. I like cheese, but we don't get good cheese often. In Moscow, we never got cheese. I dreamt of cheese, but it was war then." Wolf smiled wistfully as he put the lighter in his pocket. "Thank you. We call it the Great Patriotic War, not World War 2 like you. That was when we were both fighting the same enemy. The struggle was justified then. Now, well… sometimes I'm not sure."

As cigarette smoke curled into the air, a fragile bond seemed to take hold between the two. They were both products of countries at war with each other even if the war was "cold." Countries driven by ideologies that devoured men's souls. In that moment, the boundaries of nationality and language seemed to fade, replaced by a shared understanding of the burdens they carried.

"Were there any other people at the *Gasometer*?"

"Ah, you know where it happened."

"I heard, yes."

"No, we found four dead, no one else. I think your double or traitor, whoever he was, must have run away. Have you found him?"

"I don't know. I've heard nothing as of now."

"Ask your woman over there in the car. I think she may know. You know, we are both nothing, but pawns in a grand game," Wolf said, his voice carrying the weight of resignation. "Perhaps, in our own small ways, we can find ways to get around that."

Palmer nodded, a glimmer of hope flickering briefly in his tired eyes. "We can try, but I doubt anyone else really cares about reconciliation. Our leaders are intent on winning the game, not settling for a draw." He nodded, a final gesture, and they parted ways, each disappearing toward the labyrinth of Berlin's narrow streets. As Palmer walked off the end of the bridge, he couldn't help but wonder what Wolf would do next.

Palmer turned to look back. Wolf was gone, but in Palmer' mind, he saw that the spymaster's smile — much like the elusive Cheshire cat's — remained.

―――――――

Charlie climbed into the car and turned to look at St. John in the back. He was curled up on the seat with an OD green army blanket covering him. Maria had a pensive look on her face. She shook her head as if to say he wasn't doing well.

"You okay, boss?" Charlie asked.

Nothing, then a stir under the blanket. "I'm okay," St. John bleated. "Charlie?"

"Yes?"

"I gave up STORCH."

"What!" Charlie swiveled around quickly. "They only had you for twelve hours. Did they torture you?"

"They were going to. I only told them one name. They pushed me around a lot. One guy punched me."

"These people aren't baseball cards. You don't just trade them away like that."

"Why? It's not like they'd survive long anyway."

"They won't survive at all, now. This isn't a fucking game, Ted! We lost one man last night, did you know that?" *Jesus,* said Charlie under his breath. "Let's go then. Get him back to the office. We may have time to warn them."

Maria started the car and rolled off toward Dahlem, shifting quickly until they were barreling down the empty streets.

"He's a player, you know," she said.

"Who?"

"Wolf."

"How do you know?"

"I'm a woman, Charlie. I can see and hear how men think."

"Maybe, he is a spy-handler after all. But, more importantly, he confirmed that Kader was going to try to assassinate the president. That's what *Feuerschmied* was all about."

"How did you find that out."

"I dropped it into our talk as if it was a fact. He didn't hesitate to confirm it."

"Well, that confirms what I just heard. Myers and that colonel confronted Kader at headquarters."

"And?" he said distractedly. He was thinking about his assets and damage control.

"Kader's dead. Myers shot him. They recovered a bomb."

"I should have known it was Kader. I missed him and we almost arrested the wrong guy."

The story was too bizarre, Charlie thought. Nothing like what he thought he'd joined up for, but still better than being on the plains of Nebraska.

"Charlie? You okay?"

"I'll be fine."

"I'm impressed by you," she said with a smile.

"You're pretty damned impressive yourself, Maria." Charlie was turning pink.

56

OBERST STEINER WAS the first one through the door, pistol drawn. It was a regular occurrence these days, busting down doors and arresting traitors, counterrevolutionaries, and Trotskyites. He reveled in seeing the fear in their eyes when they saw his maroon-piped uniform and knew their future freedom was about to be severely circumscribed or abruptly ended. That depended on their first reaction as much as on the revelations they disclosed in the basement of *Haus 24*.

The call had come early, surprisingly it was direct from Mielke. "Crush them," the minister had said. The address was delivered to his section as they loaded out. They were rolling within thirty minutes of the minister's call.

It wasn't that far and it was a small place. Easy to search.

"Check everything, especially the books. Make sure the game pieces don't hide anything. Look for radios, code books, all the usual shit," he said to the entourage that trooped in behind. Looking at the books, he felt revulsion. Here was a person that lived off the state, was bathed in glory and given medals and ribbons for playing games. He knew chess himself, even enjoyed it, but being coddled by the nation without any other contribution? How was that fair? Especially now that this traitor's true allegiances had been revealed.

No warm bodies, he thought. *No cold ones either. That happened a lot these days also. People got scared and ended themselves rather than be arrested. Fieglings!* Cowards.

"Nothing, comrade colonel." said one of the searchers.

"I have something," another said, voice excited, holding a small piece of paper.

"Let me have it."

"What is it, Colonel?"

The colonel read off the words and letters, "Klaus called. He said to tell you: Qh5+" He thought a moment. "It's a chess notation." His lessons came back to him, that effeminate teacher who swore at him when he made a bad move, and then played old trick moves to humiliate him. And he remembered. "It's a warning. Greco's 1615 queen sacrifice to take the king. A chance to escape."

He looked at the ceiling and swore.

57

JOZEF WAS READY. Dispatching Kader and recovery of almost all the unit's personnel from the Soviet sector had burnished his credentials. Barksdale was happy, Barnes was ecstatic. Kader having been extinguished put Barnes in the catbird seat, maybe Barksdale would recommend him for promotion to full bird or to be a presidential aide. But General Barksdale was a hard man to please, so he knew Barnes probably had a snowball's chance in hell for anything.

Most importantly, he had the paperwork in order to resettle Maja and Roman. Once they'd seen the intelligence Roman had provided, the process was easily greased by Myers of CIC and Palmer of the Agency. Of course, their superiors agreed.

Only one missing soul hung above his head, but he couldn't dwell on that now.

It had been almost ten days since he last had seen Maja and he was concerned. The telephone call had not come and he had no other means to contact her. Going to her apartment was just too much of a risk.

It surprised him when he entered his apartment that evening and found a brown envelope on the floor, someone having pushed it under the door. He checked the rooms before he came back and hovered above it like a hummingbird considering a strange flower. Finally, he pressed it with his foot lightly down onto the floor, finding it thin, no hard objects inside. Deciding it was safe, he picked it up and held it to the overhead light but could discern nothing.

Half dreading the note, he slit the top with his pocket knife and let the paper inside fall into his hand. A single sheet of delicate paper, he smelled its scent and knew its origin.

Unfolding it, he read,

"Jozef,

Reading this now, I am sure you will have realized that I won't be able to see you again for a while. I couldn't tell you in person because it hurts. Instead, a trusted friend delivered this note from me to you.

I once told you that neither Roman nor I have anyone or anything back home. That isn't quite true. We grew up in Poland, we have each other, and we have responsibilities to our country. For you, it is different. You left when you were young and have grown up in America. Had I been at home when you left, I might have escaped too.

You are perhaps more American than Polish now. You have your responsibilities to your adopted country. That is a very good thing for you.

Roman and I heard the news of the incident at the gasworks and his friends told him the story of what happened there. We now understand why it happened and, because of that, we have realized that we all live in a most dangerous world.

There is much work to be done and we cannot run away from our duties or the motherland.

Roman has been told that after this he will be considered for a job with an Embassy somewhere, maybe Europe, maybe elsewhere. In the meantime, he wishes to stay the course and not lose that chance. I agree with him. He has a future within his service and he can do more from here than over there. At least for a while. Tell your friends that we will be ready to work with them when we come out. Maybe sooner. And tell yourself that you have done your best to help us. We won't forget that, nor will I forget my love for you. We will see each other again, maybe soon, maybe not for a while, but we will see each other again.

I love you, your sister Maja."

The letter fell to the ground from Jozef's hand like a fluttering leaf from an oak in autumn. His hands covered his face and he held them there. Then, he rubbed his eyes and sighed.

"*Bóg, Honor, Ojczyzna,*" he whispered. God, Honor, Homeland.

58

THE BRIDGE WAS the only connection Charlie had to the other side now. He couldn't cross over because the opposition knew who he was — maybe not his real name, but his face. He thought it funny that he was the man without a name. Maybe Wolf would assign him the codename of *Käsekopf*, Cheesehead, or something equally banal.

"The lie was the truth; the truth was a lie. I am a liar. Born to lying, bred to it, trained to it, and well-practiced in it," he said out loud and laughed.

He heard footfalls and turned to see Makinen and Becker approaching. Charlie's questioning look was answered by Mack, "Your secretary Maria told us you have been spending a lot of time down here."

"I would advise you not to call her secretary to her face."

"Why, what is she?"

"My secretary, but she's become our ops officer. She'll be going back to the Farm soon."

"Really? A woman case officer?"

"Not the first. One of, but not the first. Not the last either, I think."

"Well, how 'bout that?" said Becker. "How's ol' Ted doing?"

"He went home. Compassionate reassignment and probably a long security debrief. He was pretty stressed out about the whole thing. Anyway, it's his own damn fault, he ignored my signal. But, both he and Maria will get a medal out of it."

"Not you?"

"I didn't do anything. I was just an observer. I don't need the ribbons. Besides, my plan didn't come off anything like it should have."

"Yeah, plans have a way of doing that," Becker said.

Charlie had been pondering what went wrong for a couple of days and come to another conclusion. "Not only that, I think Anton knew we had the wrong guy."

"Why do you say that?"

"Remember in the safe house? Anton said that the Grandmaster told him the King's Bishop was bad. He was right, Kader was Bishop to Eisenhower the King."

They all took that tidbit in silently. Mack pulled a cigarette from somewhere and lighted it. He took a long drag and exhaled. "I heard Myers is getting a medal," he said.

"Where did you hear that?" Charlie asked.

"Our CO. He said Myers was the guy who stopped Kader. Funny thing is, he used the colonel's pistol to shoot him. Haven't quite figured that story out."

"And we probably never will. Maybe it's better that way."

"Maybe. So, who's in charge of BOB these days?"

"Me. For the time-being. Until they get some higher-ranking Ivy Leaguer to take over."

"Too bad," said Mack.

"No, it's fine. Being chief means more paperwork and less time on the street."

Becker took one last draught from the cigarette he was smoking and flicked it over the railing. "Have you heard anything from the other side?"

"No, other than talk that the *Ossies* are going to restrict travel somehow. Too many people moving west."

"See anything over there?" Becker said, nodding to the other bank of the river.

"No. I keep hoping though."

"Why don't you go over? We can't, Barksdale told us to keep a low profile until things calm down," said Mack.

"What about KIBITZ? Don't you still have that to handle?"

"KIBITZ is dead. Your boss gave it up to *Stasi*, remember?" Mack said.

"I know. We'll have to start over from scratch now. It's getting harder." Charlie dropped his cigarette and ground it out with his shoe. "But I can't go over either. What would I do? Search for him at the gas works? I can't ask the Russians, they all seem to be dead."

"You could go see Wolf and ask him," said Mack.

"Like Priam sneaking into the Greek camp to get his son's body back from Achilles?"

"Priam got him, didn't he? If you did that, then we'd know for certain," said Mack.

"It would be more like Heracles rescuing Alcestes from Death. Not sure I'm ready for that."

"The damn Greeks were too melodramatic. We need to just go over and kill some Russians." Mack said as he sent his cigarette sailing over the bridge railing and shook his head.

"We may get our chance soon enough," Charlie was already conjuring something. "But not quite yet."

"I had to tell Kim that Anton was on a long trip. Didn't know what else to say. He likes Anton a lot." Becker wasn't ready to let him go.

"I liked… I like him too. I don't know…," Charlie went silent a moment. Mack and Becker seemed to respect that. "Wolf told me four Russians went down. He thinks Kader killed them."

Mack spoke, "I doubt it was Kader. He wanted to blow headquarters up and they helped him. I think it was Anton. Funny though, the colonel's pissed. He said he may charge Anton with going AWOL."

"Really? That's kind of petty," said Charlie.

"I'm just saying that's what Ciernik said he'd do. Right before he gives him a medal."

Charlie snorted a laugh. "That almost makes the whole thing worthwhile."

"Does it? Maybe, but will we ever know?" said Becker.

"There's one thing I don't understand, why did Anton decide to go alone?" Charlie said.

"He ran to the sound of the guns," Becker said. "There comes a time when you realize something is more important than yourself."

"Was it really?" Charlie was only beginning to understand.

"Knowing what we know now, yes. It might have been worse if he hadn't." Becker said.

"Let's go get a drink," Mack said.

"I know a place," said Charlie. "Ever been to the Savoy? It's on me. We have a comrade to toast and some ideas I'd like to discuss with you."

"Sounds good," said Mack. "We heard good things about it from someone."

Becker and Makinen turned to go, while Charlie took a last look at the East.

This business, if it can be called a business, is like assembling a jigsaw puzzle without knowing what the picture depicts — imagine a blind person who must fit the pieces together only by touch and memory — even then he won't know what the final image is, only that it's finished. For the moment.

In front of him, a broken city, a place frozen in time, yet to be reborn. Still, all in all, it was better than being in Hastings.

Postscript

———◆———

ACROSS TOWN, A woman stepped out of the dreary little bar that stood at the corner of Oderberger and Kastanienallee. Dim street lights, tendrils of fog hung in the night sky, a cold bite to the air. She looked around a bit, then went back inside. A moment later she came back out, a large tote bag on her shoulder, holding the hand of a smaller version of herself. She didn't bother with locking the door, she didn't care anymore.

"It all belongs to the people anyway," she whispered under her breath. It had been nearly a month since she'd heard from Klaus. She hoped he was safe, but these days it was hard to know. What Katja did know was that she had to be careful. At this time of night, anything could happen and she'd heard the muffled thumps and what sounded like gunfire in the city several nights ago. After a while, the sirens had died down, and the city became again peaceful. At least as peaceful as one could hope for.

A shush given the child, Anya was her name, could be heard faintly as the Katja turned down the street. It was the opposite direction from how she usually walked to get home, but she knew this route by heart. After she'd received the note with the directions, she had memorized them and thrice practiced walking the route, once in the day, twice at night. Now with a bundle of

West German Marks in her pocket, a key to an address she knew by heart, what papers she possessed, along with enough clothing in the bag to begin again, she walked on.

Little Anya kept up with Katja's pace, silent now, possibly excited by the things her big sister had promised her. Maybe the stories were true. Hopefully they were, because dreams are based on hope. Anya would find out soon, once they crossed over. Katja and her little sister walked on, heading northwest, along the railway track to a path that led into the bush. She pushed through the tangled branches, pulling Anya into the dark tunnel, and walked toward the dim light that outlined the small archway at the far end.

About the Author

———•———

JAMES STEJSKAL SPENT thirty-five years as a "Green Beret" and CIA case officer living and conducting operations around the world during the Cold War and after 9/11. He has written five military history books, along with numerous articles, and received accolades for his book Masters of Mayhem: Lawrence of Arabia and the British Military Mission to the Hejaz. His fiction centers on intelligence and special operations and Ratcatcher is the fifth book in his The Snake Eater Chronicles. He lives in northern Virginia with his wife, Wanda.

DOUBLE‡DAGGER
— www.doubledagger.ca —

Double Dagger Books is Canada's only military-focused publisher. Conflict and warfare have shaped human history since before we began to record it. The earliest stories that we know of, passed on as oral tradition, speak of war, and more importantly, the essential elements of the human condition that are revealed under its pressure.

We are dedicated to publishing material that, while rooted in conflict, transcend the idea of "war" as merely a genre. Fiction, non-fiction, and stuff that defies categorization, we want to read it all.

Because if you want peace, study war.

Printed in Dunstable, United Kingdom

65470158R00201